more **men**
on my mind

Radha Thomas was born in Tamil Nadu, grew up in Mumbai and Delhi and left for the USA to pursue her dream of becoming a jazz singer. When she discovered that music wasn't going to keep body and soul together, she found a variety of day jobs, while singing in clubs at night, sharing the stage with many of New York's renowned jazz artists.

She has been a tour guide in Australia, New Zealand and Fiji, organized exhibitions in China, owned a boutique on Long Island, worked for an art publisher in New York, anchored a weekly jazz show and even written a column called 'Between the Sexes' for a local magazine. She is a trained Dhrupad singer.

Thomas returned to Bengaluru, India, after about twenty years.

She leads UNK: The Radha Thomas Ensemble—performing all over India. They released their first album, *I Only Have Eyes For You* in 2012, which was picked up for airplay in over hundred US jazz radio stations. She is presently working on her second album and a tour of Europe.

The author is Executive Vice President at Explocity.com

more **men** on my mind

Love 'em, Leave 'em
Can't Live Without 'em

RADHA THOMAS

RUPA

First published by
Rupa Publications India Pvt. Ltd 2014
7/16, Ansari Road, Daryaganj
New Delhi 110002

Sales Centres:

Allahabad Bengaluru Chennai
Hyderabad Jaipur Kathmandu
Kolkata Mumbai

Copyright © Radha Thomas 2014

This is a work of fiction. Names, characters, places and incidents are either the
product of the author's imagination or are used fictitiously,
and any resemblance to any actual persons, living or dead,
events or locales is entirely coincidental.

All rights reserved.
No part of this publication may be reproduced, transmitted,
or stored in a retrieval system, in any form or by any means,
electronic, mechanical, photocopying, recording or otherwise,
without the prior permission of the publisher.

ISBN: 978-81-291-3113-3

First impression 2014

10 9 8 7 6 5 4 3 2 1

The moral right of the author has been asserted.

Printed by Thomson Press India, Faridabad

This book is sold subject to the condition that it shall not,
by way of trade or otherwise, be lent, resold, hired out, or otherwise circulated,
without the publisher's prior consent, in any form of binding or cover other
than that in which it is published.

For Tiku, again

CONTENTS

Author's Note ix

1. The French Connection 1
2. Bon Voyage 9
3. Breaking Bed 15
4. I Love Paris in the Springtime 23
5. Operation Veronique 34
6. New York, New York 45
7. The Indian Princess 52
8. Dirty Sex 62
9. The Play's 'the Thing' 68
10. When Your Day Is Done and You Wanna Run 76
11. The Right Way to Eat a Softee 84
12. Third World Collision 90
13. Siren Song 101
14. Diplomatic Immunity 112
15. Where Have All the Virgins Gone? 118
16. Window Dressing? 128
17. Eeeeeek, a Mouse! 139
18. Does Karma Wear a Turban? 152
19. One Night in Bangkok 159
20. Toast Points with Peppercorn Infused Goat Brain 169

21. Big House, Little House	179
22. Sitar Shankar	195
23. The Magical Mystery Tour	208
24. Moshi Moshi	220
25. Get Me to the Church on Time	231
26. No Laundry on Sundays	240
27. On His Knees	252
28. Ruy Lopez	267
29. Pink Strips	277

AUTHOR'S NOTE

To my many friends who may or may not read this book, no, that's not you in here. It's someone just like you but weirder, for sure.

To Ramjee Chandran who continues to think I'm beautiful, even when I know I'm not.

To my mother, who hasn't come back to life. After twelve years, I still expect her to walk in through the door waving a copy of my manuscript, declaring it's filled with typos.

To my son Stefan who tells me that I haven't quite grasped the 'b' in subtle, as he steadfastly refuses to read any of my books.

And to my aunt Tiku, this trilogy is for you. Which means you have to read the next one too.

Chapter 1

THE FRENCH CONNECTION

A shot of romance served straight up, with a twist of desperation on the rim. It's a cocktail that can make a slightly tipsy, extremely unhappy girl do pretty much anything.

Even agree to marry a man she has only just met on the subway, because he looked and sounded so, well, French. L'amour is a très strange and très mysterious thing.

Let me back up just a little, to put you in the picture. This, by no means, is the beginning.

We were at a nameless, faceless Japanese restaurant somewhere around 50th street in New York City, each of us at least six sakes past the point of no return.

I had just said, 'I will,' to one Jacques DeVillier, a man I didn't know, who had claimed, 'I am a zhournaleeest weez a specialteee in nuclearrrr enerrrgeee.'

He may have been a, 'Seriallll keeeeelleerrrr weez a specialteee in deeesmemberrrrment.' It didn't matter. At that point, he sounded glamorous and sexy to a girl who had spent her life chasing the wrong guy, over and over again.

Leading up to that moment were several circumstances and events, much too long and way too boring to get into here (although I'd written reams and reams about it as a form of catharsis earlier), but suffice it to say that before the 'I will,' I was on the A Train, sorrowfully headed home to my lonely apartment uptown, suffused with a sense of abandonment and hopelessness. My head was coloured several shades of grey.

I had been dumped by a girl I was hoping to anoint my

standby BFF. But Christine Caldwell had turned on her heels angrily, overcome by her own sadness and disappointment, caused by, you guessed it, moi.

She had stomped away from my life for good outside a bar in Soho, all because I had unknowingly slept with her husband-to-be, a piano player named David Amarro.

Oh, I knew that I wasn't 'sleeping' with him when we were in fact wide-awake and making a huge ruckus in the pursuit of good sex at the ungodly hour of three in the morning. It was in Phoenix, Arizona, and we had the whole night ahead of us before we had to get up on stage to perform with our jazz band in front of a gigantic crowd of several thousands. Twenty thousand, we discovered later.

We were counting on fame, fortune and the assorted perks that came along once the audience had erupted into several spontaneous standing ovations after our performance. So a little pick-me-up sex before stardom seemed most appropriate.

But while we were in the throes of indescribably exciting sex-for-the-first-time, (I was very fortunate that it wasn't unspeakably awful as I'd experienced not once, but many times before) what I didn't know was that David was already having an affair with Christine, aforementioned potential BFF, whom I had befriended recently, and with whom I'd shared many evenings filled with much heart-to-heart, much gossip and lots of wine. I loved hanging out with Christine. I was hoping she'd become my shopping buddy too.

But clearly, the confidences exchanged were only one-way. I had poured my heart out while she drank it in. She hadn't confided everything in me. As a result, I foolishly assumed that she was the committed, faithful, long-term girlfriend of our band's guitar player, a rather mournful chap named Angelo, with whom she'd been living with for several years.

If I learned anything it was that one should never assume anything. Things are never what they seem.

She hadn't so much as hinted about her indiscretions to me. As far as I knew, she and Angelo were happy as two mynahs in a peepul tree (I kid of course, there are no mynahs or peepul trees in New York).

But unbeknownst to me at the time, his sad songs and droopy moustache had driven her to seek joy elsewhere. Across the stage (metaphorically) from fret board to keyboard, directly into David's ivory-tickling hands.

No great surprise there. I would have done the same.

◆

But I could only surmise all of this in retrospect. Blame it on the wine if you will, but things might have been a lot different had Christine not played things so close to the chest.

Or if David wasn't such a two-timing toad who, without the shackles of fiancé, wife, mother-in-law, etc., in Arizona, had seized the opportunity for a little pre-bachelor party. With me.

I didn't mind at all. David was very cute. He played the piano beautifully too. He'd been flirting with me for weeks during rehearsals. In hindsight, I ought to have noticed that he only flirted with me when Christine wasn't around, but I've never been too observant.

He continued putting the moves on me on the plane ride from New York to Arizona, making it very clear that we would be sharing bodily fluids. We were after all two consenting adults, I didn't object. On the contrary, I encouraged. And it was well worth it.

◆

On our way back to New York, David made an odd request.

'Let's not talk about our, ahem, encounter, with anyone,' he said. 'Let this be between us.'

'Why?' I wondered. 'Everyone in the band already knows about us David, who am I supposed to keep it from?'

'Please?' he said without giving me a proper answer.

'Ok,' I agreed, but I had no intention of keeping anything to myself. I have never been able to and I wasn't about to start then. Secrets were never ever safe with me.

What was the use of having great sex if you couldn't blab about it to a few people? What was the point of not being able to relive the whole thing, doubling the pleasure with a little flourish here and a little embellishment there?

So having bragged about David to my main BFF at the time, a Swedish girl named Shas with whom I worked in a travel company, zipping all over the globe, I felt the need to share a little more, prolong the sensation a little.

Christine was my second choice. A huge mistake, I realised a little too late.

Through her tears, Christine told me that she and David planned to 'come out' of the bedroom to reveal the truth to Angelo as gently as they could, before embarking on a lilting life of mutual bliss. That was the plan. The plan that would never see the light of day because I went and ate the forbidden fruit, or put more accurately, allowed it to eat me.

She was crushed. And I knew that the moment she got her hands around his neck, she'd crush David. As for me, I lost both a friend and a lover at one go.

Once more with feeling, I said to myself sadly.

I was familiar with this sort of tragic loss. Years ago, when I had first begun my discovery of man, I had optimistically tried dating three men at one go. It was delightful while it lasted. But on that occasion too, it didn't take very long for my depravity to be exposed.

The sister of one of the men I was dating discovered my triple cross, and in a spiteful slash, had informed each one about what I was doing. In one whoosh of the magic wand, all of them vanished.

I ought to have learned right then that hell hath no fury like a woman scorned, or something to that effect, but I hadn't picked up a thing, obviously.

I tried to analyse what went wrong.

Why was it that when it came to me, the universe's zeitgeist was acting more like a malevolent poltergeist?

All I wanted was a man. More than half the world was filled with them. Was it too much to ask for a sexy man? A funny man. A man without strange kinks and weird habits. A man with an average-sized appendage (not too big, not too small, just right) and a voice that didn't squeak. It wouldn't hurt if he had a movie star's looks and some spare change to spend on me. I was also hoping that this man would not have a wife and kids tucked away somewhere, waiting to make a noisy appearance after the 'I do,' when it was too late to say, 'Why me?'

♦

I clung to the straps of the A Train, which runs from Queens through Manhattan, 'all the way to Sugar Hill way up in Harlem,' as the song goes, but by no means is the smoothest of rides.

It is no Shinkansen (Bullet Train) in Tokyo or even the MRT in Singapore. Modern, sophisticated trains that respect the fact that people like to select whom they want to rub-up against.

The A Train on the other hand, cool as it is, swings this way and that, carelessly flinging its passengers onto one another, without a care to personal space.

I was being repeatedly flung onto Jacques DeVillier, a cravat-wearing Pierce Brosnan clone. But after the fourth, 'Oh pardonnez-moi,' instead of glaring at me rudely or moving away to another spot, he had asked me to dinner.

'Mais oui,' I had agreed without hesitation. He was very handsome.

Fate loved me.

One sake led to another. Between mouthfuls of very expensive sushi, the conversation flowed. Love grew. And something about my coruscating personality must have prompted him to ask, in what can only be described as utterly French, 'Weeeell you marrrreee me?'

I was taken aback at first. Handsome as he was, he was also a guy I'd just bumped into. My, 'Oh pardonnez-mois,' could have been met with a few, 'Pas de problem,' and that could have been that.

But it was as though the gods had shaken off their torpor to speak directly and clearly to me, 'enfin l'élu,' (he's the one).

Why the heck not, I debated in my head. I did that often. Talked and argued with myself. I always won.

This was turning out to be a Mills & Boon romance. The kind I loved reading so much back in my high school days in India, literature that had moulded my very life. (For those not in the know, these are books of love, romance, heartbreak and ultimate salvation. There are several veins or themes that these delightful books adopt. There are doctors/nurses who find love against all odds. Millionaires/secretaries. Arab sheikhs/visiting English nannies. Widowed counts/scullery maids—well, that might have been Georgette Heyer come to think of it, but you get the drift.)

Jacques had revealed between the uni and unagi that he lived in Paris. He had been married once and quickly divorced. The lady in question had been more partial to the wine produced in every nook and cranny of his country than to him. She was an alcoholic. Besides she had brought three children to their etat unis and he didn't like the little buggers one bit. I smiled at that. I didn't think very much of children either. Little snotty screamers.

Jacques wanted to take me to France.

'You weeeeeel lovvvvve Pareeeeee,' he said pulling me close to him. By that time, the waiters in the Japanese restaurant were staring at us with samurai swords in their eyes. We had been there for hours, revealing our lives to each other, getting drunk and more boisterous with each cupful of sake. It was way past their closing time.

'I think we'd better leave,' I said to Jacques darkly, 'before they force us to slice open our own bellies on the sidewalk.'

He laughed uproariously at that, 'You arrrrrre funnnneeeeeeee,' he said. 'But I am serious, ma cherie,' he continued, 'you are zee woman I 'aff been waiting for all my life. I have found zee laaadeee of my dreams. Weeeell you marrrreee me?'

I couldn't believe what I was hearing.

◆

At that point in my internal deliberations there was a loud interruption. My egos were talking to each other. The main and alter.

M Ego: Kick him in the shin and run out of there because he's a psycho killer and has a few grains of ricin in his pocket, just for you, you slut.

A Ego: Oh shut up. It's not like all the people you thought you knew so well ended up as shining examples of manhood. Where are they now? Huh? Huh? Huh? Who's waiting at home for you? Even your plants are dead.

M Ego: You can't speak French. That's all they speak in France. And if his accent sounds sexy, it could be because of the six sakes. You have no idea how you're going to feel about the French accent before coffee in the morning. And you thought the violin was painful. Put it in perspective. (The ME was referring to an old boyfriend who played the violin all day and all night long. It's true that at the beginning of our romance, I couldn't get enough of its tinkly trill, but towards the end, the self-same strings and bow sent shards of poison-tipped glass through my brain.)

A Ego: Hey! You can hang around the Latin Quarter, singing jazz. A la Edith Piaf. That's one way to learn French.

M Ego: You'll have a bunch of little Indo-French kids crying, 'Maman, maman, j'ai faim,' and you'll spend your life riding up and down the city on a bicycle hunting for French bread. There won't be any singing.

Jacques, who didn't look impatient at all while all this nasty stuff was going on in my head, right in front of him, asked me again, 'Cherie, will you marrryyyyy meeee?'

I took a deep breath, 'Why the hell not,' I said to myself. The A Ego had won the battle. 'Yes Jacques,' I said. 'I'll marry you.'

Chapter 2

BON VOYAGE

We didn't exactly run out to a gaily festooned, neon-lit chapel, clutching a couple of hundred bucks, so we could be united in holy matrimony by an Elvis look-alike.

This was not Las Vegas where such things happened. It was only New York.

The laws were different. New York laws lacked a sense of humour, that quirky impetuousness that romance required. You had to get a license in person (both parties, no proxies) at the Office of the City Clerk, and then wait twenty-four hours before you could legally be married.

You also had to provide all sorts of proof about who you were and how many times you had been married before.

This wasn't a problem for me. I probably wouldn't have been hunting men down so ferociously, the way I was, if I'd already had a taste of wedded bliss.

But Jacques, a man who had been through the mill, needed his divorce papers to convince New York City officials that his former Beaujolais-brimming bride no longer laid claim to his heart and purse, and would therefore have no objection to his repeating his folly. They didn't condone bigamy in New York.

Sadly (or maybe fortuitously), Jacques wasn't carrying a handy set of DDs (divorce documents) with him.

As he pointed out, the Metro in France pretty much stayed in a straight line and didn't toss people onto one another this way and that, so he hadn't anticipated bumping into someone as charming as moi, necessitating urgent legal documentation.

Aside from that, there was another problem.

He was headed back to France the next morning, tickets all booked and paid for. We couldn't get married even if he had all the paperwork.

So for the moment a pall of doom was settling on our nuptials.

My expression must have said it all. 'Cherie, all eeeeeeeeees not lossssssst,' he assured me. 'Eeet eeez not zee end. Onlaay ze beeegeeneeng. I will returrrrrn to Paree and send you a tickeeeeaiiiiit. You veeeeel veeeseeet meeee forr ayyy couple ovvv weeks and weee veeel make sweeeeet loooove. Zennn vee veeel get marrrrried.'

Jacques kissed me passionately on the sidewalk outside the entrance to the subway and his technique was exactly as I had hoped.

Masterful and confident. He took charge of my embouchure. No slobbering, no clanging of teeth, no smashing of noses. The kiss was never ending, waves of passion that surged and ebbed. He made my senses spin uncontrollably.

But my knees began to lock and the kiss had to end.

He also had a plane to catch. I had some sleep to catch up on. I still had a day job to go to, in the travel company, where 9 a.m. meant 9 a.m. and not 9.03 a.m. They docked you fifteen minutes of your hourly pay if you came in late. You couldn't make up for it by working fifteen minutes extra at the end of the day. Very unfair.

Jacques and I pulled apart reluctantly. He held my chin and looked deep into my eyes one last time before I watched him disappear in the direction of his hotel. The chasm between us grew bigger and bigger. Soon it would bridge the Atlantic Ocean.

Love and let go? Was that going to be the story of my life? Would I hear from him? Would he remember me in the morning? Was it a dream?

◆

But no. It was very real.

True to his word, Jacques kept up a steady stream of romantic correspondence for a few weeks and it ended in a flight ticket.

First Class. From New York to Paris. One way. No return, which meant he was very serious about marrying me. On Air France, of course. (Which some New Yorkers still referred to as Air Chance, because they lost people's luggage, skidded off runways and conducted themselves in a manner that wasn't very different from other airlines, but unfortunately, since their name rhymed with 'chance' they got stuck with the jokes.)

I didn't care. I'd have flown Air Outer Mongolia if that's what it took to get me into the arms of my amour. I'd soon be a 'Mrs' or 'Mme' if I wanted to be country-specific.

I was beside myself with excitement.

Of course, my friend Shas (Kirsten Bjornsson, whose first name was pronounced 'Sharstin', and which she had stylishly abbreviated to 'Shas') thought it was the dumbest thing she had ever heard.

'Marry a man you don't know at all? Based on what he says to you after six sakes? I mean, we're not even talking French wine! That's beyond stupid. You have sunk to new depths,' she stated, no mincing of words, no couching of contempt. 'If there was an abyss filled with morons and someone shone a light in there, you'd glow the brightest,' she analogised unnecessarily. 'A nuclear moron.'

'Big deal,' I said with a shrug. I didn't care. She rarely said nice things. It was a miracle we'd been friends for so long.

'I don't think you need to "know" a man before marrying him. You forget I come from India where it's forbidden completely to have any knowledge of the person you're about to marry. You're lucky if you get to see a photograph,' I said pompously, exaggerating for effect.

'Hrummmmmmpppphhhhh,' she snorted, flaring her nostrils like a prize-winning racehorse. 'Oh really? What about Vikram, Calvin, Monty, Aki, Martin, Peter, Arya, Mike, Dean, David,

Woody, Troy and the many others whose names I now no longer remember? And the ones you've most surely hidden from me, the real losers.'

Lamentably, I had given her an itemised laundry list of all the men who had ever entered my life (through my bed), so I could not posture elegantly (or chastely) with her now.

She was right in reminding me that my intentions had always been matrimonial in nature, as I gave myself freely and willingly, to one man after another in the hope of snagging a new last name.

The litany of names were of men I'd mostly had the displeasure of knowing, barring a few.

A DJ who wasn't in the least bit interested in what lay under my dress, ergo, I assumed he was gay. A drug dealer who definitely wasn't. A poet who was most certainly insane, a violin player who came perilously close to being 'the one', a lunatic businessman who spoke aloud to his body parts by way of foreplay, an engineer who was extraordinarily boring, a mathematician who was a total dish but already married (the louse), a philosopher who couldn't control himself, a professor who fell asleep in the middle of it all, a lawyer who wanted threesomes and foursomes which was alright in terms of having new experiences and all but whose apartment was way too filthy for me, a tattooed motorcycle man who was most likely a chain-saw killer and the last one, a piano player who had just agreed to marry my friend before having one last fling with me.

'Not one. Not even one,' said Shas with a sneer that suggested I was incapable of landing a man who would want to stick around, her eyes rolling and lips curling. If I was the type that understood insult and ridicule, I may have been offended. But I was usually oblivious to the signs around me.

'My point exactly,' I said smugly, ignoring her theatrics. 'That's what comes of "knowing", a man. I've run through all these men. Known them intimately. Some more than others. You don't see any of them pushing the baby carriage, do you now? So I'm pretty sure that the unknown is a far safer bet. I'm going to quit my job and move to Paris. You'll have to come visit me on the Champs-Élysées,' I said grandly. 'We'll do lunch on top of the Eiffel Tower.'

'I will not, and neither will you be so stupid even though it's hard for you,' she said firmly as if she was my boss. She wasn't my mother or even my aunt, two women who wielded considerable influence on my life when they chose to meddle.

I was acting all cocky because the mother was safely away in India where she had no knowledge about my day-to-day, and the aunt, while near enough on Long Island, had recently stopped asking for hourly updates, assuming, perhaps mistakenly, that I was now an adult.

Shas more than made up for the absence of both.

'You will ask for two weeks' vacation,' she ordained like a priest saying, 'Repent ye sinners.'

She continued, 'You will check out this Jacques the Ripper in Paris. You will find out if his apartment has a toilet and bathtub in the same room, preferably not in the kitchen. You will discover how disgusting bidets really are. You will meet his parents and find out if they're rich. Or old, feeble and drooling, waiting for an Indian nursemaid to wipe their chins and derrières. You'll know in a minute if they like you or not. Chances are they won't. You're not all fuzzy and cuddly you know, except around the middle. You will meet his friends and find out if they bore you out of your knickers, because they'll drone on and on in French, refusing to translate. Even though they speak English perfectly. And once you're through with all this, you'll come running back to New York in time for our next trip to Shanghai,' she predicted.

She was bringing me down to earth, reminding me of our next assignment. To ensure that about five hundred people arrived in Shanghai from different parts of the world for, 'Semi Con Carne: What's Hot In Semiconductors Today'.

That's what Shas and I did when we weren't chasing men. We

worked in the Department of Conventions and Exhibitions for a company that despatched men to China for various industrial soirées.

And once they'd uncovered the inner workings of the semi conductor industry (or steam engines, railway signals, airplane parts and so on), we were to ensure that they returned to where they came from. In the meantime, while they were in China, we would attend to their needs. Local transfers, sightseeing, hotel-related issues and so on. Hospitality services, that's what our company called it. We called it five hundred men and a couple of girls, far, far, far away from home, with no bosses and a company expense account.

Such excursions had lit up my life with joy and anticipation barely a few months ago. But après Jacques, they appeared mundane, so boring, so meaningless and so much a waste of my time.

But as always, Shas prevailed. Shas who spoke often about her far sightedness, her powers to peer into the future, her ability to predict what would happen with razor-sharp precision, especially when it came to me.

While her ESP had failed us on a couple of critical occasions, life and lock-up situations where I had accused her of being thud-brained, when it came to me and the men in my life, I had to duck. She almost always managed to hit the nail on the head with remarkable accuracy.

I agreed not to tell the mom, the aunt and other sundry people about my secret. I admitted that it was better not to kick up a maelstrom of negativity just yet.

'I'm off to Gay Paree on a two-week vacation,' I lied to them blithely. It was believable. People who work in travel agencies are entitled to a huge discount on airfares, often the hotel rooms are free.

Shas had the final word. 'I give you ten days to realise you hate Jacques and France equally,' she concluded. 'I wouldn't be surprised if you're back in twenty-four hours.'

Chapter 3

BREAKING BED

I was a little nervous as I boarded the flight to Paris. What if he wasn't there? What would I do? Was the wretch, Shas, right? Would I be back in less than a day? I sighed. I was arguing with myself a lot.

But I had nothing to be afraid of. Jacques would be waiting for me at CDG as he'd promised.

Being in the travel business, Shas and I had long stopped referring to places as Los Angeles and Hong Kong. It was so passé. We preferred using three-letter airline abbreviations such as LAX and HKG.

I discovered that Madras (now Chennai), the city of my birth, was MAA and not MAD, that honour had been bestowed on Madrid. Maybe Madrid got their airport before Madras. Who knows? I didn't like it. It made my city sound like a bleating goat. And despite the fact that Peking was now Beijing, the airline code was still PEK. If you stupidly said BEI to the ticketing agent at the airport, you'd end up in Beica, Ethiopia, which may have been a nice enough place as places go, but not to the point at all.

Speaking in TLA (three-letter abbreviations) increased our coolness quotient considerably. Especially with people who didn't know WTF we were talking about.

I was babbling (in my head) because I was excited. And nervous. And scared. I was entering Chapter Two in the saga of my life and things weren't clear at all. Not to mention I didn't know a soul in Paree except Jacques.

I spotted him. Jacques wasn't wearing either a cravat or beret.

I guess there's no need to prove Frenchness if you're already in France. Doesn't impress a soul.

But he was wearing tight blue jeans and a white T-Shirt through which I could see his body, and it was extremely sexy. He was still every bit as handsome as Pierce Brosnan, even without the benefit of sake-tinted glasses. He was also carrying a ton of red balloons. My heart soared. How could life be anything but fantastique with such a hunk?

I clung to him as we walked out to the parking lot, wondering what fancy car he'd be driving.

I did a small double take. Jacques had a modest red Peugeot 205. There were a few dents and dings both in the front and the rear. My soaring heart sank a little. Like hitting turbulence in an airplane. My heart had been subject to plenty of these up and down acrobatics in the past few years, and I hoped if nothing else, its muscles were getting strong.

What kind of an idiot would dream about a Frenchman in a BMW or a Benz? Look at his pecs, I told myself. Don't worry about his car. At least he has one. It's better than the subway, err, the metro.

We drove to his apartment in Quartier du Marais, an old and historic, chic section of Paris, right within the city itself. It was no ordinary drive and it remains a miracle that I am still alive to tell this tale.

According to my research, it would take anywhere from one hour to one and a half hours to make the journey. Jacques got us there in fifty minutes flat.

At first, while we were still on the highway, Jacques drove masterfully fast but within the limits of the law. (I learned later that it was because the gendarmes—French for cops—had installed radar traps to catch speeding Frenchmen so they could escort them to prison, which incidentally is the same word in English and French. Except in French you'd probably say 'preeeh-zohhnn'.)

I looked around the whizzing scenery to catch sight of familiar landmarks I'd read about and seen in the movies.

But all too soon we reached the city itself and then his driving became insane. I had no idea that French drivers were among the rashest, rudest and most dangerous drivers in all of Europe. I also wasn't aware that the French government gleefully collected tons of money in traffic fines, just because its citizens drove so badly.

Had I known, I would have most certainly taken a taxi. But as it was, I clutched desperately to my life's as yet unfulfilled hopes as Jacques laid bare his driving skills and road etiquette.

'Can't we slow down,' I begged as the contents of my stomach came dangerously close to being disgorged onto his dashboard. My stomach has always been delicate and it takes very little for me to upchuck. The sight of someone eating a banana with his mouth open, the sound of someone vomiting, reading in the backseat of a car… The list is endless.

He just smiled raffishly and patted my knee. 'Relax, ma cherie,' he said soothingly as he stepped on the gas. The light had just turned orange. Normally a signal that one should slow down. But despite his vroom, we missed the orange and squeaked through the red light, almost slamming into a few pedestrians legally ambling across the stripes. Jacques screamed at them to hurry up.

If that wasn't enough, he stuck his middle finger out at people who overtook him (the ones with fancier cars), leaned out and yelled at bicyclists who annoyed him and if not for the steel posts placed strategically at intervals on the sidewalks, preventing Jacques from mowing down baby carriages, the sick and the elderly in wheelchairs, we would have left a bloody pile of road kill all over Paris in our wake.

To tell you the truth, if I hadn't been so terrorised by this behaviour, I may have savoured the nostalgia, the familiar feeling that overcame me as I sat in his car, awaiting certain death.

It felt so much like India, and Jacques was behaving exactly as any normal, curry-blooded Indian in Mumbai or Bangalore would, with murder in his heart and a steering wheel in his hand.

The buildings, roads and trees; the scenery of Paris went by in a blur as I turned once again, as I always did when all else failed, to the myriad Indian gods and goddesses, especially the ones with multiple hands and heads, to keep me alive and in one piece.

◆

One of the main reasons I was in France was to get some serious experience at La Petit Mort, which is the French metaphor for the orgasm. It translates literally to 'the little death'. The idiom alludes to the release of oxytocin in the brain once the deed is done and the feeling of spiritual aloofness that follows orgasm. The French are darkly poetic about everything. Very Françoise Sagan.

I was praying that my Indian gods understood that 'mort' was only a figure of speech, poetic license so to speak, and not to be taken literally. I wondered if Indian and French gods ever chatted with each other.

Happily for me they did.

It must have been their quid pro quo, because soon we found ourselves in his neighbourhood, still alive.

The street where he lived had storefronts, cafés and bars at eye level and people lived in the apartments above. Very civilised. Similar to many areas of New York City, especially the avenues on the Upper West Side.

We finally found a parking spot, and I stumbled out of the car, shaken and stirred, unsure if I could stand at all. My hair was a mess. Most of my mascara was on my cheek and all my lipstick on my chin. Jacques took me in his arms as if I was a freshly powdered princess and kissed me intensely and fervently right under the noses of his neighbours in the apartments above. It was as if he was picking up where our kiss had left off on the streets of New York.

Parisians passing by smiled appreciatively, unlike New Yorkers who will ignore you completely, or glare if they're loveless themselves. They don't care a centime for young love in New York.

We went directly to his bedroom, leaving a trail of luggage, handbags, shoes, bra, blouse, white T-Shirt, blue jeans, sexy briefs and so on all the way from the front door. Passion in Paree. We fell on his bed, finally naked, and got down to business. Loud and satisfying business that included several petit morts. Somewhere around my eighth PM, I heard a faint creak.

I didn't pay much attention to it. I wasn't up on French sounds yet, so there was no point in getting frazzled.

'Focus,' I told myself sternly. I didn't want a repeat of the Woody incident.

On that occasion, in case you missed the prequel, I was on Woody's undulating waterbed, trying hard to concentrate on his tender ministrations so I could reach nirvana (I didn't know French back then). It was extremely difficult. I was constantly being brought back to earth by the sights and sounds of small furry animals that darted hither and thither on the floor in-between the debris from Woody's day-to-day life which consisted of left over food, clothes, drink, packaging, newspaper and dust. His house was filthy and dirty.

Unfortunately for Woody, the sneeze that I had been trying to control for about ten minutes, finally erupted from the bottom of my soul, which at that moment was hovering between my legs. And as I sneezed, I involuntarily contracted all the muscles in my body at the same time that Woody was about to touch the stars.

Poor Woody! The only stars he saw were the ones in his eyes as I almost broke off his you-know-what. I had been doing my Kegels religiously, so I was pretty firm and strong down there.

But back to the present, I wasn't thinking about Woody at all. I was having too much fun. Like M&Ms, you can't stop at just one PM and I wanted to try and set a world record. Maybe a dozen. A baker's dozen.

'Creeeeeeeeaaaaaak,' came the sound again. It was louder and more insistent and it was under the bed. Very close by.

'Deeeed you 'earrrrrr zaaaaat?' he asked, pulling apart from me.

Ah. I was right. There was a sound, I said to myself. Was it an earthquake? I'd been in an earthquake once, when I was about seven or eight in Mumbai. I was fast asleep when everything around me started creaking and groaning and shaking. The mom and dad had grabbed the brother and me and we'd run out of our apartment into the car. I never understood why the dad felt it would be safer to drive around the city as it rattled and rolled, but he was right. When we came back home, after the shaking had stopped, we were safe and sound, with life and limb intact, while our balcony had fallen down to the ground and the bathroom was in shambles. I thought it was pretty cool at the time. But now, older and wiser, the memory scared me.

'I hope it's not an earthquake,' I said nervously, as I sat up in bed.

'Mais non,' he said reassuringly. 'We nevvvvvvverrrr get 'errrsssssquakkes in Paree… ma ch…' Even before he completed his sentence, the bed that could have been immortalised by a world record came crashing to the floor, the centreboard cracking apart, the legs splaying and splintering. The headboard went toppling off to one side, smashing the pretty table lamp that stood on a bed stand. We landed on the floor, fortunately on top of the firm and springy mattress, which protected our delicates from being sliced up into slivers. We could have spent days hunting for little pieces.

We looked at each other, eyes crinkled.

Ah the infamous French Bed. This was not the first time I'd been exposed to comi-cruelty.

Back at St Luke's, the convent school I'd been banished to as a young child, I'd been introduced to the French Bed shortly after my incarceration.

One night, after lights out when we had all modestly switched from school uniform to PJs in the dark, after we were done with kneeling on the cold stone floor to pray for sins we would soon be committing, I kicked off my slippers and sat on my bed, ready to say nightie-night to the day. I swung my feet over into the neatly folded blanket-and-sheet ensemble that I had created myself earlier that morning. That's how it was in St Ls. You learned how to do everything yourself. It was their way of churning out self-sufficient human beings. No servants and no nannies to ease the mindless burden of daily grind.

Normally my feet would slide down to the bottom of the bed and my toes would tickle the tucked-in corners of the blanket, all warm and toasty. My legs and torso would soon follow and then my pretty little head would be nestled in the contours of my some what hard pillow, while I awaited the call, 'lights-out'.

Normally.

But on that fateful night, the more I tried to push my feet down to the bottom of the bed, the more nothing would give. I kept pushing and shoving, shoving and pushing, and very soon had worked up quite a sweat. Finally, I screamed in frustration as my feet ripped right through the bed sheet.

It takes superhuman strength to rip through the three hundred-thread count Egyptian cotton that my mother had lovingly purchased for me. We, of the high thread count lineage.

Of course, the girls in the dormitory, all fifty of them cackled and hooted as if it was the funniest thing on earth.

I realised I'd been had. It was a right of passage. An initiation. My welcome to boarding school.

It was a simple and effective gag.

Here's how it worked. After laying down the under sheet and tucking in the corners envelope-style around the bed (they make beds this way in the military too), you laid the top sheet down and folded it back up halfway. You laid the blanket over the sheet folded in half and made the rest of the bed in the regular way. The bed would pass inspection by the most eagle-eyed drill sergeant.

It's only when you actually tried to get into bed that you realised it wasn't possible.

The French Bed ranked right up there with chewing gum in the hair and toothpaste in the shoe.

I related the bed incident (not the Woody one, which may have put a damper on our love life) to Jacques. We burst into laughter and didn't stop laughing for ten minutes. It was a great way to inaugurate our love life, I thought. What a tale to tell Shas. 'He made love to me till the bed broke.'

Chapter 4

I LOVE PARIS IN THE SPRINGTIME

'Zzzerrrre eeeeez no bed zaaattt can 'aaaandelll our paasssssion,' declared Jacques. We agreed it would be safer to continue our romps on the mattress itself, which was now directly on the floor. No chance of any mishap, unless the floor itself fell through.

It was a possibility, since I was in France.

I was reminded of Chief Vitalstatistix (Abraracourcix in French, meaning, with arms up ready to fight), a French cartoon character who constantly worried about the sky falling on his head. Maybe one acquired strange phobias when one was in France.

I brushed silliness aside and settled into a routine. I was here to get used to France and all its oddities. There was no time for paranoia.

Jacques went off to work in the morning, to find out all about nuclear energy and how it was going to enhance the lives of the French. He would come back in the evening and take me out to restaurants, jazz clubs. He'd introduce me to his friends. He did all he could to integrate me into his life.

It was new. It was fun. Sort of.

Once or twice he had said, 'I will be late ziss eveneeeng. I 'ave to see zee lawwyeahhhr.' I didn't really pry. I assumed it had to do with the safekeeping or promotion of nuclear energy. Such things couldn't be left carelessly on one's desk, I imagined. They had to be locked up in legalese before being stuffed into in bank vaults.

His friends were nice. But none of them spoke English very well and they would often launch into lengthy conversations amongst themselves without realising I didn't understand a thing. It is also true that even if they'd been speaking in English, I probably wouldn't have caught more than the barest of gists, since they mostly spoke about heavy water, rods, mass-energy equivalence and other topics that floated way over my head like the water vapour you see coming out of the cooling towers in a nuclear power plant.

Every once in a while, they'd stop to try and translate, but it wasn't fun. Not for them and not for me. I felt pretty dumb. It was frustrating not to be able to show off my sparking wit and cynicism. My allegory and alliteration. My vocabulary and idiom. 'Please, thank you, I'm sorry, where's the loo and pass the butter,' hardly showcased my intelligence.

Jacques didn't know any musicians or fashion designers.

I guess I could have gone job hunting, or even friend-hunting but Jacques wasn't keen on it.

'You can looooooooook forrrrr a zhobbbb laterrrr,' he said kindly. 'I veeeeel take carrrrre of youuuuu. Zerrr is sommmesiing I am waittinggg forrr. Weee villll tallllk of eeett laterrrr.'

He was being sweet.

Or careful.

Maybe he didn't want me to get too comfortable in France. I'd have to get a working permit anyhow. This would take time. It wasn't like old US of A where any old immigrant, legal or illegal, found easy employment.

So I focussed on my nesting instincts.

I remembered that when I'd moved into Aki's apartment (he almost became 'the one'), I was filled with a sense of purpose and resolve. I had wanted to redecorate every square inch with my personality and stamp every available surface with my mark, as quickly as I could. Peeing on the tree, so to speak. And all the branches too.

Jacques had a living room, a small kitchen, a bedroom and yes; the shower and toilet were miles apart. It was a little disgusting. At least the toilet wasn't in the kitchen, I comforted myself.

I poked around waiting for inspiration to strike. Where were the visions of tulle, lamé and jacquard in shades of ecru with aubergine accents hiding?

'Give yourself time,' I said to myself. He was so fabulous.

But nothing happened. I didn't even feel like dusting.

So I decided to do some exploring on my own. The Paris Metro is pretty clearly marked and it's hard to get lost. As long as you know which direction you're headed, you can get from point A to point B and back to point A again.

But it was no fun sightseeing all alone. Unlike New York where everyone speaks English, or at least tries to, so you can strike up friendship with a total stranger 'sans souci' (without worry), in Paris, you have to speak French. People will refuse to speak to you in English, even if they know eeet verrrrrryyyyy welllll.

I wondered why.

And then I found that it was an old feud, a Montague and Capulet kind of ancient insult. The story goes that Charles de Gaulle, the famous French General, was trying very hard, right after World War II not to look like a puppet of his allies Roosevelt and Churchill (English speakers both), while they set about re-creating the world as we know it today.

They didn't give a fig about CDG and took to dissing him routinely, without a care. It may not have mattered if they were just two blokes on the street corner gossiping about a third chap, but they weren't just blokes.

They were heads of state. And being heads of state, their every word was faithfully reported in the world press.

CDG took umbrage that his name was being maligned and his reputation eroded.

'Damn and blast the English, even if they rescued us from the Germans,' he would have said to his aides. 'We will not speak their language here in this country. Not a word. Never. Anglais est terminé.' And with that English was banned, unofficially, from France.

The tone he set back then remains to this very day, even if no one in France can remember why it is that they hate English so much and won't speak it. The fact is that they just won't.

The few that relent and speak English, cling to their French accent so dearly that they may as well be speaking French. It's a dreadful imposition on the ears of non-French speaking people.

It is another story that almost seventy years later, one Nicolas Sarkozy (not a true Frenchman, but one of Hungarian origin) realised that CDGs peevish attitude had bred a nation of language-deficient citizens who couldn't get jobs outside France. He began a movement to push English, the language of Shakespeare, down the throats of its people, as early as age three. Naturally, he was met with plenty of French resistance.

◆

While all this history was creating a din in my head, I came to the sad realisation that my understanding of the language was mostly restricted to 'ala carte' and 'Chateau Neuf de Pape', and lingerie, and of course, 'la petit mort'. Important words that had to do with food, drink, clothing and sex, but a lexicon that was pretty useless in casual conversation.

Riding the Metro, ambling in and out of museums and cafes, strolling along the Champs-Élysées all by my lonesome, was pitiful. There was no one with whom to share the occasional 'oooh', or 'aaah', or even, 'ewww'. Enough to make a girl's heart weep in sorrow. Bonjour tristesse.

I felt like an unwanted visitor. An alien.

I tried exploring my immediate surroundings. J's apartment. I went through his closets and cupboards, cabinets and even under the counters. I'm not sure what I was hoping to find, but it definitely wasn't there. No fun and excitement, no glamour and mystery.

He had books, clothes, very little in the way of interior décor but a nicely stocked liquor cabinet, which I found pleasing.

I'd wait eagerly for Jacques to come home every day just to have someone to talk to. Even though his accent, as the irritating Shas correctly predicted, was beginning to grate. On the plus, the sex was excellent.

Cole Porter had certainly led me up the garden path with his song, 'I Love Paris'.

Every time I look down on this timeless town
Whether blue or gray be her skies
Whether loud be her cheers or soft be her tears
More and more do I realize
I love Paris in the springtime
I love Paris in the fall
I love Paris in the winter when it drizzles
I love Paris in the summer when it sizzles
I love Paris every moment
Every moment of the year
I love Paris, why, oh why do I love Paris?
Because my love is near.

Utter bunkum. Songwriters will say anything to make a buck.

◆

While I strolled the banks of the Seine and came home to be ravished by Jacques, I noticed a subtle but definite change in his behaviour. He was beginning to look dejected.

Finally, one evening he asked, 'We weel go to my fazzzzzer's appartmonnn?' It was a request.

The French usually don't ask, they declare, and merely by turning the inflection up at the end, assume you'll understand it's a polite request and not a, 'you'd better come along to my father's apartment with me when I say so or else.' You get the hang of it after a while, and it ceases to sound rude. Besides he sounded distraught.

It was a surprise.

It was the first time I'd heard of the father or the apartment. Odd, coming from a man who wanted to share the rest of his life with me.

All I'd heard in terms of his ancestry until that point was that he had no siblings and that his parents had passed on. He had elaborated a little about his contempt for the alcoholic wife with the nasty temperament and children to match. Other than that I knew nothing.

To be fair, I hadn't rattled on about my family back in India either. I somehow assumed that the French didn't care about aunts and uncles and cousins and soon and so forth, the way we did back in India where families never ended. Cousins, second cousins, fifth cousins, their husbands, their siblings, everyone was considered a close relative.

'Sure,' I agreed. It's not as if I had something pressing to attend to. 'What are we going to do there?'

Jacques sighed sadly.

He explained that this could be his last and final visit to the apartment, the one he had grown up in. He wanted to pick up a photograph of his mother. While he still had the chance. Maybe a few other knick-knacks.

The story tumbled out.

The sad saga of what happens to a man who pays more attention to nuclear energy than to his father.

◆

Jacques' mother had passed on some years earlier and his father had finally exhaled his last breath only a few months earlier (just before we'd met) in an assisted care facility, where his memory had finally vanished completely into thin air on account of Alzheimer's.

But that was not the problem.

It was his fortune. Roughly a million US dollars distributed across various negotiable instruments and a three-bedroom apartment (each with its own toilet and shower in the same room) in the heart of Paris, had also gone, 'pouf', on account of a beautiful young lady named Veronique.

◆

Jacques' father Thierry and his mother Giselle had lived in comfort and elegance on Rue St Martin, back in the day, when Giselle was still hale and hearty and Thierry was at the top of his profession. He headed up circulation for Le Monde, a popular evening newspaper. Thierry travelled the length and breadth of the country, ensuring that every little roadside kiosk and bookstore carried his beloved paper, leaving Jacques and his mother alone for long stretches. When he eventually came home, he was usually brusque and short-tempered.

A man on the road gets used to his solitude.

Jacques did not like his father very much.

His mother was the glue that had kept the family together.

When Giselle had first taken ill, she had been sent to the hospital where they tried to drive out the cancer with several rounds of chemo and radiation and surgery, but eventually the dreaded disease came back. There was nothing more the doctors could do, so she was sent home to await the inevitable.

It broke Jacques' heart since he was very fond of his mother. 'She wouldddddd luhhhhvvvvve youuu ma cherrrieeeee,' he told me. I doubted it. I was not the 'lovable' kind and parents, even my own, had a hard time with my antics.

Thierry and Jacques had taken care of her as best as they could, till she finally gave up the fight. It was a sad time for both of them and for a while it looked as though her death had actually brought the men close.

In the days immediately following her death, Jacques would visit Thierry often. But soon, the visits dwindled down to once a week, then trickled down to once a month, finally settling to a couple of times a year, usually at Christmas and on birthdays.

He had noticed that his father was forgetful, but put it down to senility and left it at that.

◆

Enter Veronique.

Every single day, the lovely Veronique, age twenty-three would stroll up and down Rue St Martin in her short skirt and bouffant (a hairdo that will never go out of style), checking out her reflection in the storefront windows that lined the street, when she wasn't checking out the cars that slowed down for her, or the men that stopped to find out if they could afford her dazzling presence for an hour or two.

She stood out from the ruck of the other ladies of the street. For one thing, she didn't wait till the sun went down, she was just as happy to be prancing about in the morning or the afternoon. For another, she was enchanting, with large eyes, dark hair, long legs and an enormous bosom.

If all that didn't set her apart, then there was her little French poodle with its rhinestone collar and golden chain. It followed her everywhere. The little yipper had been trained to snap at the heels of hagglers and bargainers who tried to beat down her price whenever she shouted, 'bordelle a merde', which translates to, 'whorehouse of shit'. Some men just didn't appreciate that quality came at a price.

They were a familiar sight on the street, Veronique and her little chienne.

◆

The seventy-something, lonely Thierry found that life was a bore in the beautiful apartment on Rue St Martin, where no one was baking spinach quiche or making warm goat cheese salad with walnuts. Where the coq au vin wasn't simmering on the stove and the pâté wasn't getting nicely browned in the oven. Where no one would share a glass of cool Chardonnay in the summer or hearty

Bordeaux in the winter while watching television. He missed Giselle.

T's friends and relatives were either too old or already dead. There was just no one to talk to. Not even his only son and legal heir who, confident that the inheritance laws in France would not cut him off from what was rightfully his, was more or less counting the days to his father's funeral.

A cheap one, J had decided. He was sure Thierry had cheated on his beloved mother Giselle not once, but several times.

Thierry DeVillier, all alone and on the wrong side of seventy, with snowy white hair and a cane to steady his gait, would nod at Veronique gallantly, as only a Frenchman can. He may have been old and batty, but there was nothing wrong with his eyes. He knew a beautiful lady when he saw one.

Veronique, young as she was, had set no age limit for her customers so she tittered back coyly at him, wishing him Bon Jour and Bon Nuit, depending on where the sun was positioned at the time.

Thierry loved it.

He had begun carrying expensive little doggie treats for her pooch as an excuse to stop and chat. He loved the fact that Veronique had named her dog Vivi (which means 'penis' in French) and told her so. He still had enough 'man' in him to appreciate the naughty.

It wasn't long after, one morning, when Vivi had been fed his daily quota of Royal Canin, that Veronique admitted shyly to Thierry that she was actually falling in love with him. Even though they hadn't held hands or kissed and certainly hadn't made love. Even though she knew nothing about him. And despite their obvious age difference. It was his eyes and his fondness for the dog, she revealed, bending down to pat the pooch's head, giving Thierry a good look inside her generous cleavage. She had a little heart tattooed on the swell of her left breast.

That's all it took. Thierry was hooked.

♦

He was not to know that Veronique was no innocent streetwalker tempting the young buck or passing geriatric without discrimination, using her wiles and charm.

He was not to know that she was closely acquainted with one Mlle. Ondine, the very maid who came in every day to clean up his messes.

He was not to know that Ondine was betrothed to Etienne, Veronique's brother and also her pimp. There was no shame there. The money had to stay within the family.

He was not to know that it was Ondine who had cased the joint, as it were, and discovered the opportunity there, spilling the haricots to her boyfriend and his sister.

Thierry had no idea that he was being described as a terribly lonely old man with no one to take care of him. A man who needed to be avoided at all costs, under normal circumstances because he was a slob and tended to spill everything he ate and drank. A man who drooled and wasn't too careful with his aim in the toilet. It was hell to clean up after such a man and Ondine felt she would certainly go to heaven for all the penance she was accruing.

And he certainly didn't know that the trio was in cahoots to relieve him of the aforementioned million or so US dollars he had saved.

Ondine, who also brought in the mail every day, found plenty of time to go through it.

She had a pretty good idea of Thierry's financial assets. Jewellery, stocks, shares, bonds, cash and so on locked in a safe in the apartment, bolted down to the floor, with a combination lock. All one had to do was get the sequence of numbers out of him.

There was also the apartment itself, all paid for, free and clear from mortgage, with a lovely view of the garden downstairs. Who knew what else there was?

She knew there was a son somewhere in the picture, but the bastard almost never showed up. And when he did, it was only for a few minutes. Ondine had met him once. Nothing much to worry about, she assured Etienne and Veronique. He was a tad too good-looking to be dangerous. She was certain that in a hand-to-hand, Etienne would win.

Then there was the clincher. Thierry was forgetful. Getting more and more so. Alzheimer's without a doubt. Optimistically, Ondine gave him another two years to go, most likely less, she guessed.

She gleefully informed the pair that he had no idea if things went missing from his home. She had already filched a couple of antique silver picture frames, several Lalique crystal vases, some Lladro figurines, a couple of oil paintings and other bric-a-brac decorating the apartment. But she knew all this was peanuts compared to the real moolah Thierry had stashed away.

One needed a proper plan, and if the trio put their heads together, they could all be very rich and live happily ever after.

Chapter 5

OPERATION VERONIQUE

Thierry continued missing the toilet when he peed, drooling down his chin as he ate and increased the frequency of expensive doggie treats for Vivi. Meanwhile, Veronique, Ondine and Etienne got down to business.

The MO was simple.

Veronique would spin her magic web around Thierry so he would fall hopelessly and irrevocably in love with her. She would tempt and tease him until he could stand it no more. The three of them didn't believe it would take too long before he'd be 'de mastic' (putty) in her young but very experienced hands.

They had even planned the wedding march. She would cling to him like a limpet as he limped along to the registrar's office, Vivi by her side, to seal the deal with a wedding ring and a marriage certificate. Ondine and Etienne would be witnesses. Once Veronique had secured the rights to his estate, the trio would slowly but surely disengage from Thierry's yellowing life as he awaited his death.

It would be all daisies, sunshine and blue skies after that.

The clever trio also realised that using sex as bait, while a powerful and alluring tool, also had the potential of backfiring. The codger was old. If he couldn't perform to satisfaction (the little blue pills could only do so much) there was a chance he'd get frustrated and retreat.

So they worked out a Plan B.

Etienne would befriend Thierry and provide masculine companionship. Take the bugger out to play Pétanque when the weather was good; drink wine and cognac with him. Discuss politics, or plants or peregrines for that matter. Anything to keep him happy and occupied between the stomach churning sex that poor Veronique was stuck with. Everyone would share the responsibility equally.

Ondine would continue to wash and clean as she always had, without breathing a single word about her connection to the loving siblings who had miraculously entered old Thierry's life, just when he had given up all hope. When he had all but resigned himself to a fate in which his rotting corpse would be discovered by neighbours on account of the stench.

He was overjoyed.

He was also very much entrenched in what is known as the long con.

◆

The plan was tweaked and re-tweaked so that all possible contingencies were covered. Then the trio set about turning their plans into reality.

Veronique trilled and cooed. She batted her eyelashes and flashed her bosom at Thierry with renewed vigour. He, already feeble, was no match for her wiles.

So to no one's great surprise, in a matter of weeks, Veronique and Vivi had taken up residence at Rue St Martin in the former Mme Giselle DeVillier's home. Amidst her potted plants, her lace doilies, her pretty curtains and bric-a-brac collected over the years.

Dainty and delicate, classy and understated, it was an anathema to the louder and brassier Veronique who couldn't stand most of the stuff the old lady had collected.

Everything smelled of old biddy.

And she didn't see why Thierry's son Jacques needed a room anymore. He didn't visit and had no use for his rocking horse and toy trains, still lovingly preserved by his wistful maman. Perhaps hoping for a little grandson to hand it over to, never mind that little boys these days preferred video games.

Ruthlessly, Veronique tossed all of J's possessions either into the trash or sold it for cash. She turned his room into a studio where she pursued a newfound interest in painting. It was a pastime she had taken up now that she had the entire day to herself, there no longer being any need for her to pound the pavement.

Vivi was her favourite model.

The fortunate pooch, filled to the brim with designer doggie food, obligingly slept all day long, making it easy to paint him. There were several unfinished canvasses of Vivi around the room where he varyingly resembled a drowned rat, an opossum after a huge meal, a rabbit and other rodents and marsupials.

Veronique was no Cezanne or Rodin or even a Vigée Le Brun. (Louise Élisabeth Vigée Le Brun, whom you may not have heard of, but who was the talk of the town around the 18th century. She was the official painter of one Marie Antoinette, whom you most certainly would have come across.) She hadn't quite got the essence of the French poodle down to an art form.

Etienne became a regular visitor, staying often in the spare bedroom, which was always made up. Ondine would sneak in after Thierry's sleeping pills took effect and together they would polish off his wine before making whoopee.

The preying trio was circling Thierry's life as if he was already carrion.

◆

When she wasn't painting Vivi or attempting to make love to Thierry (which was a complicated and physically exhausting activity, because the poor man often forgot what he was doing right in the middle of doing it), Veronique went shopping.

Thierry's apparently limitless credit card was put to excellent use. She bought diamonds from Cartier, the latest fashions from the House of Dior and Chanel. Even a Swarovski crystal-encrusted collar for Vivi.

Thierry was ignorant of any of this. The credit card was linked to an auto-pay bank account that took care of everything.

He was also blissfully unaware that he had gifted Etienne an enormous television set and an expensive fishing tackle. Such was the unconditional nature of his love for Veronique. It made him blind. The A'heimer's helped a little too.

Ondine continued to take what she wanted from the apartment when the fancy struck and sold it as freely as if it was her own.

Jacques, who could have popped in for a visit to stop Act II, and then III and IV of this drama, just didn't bother.

The nuclear stuff took up all his energy.

All in all, the trio were at the very heart of the good times. Mostly.

Once in a while, following a particularly exhausting bout with Thierry, Veronique would curse and stomp after the codger had shuffled out of earshot or fallen off to sleep.

'You bastarrrrrrrrd,' she would say to her brother as if it was all his fault. 'Youuuu 'affff no ideeee how my mousssse achesssss. I am doing alllll ze worrrrk. You onleeey deeseerrvve a quarrrrrrter of zeee moneeeey.'

But the split was going three-ways. That's what they had decided. Veronique could do nothing to change it now, no matter how disgusting the task at hand (or anywhere else) grew. So she decided to take it out on Thierry's chequebook.

Her demands grew weirder and more fanciful with each passing day.

One particular object of her desire was something she had seen in a magazine. A pair of genuine, elephant leg bar stools, from an African elephant that would have undoubtedly preferred to have been trumpeting around Kenya, minding its own business.

Purchasing such things was highly illegal, but Veronique couldn't care less about the law. The lust-led Thierry agreed to procure the stools from a dealer of questionable repute, who claimed that the vintage items were purchased years ago from Africa, and had been in his family for at least one hundred years. He guaranteed they were one-of-a-kind. For $25,000, they were a real steal according to Veronique.

The legs received pride of place in the apartment, replacing the Louis XVI chairs with matching side tables that Jacques' mother Giselle had bought years ago. Ondine had located an antique shop that was most happy to cash them in for her.

On the plus side, with each well-deserved, valiantly-fought struggle to petit mort, Thierry fell more and more in love with Veronique.

'Weee musssst marrrreeee immediatement,' he declared.

◆

It was around this point in the relationship between Thierry and Veronique that Jacques decided to visit his dad. It had been more than a year since his last appearance. He had been travelling the globe chasing the twists and turns of nuclear energy, and his father wasn't topmost on his list of priorities. He had also just been through a divorce.

It's not as if Jacques had completely ignored him, a few token phone calls had been made and the old coot had seemed happy enough, he felt, so it was without a care in the world, whistling La Vie En Rose (France's favourite song), that Jacques rang the buzzer on the door to his father's apartment, the place he had once called home, in happier times when his maman was still alive.

He was met with the loud and shrill yipping of what sounded like a small dog, the kind he detested with a passion.

Maybe some old lady was visiting, he deduced. Old French ladies had a penchant for tiny animals. Poodles, Chihuahuas, even little turtles, although turtles didn't bark. Good for him, he thought. The bugger has a girlfriend. Well, why not?

Ondine, whom Jacques vaguely recognised, opened the door. But when he stepped into his familiar old home, the one where he had played with his choo-choo trains and marbles, learned how to go potty and so on, he got the shock of his life.

He could barely recognise it.

Gone were the familiar, subtle and elegant furniture and paintings, the tasteful, comforting, upper-crust stamp of his mother Giselle.

And in its place was a mish-mash of neo-plastic and African jungle.

Surveying the intruder at the door, draped across an ornate sofa, wearing the barest of skirts and a lot of make-up, was Veronique, smoking a cigarette through a long holder.

One of her feet was on the floor and the other was tickling Vivi in the neck. The dog continued barking. Veronique's red toenails did nothing to calm it down.

'Wherrrre is my fazzzzer, M. DeVillier?' asked Jacques, wondering if he had walked into the wrong apartment.

'I am Madame DeVillier,' said Veronique, in reply. 'Ooooo arrrrrre youuuu.'

At that point, Thierry DeVillier, perhaps recognising his son's voice, came out of the bedroom, dishevelled, eyeglasses askew, with claret-coloured lipstick smears around the crotch area of his trousers.

'Allo, allo,' he said happily. 'Viquie, c'est mon fils Jacques. Jacques c'est ta maman, Veronique.' He then clapped his hands gaily as his cane clattered to the floor. He looked like a little child with a new toy.

A lot of French flew back and forth. Between Jacques, his father, Etienne and Veronique. At the end, Jacques understood that the con artist brother and sister pair had taken his frail and fragile father for a very long, fun-filled, expensive ride that had put a crater-sized dent in his inheritance. He would have to do something about it right away, if there was to be anything left for him at all.

Just one glance at the baubles and beads on his new stepmother Veronique told him that at least a quarter mil had already gone. Even the cigarette holder looked expensive. And bloody hell if those weren't Swarovski crystals on the dog.

Could more than half a mil be gone already? How much did the bugger actually have?

◆

Jacques went out the very next day to consult a lawyer.

He wanted to find out if he could declare his father incompetent and prove that the woman claiming to be Mrs DeVilliers was a prostitute who had taken advantage of an old man. He was hoping the lawyer could establish that the brother and the maid had been in cahoots and that his father's state of mind, tenuous at best, was an easy target for the trio. Was it not? Was there anything he could do to get them out of his life? It wasn't over, was it?

He was met with a resounding, 'Non, non, non est non,' for each question.

Not only had the beautiful Veronique obtained the most legal of marriage certificates, to make doubly sure, she had also ensured that she had a written will, signed on all pages by Thierry himself, in a spidery quiver, in front of a 'notaire', whose signature is even more binding than your average American notary public. The documents declared that he, Thierry, being of sound mind and body (what a laugh, thought Jacques) was making Veronique his sole, legal heir.

To his son Jacques who had never bothered to visit, he had left a framed family portrait.

◆

The saga was far from over.

While Jacques was running from lawyer to lawyer, getting only the most negative of responses, digesting this chicanery as he discovering the depths of his father's duplicity (the man was fully capable of being a bastard with or without Alzheimer's), Veronique and Etienne quietly had Thierry admitted to an assisted-care facility.

The old man had become incontinent by then and completely forgetful. The French authorities agreed that only professionals could provide the sort of end-of-life care he needed. It would be the equivalent of geriatric abuse, to try and take care of him at home. And in any case, the government would be paying the bill.

So off Thierry went meekly, without protest. He had no idea what was going on. 'Zoo, zoo,' he is supposed to have said as he was loaded into the ambulance. No one knew if he was referring to a cat his wife Giselle once had named Zuzu, or if he thought he was being taken to the zoo (same word in English or French) for a visit.

Jacques switched lawyers, appealed to higher courts, threatened Veronique and Etienne with dire consequence and tried every trick in the book to win back his inheritance.

He even began visiting his father at the nursing home hoping to appeal to his sense of fair play and reason. But Thierry was too far gone by then to even remember his son, let alone wills, legal documents and so on. 'Zoo, zoo,' he would say and smile happily.

Jacques tried asking the doctors if there wasn't some 'memory shocker' shot he could be given (he'd seen something like that on CSI) but les docteurs assured him that such things worked once in a while for people in shock. It did not move the needle at all for Alzheimer's patients. Incidentally, didn't he know there was a big difference between television and real life?

Thierry couldn't remember Veronique either, which was a big reprieve for the lovely lady who had already found another boyfriend.

She stopped visiting her husband.

The hospice was a dreary place anyhow and there was nothing more she wanted from him. She had it all.

None of Jacques' legal efforts at winning the case worked. And not having any connections with the underworld, he wasn't able to have the trio whacked. It was all too late. And as if to prove it, Thierry gave up his ghost one fine afternoon, on Jacques' mother Giselle's birthday.

The lovely Veronique and her dog Vivi, her brother Etienne and his girlfriend Ondine didn't bother with funeral arrangements even though 'Viquie' was his legal widow, with a jangly chunk of change (including a bejewelled hatpin worn by Jacques' mother) to prove it.

So Jacques paid for a modest cremation (the cheapest kind of funeral) that no one attended. At the end of it, he was handed an urn filled with his father's ashes. He put this in the trunk of his car, intending to toss it into the Seine when he got around to it but for some reason, just hadn't found the time.

◆

I was brought back to the present with only one terrifying thought. Was Thierry being flung this way and that along with my luggage as we drove home from the airport? Was he airtight?

I didn't have too much time to ponder, as J wanted me to hurry up. We had to get to Thierry's apartment. Veronique had allowed Jacques one last visit to pick up any items of a personal nature that she didn't want.

Jacques had been such an eloquent storyteller that I could clearly visualise the elephant leg stools, Veronique and Vivi, her pooch. I felt I was in a Woody Allen movie.

I was right.

Veronique, every bit as breathtaking as I had imagined, opened the door in her high heels with the shrill Vivi at her feet. I stepped behind Jacques, for protection.

The apartment itself was lovely. Moonlight streamed in and you could see trees here and there. I might have had a nice life in there with a few Indo-French enfants, were things a little different.

I stopped daydreaming. The elephant leg stools stood there incongruously, amidst a pile of packing boxes, a reminder of what was never going to be.

Veronique had sold the apartment to a rich American, and she was moving to Rio de Janeiro with her new boyfriend. Ondine and Etienne were moving to Provence, where they were opening a bed-and-breakfast.

Jacques and I hastily went through the rooms scavenging for anything salvageable, but there was precious little. He picked up the framed photograph willed to him by his father's hand and off we went into the dark, French night in search of a nice bar where we could drown his sorrows.

I was beginning to get spooked by the whole thing. I saw a few moist droplets trickle down the corner of Jacques' eye. This I found disturbing.

For a fellow who didn't care a centime about his father while he was alive, he certainly exhibited a lot of passion and grief after his death. What was he weeping about? Lost treasures? Lost opportunity? What about his father's ashes that were being smashed around the trunk of his car as he drove maniacally through the arrondissements of Paris? What kind of a man would do that? What would he do to me if I got ill? Shove me off La Tour Eiffel? Dump my remains dans la poubelle (the garbage can)?

The way I saw it, Thierry was very lucky to have met Veronique. His dying months were spent in the mouth of a woman prepared to make him happy, even if it took her two hours of hard labour each time the birds met the bees.

That deserved its righteous reward. Any court of law could see that.

'Liiiiiiifee eeeeeeees like zaaaaaat,' I said to Jacques philosophically, once we had sat down at the bar.

Rather than agreeing with me pragmatically, he burst into

tears. It was very embarrassing.

To be trapped in a bar in France with a sobbing Frenchman, unable to explain what the ruckus was all about in the local language, has got to be one of the worst situations one can find one's self in. People were staring at me as if I was the villain. There wasn't a thing I could say or do. I patted his head like he was a puppy. The way I imagined Veronique would have patted Vivi's yappy head.

It didn't do the trick. If anything, his sobbing became more uncontrollable.

And in that moment, while Jacques was being consumed by utter despair, as all hope of inheriting his father's wealth had departed with a wag of French tail and he faced endless years of dreary nuclear energy, making it possibly one of the most pathetic points in his life, I realised he was not the one for me.

I liked successful people with joy ahead of them.

I didn't want his enfants.

Or the sound of his ablutions du jour.

France wasn't the place I was going to spend the rest of my life, despite the fineness of its wine, oysters, caviar and cheese.

Chapter 6

NEW YORK, NEW YORK

Once I'd made up my mind (which took a split second) it didn't take too long for me to disengage. I'm good at that. It unnerved me a little to think about how dangerously close I had come to infusing my offspring with Jacques' genes. It would not have ended well.

If I'm to be honest, I think J was equally relieved to be rid of me.

My whining about the French language had amplified at roughly the same rate as his stock of liquor was depleting. He had a bed to replace. Not cheap. The fortune he had expected (which may have kept me in good humour and his liquor supply refreshed) had vanished. All in all, he knew he needed to seriously re-evaluate his life.

He swallowed a couple of times as he handed me an economy flight ticket to go back. It must have been embarrassing. He had been blowing up money he didn't have.

I said adieu as sorrowfully as I could. He kissed me probingly. His French-kissing was above average. I wondered if all French men kissed like that. 'Stop it silly,' I said to myself, with an imaginary thwack to my head. 'That's as idiotic as saying all Indians are non-violent, Kamasutra experts.' I lingered a second in the kiss. Who knew what sort of slobbery creature lay ahead of me in New York. If kissing was the only criteria for judging a man, Jacques would be right up there on top of the list with the best of them. But there was so much more a man needed to be in control of. Starting with a respectable bank balance.

I broke it off. Poor Jacques. Poor me. Poor Thierry.

I couldn't wait to get back home to America. I had stopped feeling that India was my home about the third or fourth month after my arrival in the USA. New York has a welcoming bosom and if you're not too picky or squeamish, you can have a bang-up time.

I longed to get back to my own apartment on the Upper West Side with the questionable view of the Hudson River. I couldn't wait to ride the subway and push past surly commuters as they tried to exit the cars.

I ached for souvlaki, sushi, tacos, nachos, pla lad prik and other native New York dishes.

I would be speaking English again. 'Fuhgeddabouddit' and 'whaddyamean' and 'gimmeabreak'.

It sounded like such sweet music to my ears. No more, 'Ooo la la,' for me unless a gun was put to my head, I swore.

◆

Shas was waiting for me at the airport, my one and only true friend. She had a welcoming smirk on her face. But I expected it. I put up with it since I had lots to tell her. Which I proceeded to do, as her judgemental finger wagged, punctuating key points in my story. What's the use of an adventure if you can't blab about it? Remember, there was no Facebook back then.

I settled back to work, feeling a little deflated, as I usually did after an adventure. It was always a bit of a let-down. Although, hope still existed in the form of 'Semi Con Carne: What's Hot In Semiconductors Today', an exhibition in Shanghai.

I got a few flowery messages of sorrow and regret from Jacques. What-could-have-been-if-only-fate-wasn't-so-unfeeling. Even a Hermes scarf with an Indian elephant on it. I guess that was a joke.

Maybe my expectations of him were unreasonable. Maybe I ought to have made a serious effort to learn French, instead of poking fun at it. As they're fond of saying in New York,

'Shouldawouldacoulda.'

So I began to pay attention to my immediate surroundings instead of dreaming about somewhere else.

I'd heard that serendipity could strike anywhere, when you least expected it and in the most unlikely of places. It was a pleasant way to go through life, the light of hope shining perpetually in my eyes. Shas thought it made me look daft, but Jerry Lowe (Jeremiah Lowenstein) didn't.

♦

Shas and I had gone to the Bottom Line (now sadly closed), a marquee club in the Village. It was early fall, the weather was turning and that particular corner, on West 4th between Mercer and Greene, could get very windy. You could turn into an iceberg if it was in the dead of winter. At least I could, because I have very low tolerance for the cold.

My hair was blowing here and there and despite the tons of hair spray, my carefully constructed 'look' was coming apart. Shas the louse, who had long straight blonde hair looked like a model no matter which way the wind blew. Most unfair. But she hadn't been to India yet, and I wondered how she'd fare in the hot Delhi summer. How would Shas look after she'd wilted?

We were on line (no one ever said queue in New York), waiting to listen to Larry Coryell or Ralph Towner or some jazz guitar player, I really can't remember. Since the Bottom Line didn't have a lot of seats, no more than four hundred, people stood patiently in all kinds of weather—winter, spring, summer or fall—until they were let in.

When we finally entered, shivering a little, most of the seats were taken. We scanned the club, looking for a spot where we could sit together. I thought I spotted one. I leaped across the distance dragging Shas, and while I did, I knocked over Jerry's red wine all over his white shirt.

'Oh noooooooooo,' I wailed, 'Klutzy, clumsy, clodhopping oaf.' I was yelling at myself. He was a mess. A handsome mess. 'I am so sorry, so sorry,' I howled, pulling out a twenty from my purse, thrusting it into his wine-soaked pocket. 'That's for dry cleaning,' I explained. 'And to buy another drink. But before that, here. Here's my chin. Punch it. Go on. Give it all you've got.'

Shas dashed off in the quest of napkins. She returned triumphant, and began dabbing at his chest. We were attacking him. A blonde girl and a black haired girl. Fantasy? Nightmare?

He smiled at me, a crinkly, heart-stopping smile, as he brushed Shas away. 'It's ok, it's ok,' he said to her. He had a few salt-and-mostly-pepper-curls and wore round, John Lennon-type glasses. He was about 5'11. I'd say he was in his early thirties. A man in his prime.

'Don't be silly,' he said to me, shoving the twenty back into my hand. 'It's all right. I'll survive. It's no big deal. How about I buy you girls some wine and we listen to some jazz guitar. That is, if you can ignore the wine stain.'

A funny guy.

I was more than happy to accept his offer and Shas agreed. Free booze overwhelmed her Swedish fear of strangers whom she was not technically free to pick up anyway, since the boring Klaus (her long-time fiancé) was waiting for her in their apartment, twiddling his thumbs.

She often left him home alone and roamed the streets of the city with me. She was protecting me from harm, she claimed. I think she was just plain bored.

We found three seats together, and in-between tunes, I found out that Jerry was what one called a general physician in India. He specialised in family medicine. A doctor who could treat you from head to toe no matter how old or young you were, regardless of sex.

I didn't care if he was a proctologist.

He was a single Jewish doctor.

That's Beluga in New York date parlance. There was not one girl, single or otherwise, in Manhattan who would have let him slip away. I was no exception.

He worked at The Brooklyn Hospital where he was completing his residency, and once that was out of the way, he'd be joining his father's lucrative private practice, but he also wanted to go to third world countries and help the needy, he said earnestly.

I visualised his life. A fancy, newly renovated apartment on the Upper West Side, facing Central Park. A country home in the Berkshires, a vacation home in Aruba and a few other sundry goodies. A nice car. At least a Lexus.

'Can I buy you girls dinner, after the show?' he asked us, but he was looking at me. 'Not here, I mean somewhere else,' he added hastily. The Bottom Line's selection of greasy cheeseburgers and mozzarella sticks wasn't exactly what made them famous.

'Oh sure, but we'll split the bill,' I said cutely. I didn't want him to think I wanted him for his money.

'Yeah, right,' he agreed grinning. He wasn't about to split any bill with two girls who worked in a travel agency, even if they were in the Department of Conventions and Exhibitions. By then I had fallen one-quarter in love.

Shas was kicking me under the table, her way of telling me to go slow. This is how all my romances started. With a flutter in the pit of my stomach. They usually ended with the runs. Me running away.

He took us to Delmonico's on Beaver Street, a famous New York eatery with a colourful past, many owners and much history. No Lexus. We took a cab. Even the rich had problems finding parking in Manhattan.

Shas and I hadn't ever been there before but had heard tales that many American classics such as Eggs Benedict, Baked Alaska and Lobster Newburg had originated in their kitchens. It was certainly elegant and pricey, at least by our hot-dog-from-the-street-cart standards.

'Lobster,' said Shas, to annoy me.

'Good choice,' said Jerry, as if to assuage my embarrassment. My friend was a bloody pest, but he was a gentleman. 'You too?' He looked at me.

'No,' I said sadly. I was genuinely allergic to shellfish. Also cats, rodents, lizards and many other creatures, besides dust, rust, mould and so on. It was a miracle I was still alive, in a world filled with potential fatality in its every nook and cranny.

'Eggs Benedict,' I said, even though it's a breakfast dish, beginning a life-long love affair. A warning though. EB is extremely fattening and does to your arteries what long hair does to the drain in your bathtub.

We had a lovely dinner, the food was delicious and Shas managed to stay under the level where quirky ends and obnoxious begins.

Jerry offered to drop us back. First Shas who had recently moved to an apartment on the Lower East Side bordering the infamous Tompkins Square park. The same park where years ago, one Daniel Rakowitz had chopped up one Monika Beerle, made a soup out of her remains and served it to the unsuspecting, unfortunate homeless who lived there. I wondered if the homeless human soup-eaters ever recovered from that experience.

I always shuddered when I thought of this gruesome tale and wondered why Shas chose that very spot from all the spots available in Manhattan to make her nest with Klaus.

'It's cheap,' said she, ever practical. She never worried about ghosts.

Then we drove all the way uptown to my humble lodgings on 84th Street between West End and Riverside. Was Jerry looking to come up? Would I say yes? Of course I would. Where was the question? I had no qualms.

How could he be an axe murderer? Axe murderers didn't

keep the meter running while they drove uptown and downtown dropping their victims off, now did they? The cabbie could easily ID him, as any self-respecting perp knows. I felt safe.

But Jerry didn't suggest either coffee or nightcap. 'I gotta work early tomorrow. But can we have dinner tomorrow night?' he asked. I liked that. Direct and believable. He didn't say, 'Give me your number, I'll call you,' which is the worlds biggest blow-off. It is very stressful to sit around waiting for the phone to ring.

'Sure,' I said.

'You like French food?' he asked me.

'No. Absolutely not,' I said firmly. 'Can't stand the stuff. Anything but.'

He looked at me oddly, but may have put it down to my being exotically Indian. 'Indian?'

'Nah. How about some nice pastrami on rye with a little mustard at Katz's?' I replied. Honestly, I had just about had it with fancy cuisine.

'Sounds marvellous,' said Jerry happily and kissed me soundly. We made arrangements for him to pick me up from my office the following day.

Chapter 7

THE INDIAN PRINCESS

He was a contradiction, that Jerry. Quiet, reverent, shy and dedicated one moment and a non-stop, manic talker the next. It was as if he couldn't decide who he was.

He loved his work at the hospital and cared for his patients deeply and sincerely. He knew the nuances, the details of their ailments even without looking at the charts. He made it a practise to memorize the names of their family members. Children's names, parent's names. His bedside manner was heartfelt and sincere. It was quite amazing. No wonder he specialised in family medicine. He was good with people of all ages. A family man.

If that degree of saintliness wasn't enough, he also volunteered at a soup kitchen on alternate weekends. With moonglow in his eyes he told me it was his dream to set up free hospitals all over the world one day, so he could spend time in the wilds of Africa or India (or both), treating the sick and dying under the hot, tropical sun.

'What about joining your father's medical practise?' I asked him. That's what he'd told me when we first met.

'That's my dad's dream more than mine,' he said through his shiny aura.

I listened to him nervously, parched and sweaty from the mere imagery. It was not the life I had imagined for myself.

I didn't care much for the sick and dying under the best of circumstances, even in air-conditioned comfort. There was no question of my volunteering a single second of labour under the hot sun.

Back in Chennai where I had spent many a languid summer with the grandparents, the brother and I were not allowed out in the hot sun under any circumstances. Especially not in the afternoon. People walked around with umbrellas that never saw a drop of rain. It was not so much to avoid heatstroke, as it was to protect one's delicate complexion from the sun.

The grandmother would have locked me up in the bathroom, if she found I was loitering in the sun, allowing my skin to darken.

There was (obviously) no concept of the 'tan' in India where in fact, people ran into the shade and into darkened rooms as fast as they could on a clear day, which was most days, except during the monsoon.

As a result, despite being hot and sunny almost everywhere, many Indians suffer from a deficiency in vitamin D. It's a vitamin that you get mostly from direct contact with sunlight.

I didn't like the hot sun one bit.

Maybe, I could talk him out of it. When I got to know him better. I'd have to work on that. How does one change a man's dreams? Alter a man's destiny?

Shas and I would have to discuss this soon. She was sure to have some helpful hints.

◆

Jerry's apartment, as I had predicted, was sunny and bright. It faced Central Park on the West Side, and the walls of his living room were lined with books. Medical books mostly. There was food in his refrigerator and the toilets were clean. There was no mess anywhere. He had no pets. I had to pinch myself to make sure I wasn't dreaming.

Things progressed very well with Jerry, who seemed to love being with me. We began seeing each other regularly.

'When can I meet your family? Your parents. Your aunt. Your brother,' he asked. He wanted to get to Level 2 in the game.

'Soon,' I said. I wanted to be sure. 'They're in India you know, except the aunt. She's right here on Long Island.'

I met Jerry's parents and sister one evening at Tavern on the Green, possibly one of the most famous restaurants in the world at the time (unfortunately, no longer in existence), located right in Central Park. There were tiny little white fairy lights here and there in the foliage and it looked magical as the sun went down.

It was a fabulous experience. The food was divine. So was the accompanying wine between courses. And Jerry's family seemed to like me a lot.

A little too much, in fact. They were fawning over me in a most obsequious manner, so very uncharacteristic, so very unlike people of their stature and age, that I grew suspicious.

I discovered that Jerry had lied barefaced to them about me.

They were under the delusion that I was as close to being an Indian princess, as humanly possible, without actually being one. He'd told them that I was more or less slumming it in New York, to see how the peasants lived, before I returned to my palace and slaves and pet peacock.

He had gone to the absurd extent of telling them that if I didn't want to shake hands or air-kiss, they ought not to be offended, since I may have considered them untouchable. It was a religious thing, he had lied, adding they ought not to take it personally, since my family owned jewels from the collections of Maharajas and we often loaned them out to museums around the world.

I was quite a catch, he had said, titillating his gullible parents.

He explained all of this hastily to me, a few minutes before I met them. Bloody hell, I thought. Why wasn't it true? It sounded so marvellous. I'd have loved to lead the life of a princess, even an almost princess. And I'd have definitely asked for a pet tiger to feed the peacock to.

'Why would you feed them such crap, Jer?' I asked. It was going to be a very tall task, living up to such expectations.

'Oh! They're snobs. They'll love it,' he smiled. 'Think of what they can tell their friends at the country club. Nothing like a little mystique from the Orient to get their boring Jewish hearts racing,' he said raising one eyebrow, in what he thought was a theatrical way.

'But I'm from Asia. Not the Orient,' I tried. His geography wasn't up to speed for sure. I hoped his knowledge of medicine was more au courant. Maybe it was time he hit the third world, if only to know who lived where.

I ended up loving the subterfuge.

It was nice to play the starring role in a real-life drama. I hammed it up to the hilt.

By the end of the evening, after accepting invitations to their homes, both in the city and in the Berkshires, I wondered if I was good enough to take up acting seriously, perhaps even move to Hollywood. Were there any roles for Indian girls who sang jazz and could do French and Chinese accents?

◆

'You have the most beautiful breasts,' he told me once. I knew this to be true. It wasn't the first time I'd heard that. My 38Ds had earned me many compliments over the years while journeying from 34B to 36C and finally, to where they were now, twin mocha glories. Men would whistle appreciatively at me while women would tell me I was fat. Beauty, as we all know, is in the eyes of the beholder.

On Jerry's birthday, I bought him a cake shaped in the form of a woman's breasts, from a place called the Erotic Bakery. Pale chocolate with raisin accents. He was delighted. The cake and its bearer were both equally delicious, he said.

While Jerry was unpredictable and fun, caring and solicitous, wealthy and generous, he was also oddly disconnected when we had sex.

I was used to men who mostly grunted, panted and groaned until the final roar, with the occasional 'baby, baby' and 'don't stop' by way of variation. I'd received unequivocal confirmation from my girlfriends that 90 per cent of mankind subscribed to this MO.

Of the balance ten percent, a few were poetic, which is not exactly a turn on. 'Poetry should never be uttered during sex,' I had overheard the mother telling the aunt once. She was right. Rose petals, daisy chains, billowing curtains, tinkling harps and twinkling stars were deal breakers.

The rest liked to talk dirty.

Sex-related conversation that could get you into the spirit of things, depending on the story being told. Sometimes I'd listen, sometimes I'd tune out. I preferred my own fantasies. They weren't restricted to sex. Often they'd involve redecorating, new clothes, new make-up, new hairstyles and so on. Lovely stuff.

Jerry was different. He didn't fit into any of the categories mentioned above. Oh he wasn't a pervert, with rusty nail-encrusted whips and chainsaw at the ready, but it was close.

He would talk incessantly while we were in the throes of passion.

About the rise and fall of the Roman Empire, the stock market, El Nino, probability theory and so on. Rattling on and on without expecting a response from me. It was bizarre and disconcerting, definitely off-putting. I needed every ounce of my focus to stay on point.

Other than the sex, there were many things about him I rather liked.

His ability to patronise fine dining establishments. His car. His sunny disposition. His family's lovely cottage in the Berkshires. Especially that. I enjoyed the drive up there, with autumn leaves of red and gold drifting by my window. It was a part of the American experience.

Jerry's mother had made a civilised set of rules that she had framed and hung on the wall in the kitchen by the fridge, where she was sure her guests wouldn't miss it.

One of the mandates of the house was that you had to leave

things as you found them. Clean and stocked. So if you made a mess in the bathroom and all over the sheets, you had to clean, scrub and wash it all out. If you ate four steaks, three boxes of cereal, eight bars of chocolate and drank six bottles of wine you had to replace all of it before you left, so the next person visiting wouldn't get a rude shock in the morning when he was pouring himself coffee to discover there was no milk.

It was a novel experience for me since such courtesies did not exist back in India where the 'next person' was somebody you terrorised and tormented as much as humanly possible because he'd trample all over you in a heartbeat. The next person was someone you:

- Cut in front of at the bank, even though everyone could see he arrived there first.
- Stood as close as possible behind in line for a movie, so that, as the brother once told me, 'I could feel his crotch against my bum.' The brother had turned around angrily and shoved the fellow, who then fell against the person behind him. Pretty soon there was a line of men who fell like dominoes. It was very funny according to the brother. It must have been.
- Honked at relentlessly if his car stalled in front of you. Even if it was evident that he was having starting trouble.
- Pushed aside rudely if he happened to be blocking your way in his wheelchair. The handicapped were annoying.
- Didn't stop at a pedestrian crossing even if he, wife, child and ageing grandma were crossing legally, on green.

In India, there was no concept of courtesy. It was not part of the Vedas. The ones rigged to suit the upper classes mainly. It was sad. Men in India urinated, spat, tossed their garbage just about everywhere and generally didn't give a hoot about walls, corridors, streets, garbage bins and so on.

If Mrs Lowenstein had wanted to become Prime Minister of

India, I'd have been the first to vote for her.

◆

One day Jerry asked me if I'd like to accompany him on his rounds at the hospital. I didn't jump for joy, because as I said earlier, the aged, the infirm, the underprivileged and other such unfortunates held no fascination for me.

Despite great advances in the medical sciences, no one had ever escaped the dreaded 'D' word. Death. The hospital was where the sick came to be informed of the inevitable, 'Sorry chum. It's curtains for you.'

Accordingly, as far as possible, I gravitated towards the healthy and the happy.

'Oh don't be silly,' said Jerry and dragged me off to Brooklyn. I don't think he believed that I was really so callous. 'I want you to see what I do, meet my patients, get to know the real me. And besides, I have a surprise for you.'

Oh no, I thought to myself. I didn't want to meet his patients, not at all. Hospitals weren't like street corners where you could lean against the lamppost, smoke a cigarette, shoot the breeze, exchange pleasantries with a stranger, and whistle a cheerful tune.

There were no laughs to be had in hospitals. Except once at a hospital in India where I had seen a sign that said, 'No parking aloud.' It wasn't a mental hospital either.

I didn't like surprises. The pleasure one supposedly derived from the surprise was almost always skewed in favour of the surprisor and not the surprisee.

'Jerry. I have a headache. I need to go home,' I tried valiantly.

'I'm a doctor and I can fix that,' said Jerry immediately. 'Come on, be a sport. Really, I've got something I want to show you.'

'What is it?' I persisted. 'Tell me now. I hate surprises.'

'Well, this one you will,' he insisted. 'You'll love it. I promise.'

That was another thing I didn't like. Somebody assuming they'd know what I would and would not want. It ranked right up there with ordering my meal for me at a restaurant. 'She'll have the broiled fish, no sauce. The tossed salad, no dressing. No wine, just a Diet Coke.' Embarrassing stuff.

It was hard enough to make my own decisions and not regret them without having someone else's opinions thrust on me.

But my resistance and resolve, which have always been in short supply, were squashed by his enthusiasm and we whizzed down to the Manhattan Bridge. Pretty soon we were at the hospital.

Jerry put on his lab coat and stethoscope, sending a few frissons down my spine. I like a working man. A man in uniform.

He took my hand as we walked in. He wanted people to know he had a girlfriend. That I was his. I was flattered. People, mainly nurses and other staff nodded at him. They were checking me out too. I liked that.

After going over some paper work, 'We're doing rounds,' he said.

'Shall I stay here?' I asked. The doctor's lounge had magazines and a vending machine. I didn't mind waiting.

'Oh no, we're taking you in disguise,' he replied and made me put on a lab coat. He also gave me a notepad and a pen and told me to doodle a little bit in each room. Pretend like I was taking notes.

It was definitely illegal, but I was up for it. I had to fool both the nurses and the patients. I could do it.

We'd knock on a patient's door politely and wait for the, 'Come in.' (Another alien, American custom. In India people just barged in unless they were entering a temple, in which case they'd ring the bell loudly, as if to wake up a snoozing god.) There would be someone on a bed, nervous and sad or asleep and alone.

He or she would brighten up hugely as Jerry came over to take their hand, and assure them they'd be fine. He would give the accompanying nurses some instructions before we moved on to the next patient. But not before he cracked a joke or said something encouraging to the poor sicko on the bed.

Once in a while, there'd be family visiting the patient. Jerry would patiently answer the barrage of questions put to him and only leave the room when all questions were answered.

One got the feeling that Jerry's words, his presence, his smile and his confidence made a big difference. Much more than, 'double the dosage of Thorazine,' which would have been quicker, certainly.

We must have visited at least ten patients that evening. My respect and admiration for Jerry grew greater and stronger with each interlude. This was no ordinary mortal. He was a guru, a mystic, a healer and he left a trail of happy, smiling people in his wake. I had much to learn about Jerry. He was so interesting. So diverse. So caring. He'd be a cool breeze in the hot sun in Africa or India.

Pretty soon the nurses bid him goodnight, and we were alone.

Well, as alone as you can be in a hospital filled with people, sick and healthy, the latter bustling up and down corridors, with the PA summoning this doctor and that to this ward and that emergency. All of it settled into a dull whirr after a while. Just another day at the office.

We stopped outside a door marked 'OB/GYN' and Jerry pushed the door open, smiling at me broadly, in a most un-doctorly way. He shoved me in quickly. I didn't pay too much attention to the fact that he locked and then double-bolted the doors behind him; I was still blinded by his god-like aura and Hippocratic sensitivity.

A few seconds later I observed that there was no patient in the room. No nurses either.

There were no windows, but who had windows in an exam room created for the pursuit of obstetrics and gynaecology? Hospitals could get sued for encouraging peep shows.

'Why are we here?' I asked, a little unnerved.

He didn't answer. He took off his Doctor's Coat and hung it up. His tie came off next.

'Jerry, what the *&%$ is going on?' I asked him, a little more insistently. 'I don't like being here. Can we go now?'

'Relax,' said Jerry calmly, as he began unbuttoning his shirt. 'Take off your clothes and get on that table,' he ordered, using the same commanding voice that dentists use when they say, 'Open wide,' just before they stick it to you with the drill.

'Put your feet in the stirrups. Let me show you how doctors do it.'

Chapter 8

DIRTY SEX

As far as I know, there are two kinds of sexual fantasy.
1. One's own: Without a doubt the best kind. Since the fantasy is inside in your own head, you have ultimate control of the outcome, not to mention the 'repeat' button right there at your fingertips.

2. Someone else's: Always risky, because you never know if your mutual interests are going to coincide.

Men usually like fantasies where two or three women will drop whatever else they'd rather be doing in order to please them, in costume of course. A chamber maid's outfit, a nun's habit, a Xena the Warrior Princess get-up, a policewoman uniform—the possibilities are infinite. Shas told me about a guy who had wanted her to be Angela Lansbury, I kid you not. In these short-films, the women are obedient and supplicant, never speaking unless specifically instructed to do so with a clear and direct 'say my name' or 'say you love it' or 'say you're sorry.'

Men like fantasies where they don't have to worry about how a woman is feeling.

This is where the male and female fantasies collide.

The average woman can easily achieve four or five PMs (petit morts, as you know by now) under normal circumstances, but will accept twelve or thirteen graciously, time permitting.

I have never heard of a man who had a sexual fantasy that involved rewarding a woman thirteen or fourteen times.

In my experience, a man's attention span is severely limited. When it comes to sex, it lasts only as long as is absolutely necessary.

And when a bored or testy man is trying to please his partner, it can get ugly. I learned very early on in life that the 'oooh' and 'aaah' and 'yeaaahhh baby' are critical in the language of love. Verbal encouragement.

As fantasies go, for a while both Shas and I had added The Mile High Club, to the top of our 'to do' list. We had decided that with all the air miles we were racking up, we'd be complete idiots if we couldn't pull it off at least once.

What tales would we tell our grandchildren? That we sat tamely in our economy seats staring down at the clouds, while everyone else on the plane was disappearing into the loo in twos (and threes, once in a while) only to reappear looking trés content?

I looked at the opportunity that lay in front of me.

The OB/GYN table.

In stirrups?

Hmmm.

There was definitely something evil and sexily Marquis De Sade about the pile of ominous-looking instruments, gleaming by the side of the exam table on which I was supposed to position myself, my unmentionables exposed to the naked neon light.

Immoral and pagan.

The instruments were harmless enough in sterile repose, but I knew that in the twitch of a Kegel, they could rip you to shreds.

Sure it was fun to see people being dismembered, impaled, scalped and tortured on television, but becoming the subject of such experimentation made me want to pee in my pants. And poo.

For a brief second I wondered if Jerry had stashed a nurse in the closet. Would she pop out, blonde wig and orange lipstick askew, smiling maniacally while he said, 'Scalpel please?'

I pushed away those thoughts. I tried to ignore the smell of disinfectant. I focussed my attention on Jerry who was now down to wearing only the stethoscope and nothing else.

I hastily shed my clothes and clambered unglamorously on to

the table and slipped my legs into the stirrups. Left leg, left stirrup. Right leg, right stirrup. They were too far apart to be able to cross my legs, even if I was having a last minute change of heart.

'I need you to scoot down a little,' said Jerry.

I shimmied down obligingly.

It was scary. Also strangely seductive. I was literally on edge.

'This won't hurt a bit,' he said encouragingly. 'You'll feel some pressure, that's all. Take a deep breath.'

I played along. It was kind of fun actually.

Happily, he didn't talk about either Mother Teresa or the works of Philip Glass. He stuck to restrained grunts (there were people milling about outside after all), controlled growls and breathy panting.

It was not a lengthy procedure and I didn't have to stay under, too long.

◆

The next day I woke up with a slight fever and a dull ache below the belly button.

I didn't think too much of it and went to work as usual.

I couldn't shake the feeling that I had to pee. All the time. But when I tried, nothing would happen. I wasn't alarmed, because the pain wasn't unbearable.

I thought that maybe I had caught a bug. As the day wore on, I felt worse. By lunchtime the fever was full blown and the peeing was nasty.

I felt as if an unforgiving, evil demon had taken up residence where, until then, only the most blithe, carefree of fairy spirits had flitted about, gaily enjoying the delights available.

I thought I was dying.

It was as if all my unpardonable activity had caught up with me and I was being punished for a lifetime of loose morals and wanton behaviour. 'My mother was so right. I have no scruples. I deserve to die,' I bawled to Shas when we took our lunch break. 'But does it have to be so painful? Please, please get me some morphine. I'll never, ever have sex again. With anyone. Even myself. I swear.'

I had of course given her the blow-by-blow of my hospital visit the previous night, but there was no joy in the storytelling. I was in such agony, I could speak only in gasps, tears streaming down my face.

'Stop being dramatic and call that idiot doctor right now,' said Shas ever the realist. 'Or better still give me his number. I'll have a word with him.'

It didn't take very long for Shas to develop an attitude, usually a terrible one, about any man that I happened to be seeing. It was my fault mostly. I never fell madly, blindly in love with anyone. So I would complain about this, whine about that, lament this and bemoan that at the various twists and turns of my many courtships, instantly prejudicing her opinions.

But while I forgave and forgot quite generously (it was very easy to make me happy. A nice dinner. A bracelet. Chocolates. Even a simple, 'oh you look so beautiful'), Shas harboured grudges like an elephant.

In this case, maybe she was justified.

'That would be so embarrassing,' I wailed. 'How can I tell him I've got a problem er-well-er-down there? How can I face him again? I won't do it!' It didn't matter that I was banging on hell's door. I still had my dignity to protect.

'Don't be stupid!' Shas said sternly. 'He's a doctor. And what's more, I bet he gave it to you.'

'Gave me what?' I asked stupidly.

'STD, you dumb-bell. Your symptoms sound like Trich.'

'Trick? What trick?' I asked stunned. Was she accusing me of turning tricks? Selling myself for money? Aside from the one time when I had performed (singing jazz I might add) in the Village with my band, when one of my aunt's sleazy friends from India had tried to shove hundred dollar bills into my cleavage, no one had ever paid me for the privilege of my company. I was dishing out my favours for free.

But while I may have thought I was sexually sophisticated, there was much I still had to learn.

STD = Sexually Transmitted Disease.

Trich = Trichomoniasis.

A non-fatal, easily curable infection that can only be transmitted from one person to another through sex. A bacteria that men carry, but that leaves them untroubled, unharmed, feeling all jolly and chipper, while the women they infect almost always develop agonising symptoms.

The awful truth began to sink in.

Until I met Jerry, I'd been a healthy, hearty girl with no problems more severe than a hangover, cured effectively by the hair of the dog and when that wasn't possible, a simple aspirin from the friendly neighbourhood drugstore.

Jerry had given me the clap.

Which he'd caught from someone else.

Who had caught it from someone else.

And so on and so forth.

It was frightening to think of this friendly, tiny, deadly bacteria that travelled from person to person, rapidly, making connections and networking silently, like a poisonous Facebook, long before such a word existed.

Who knew how many 'Likes' and 'Friends' I actually had? It was enough to make me want to scrub my insides with Clorox, which I did not do, because I was already in such pain.

'Bloody right I'll call him,' I said to Shas. I didn't care what he thought of me by then. The important thing was what I thought of him. Which at the moment wasn't very much at all.

'What have you done to meeeeeee?' I screamed down the phone.

Jerry understood immediately. He was most repentant. Being a doctor, he couldn't hide behind, 'I have no idea how that happened,' and excuses of that nature, which you could expect from a lawyer or a drug dealer, a semi-conductor salesman or even a musician.

'It's not a big deal,' he said soothingly. 'I'll give you a couple of tabs and you'll be fine by the evening. Please come and see me at the hospital. Take the afternoon off. I'll examine you just to be sure,' he pleaded.

'Oh no, no, no, no. Not again,' I said with a sharp intake of my breath. 'There will be no more examinations of my body parts, Jerry. At least, not by you. My organs will forever be out of your reach, now that I know what you're capable of doing to them,' I said haughtily but when I hung up, I was cringing with pain.

I didn't think I'd ever want to have sex with anyone, ever again.

As it turned out, there was a gynaecologist very close to where we worked in Midtown, and I popped in to see her. I asked Shas to tell the bosses that I'd become violently sick after eating Chinese. I felt vicious. China was the source of almost 90 per cent of their income.

'All you young girls are the same,' said Dr Ludmilla Mraz, from Eastern Europe, sternly, shaking her grey head. 'Why can't you use a condom? You could avoid all sorts of problems.'

With that she handed me a prescription for two tabs of Flagyl. 'Go home and drink lots of water. No sex for a week,' she said.

'Sex? That's a word I've just erased from my dictionary, Ma'am,' I said earnestly.

She didn't respond. She'd heard that before.

And abracadabra, if by the time night wiped out the day, I wasn't fine.

She was a miracle worker, that Dr Mraz. I wanted to compose a song for her.

◆

Of course, it wasn't too long before thoughts of sex and men once again returned to my brain, gratefully hanging up their hats and coats where they belonged. That's the kind of girl I was.

Chapter 9

THE PLAY'S 'THE THING'

My loins, now spring-cleaned and spruced up, I was ready for action again. But as always, action took its own sweet time getting ready for me.

Shas and I had spent a couple of weeks in glittering Shanghai, returning with nothing more exciting to scrapbook than a few nights of anonymous sex with men whose names we did not remember the next morning.

It was odd, because our previous trips had been fraught with danger, excitement, handsome men who had named their wee wees and other interesting stuff. Either we were getting too blasé to enjoy meaningless sex or 'Semi Con Carne: What's Hot In Semiconductors Today' attracted only the dullest of men.

It was hard to tell.

I was back to the ho and the hum once more, searching for that gentleman (or boor) who would wrap his arms around me and never let me go.

I was just about to breach the subway turnstiles at Grand Central, to board the shuttle to the West Side so I could go back home uptown when I heard someone, a high-pitched female, screech my name in a way that pierced through the din of New York rush-hour pedestrian commute.

This is pretty hard to do. New Yorkers aren't quiet by nature, and Grand Central is a cavernous hall that echoes a lot. But if you're from the by-lanes of Byculla, a roughish neighbourhood in Mumbai, your ability to yell for help could be the difference between life and death. The accent was definitely Indian.

I turned in the direction of the sound and saw her waving her hands at me. I rushed over and we fell into each other's arms, like long lost friends. Truth is, we were. We had been at St Luke's together many moons ago, a boarding school I had been banished to by parents who had wanted nothing to do with a hormonal teenager.

It was a nunnery where I had spent most of my impressionable, formative years, kept as far away as possible from the company of anyone of the opposite sex, which was most likely the reason why I was the way I was, ready to jump into the sack with the passing Joe or Moe. I was no psychologist, but it was plain to see.

The voice belonged to Rue, short for Aruna. Although why Aruna needed to be shortened, I never understood. It was the fashion to have nicknames, or 'pet-names' as people in India insisted on calling them. As if people were Labrador puppies or Siamese cats. Everyone with any kind of name got an abbreviation. Leena was 'Lee' and Sandhya was 'Sandy' and so on.

Rue and I weren't close in high school, but meeting her out of the blue in Grand Central made me gush like a joyful geyser. After hugging, kissing and doing mile-a-minute instant replays of each of our lives, we slowed down a bit.

'I want you to come with me just now,' she said. 'Right now. Drop whatever else you're doing.'

'Which bar?' I asked. I didn't have anything very exciting to do, and tossing back a few with Rue sounded like a great way to spend an evening.

My eloquence grew with each 'down-the-hatch' and it would have been nice to impress someone new with my tales of glory, travel, conquest and adventure.

'No not to a bar. To the theatre,' she said.

I should have guessed.

Rue had always been into theatre, back in high school she was pretty good at it too. She always got the starring role, the lead part. No one else ever stood a chance at auditions, she was a convincing actress who had the ability to cry on the spot. Real tears, she knew how to conjure up at will.

Ours was a convent school, a strict, no-nonsense environment where only Shakespearean plays were permitted. A rule written in the bible, no doubt.

Hamlet, Othello and the like. Boring stuff as far as I was concerned.

I stayed clear of those auditions while Rue lived for theatre season in Panchgani.

Sadly for her, since old Will almost always cast men in his leading roles, she was forever doomed to wear tights, boots, stiffened balloon-like bloomers and a hat with a long feather stuck in it, a fake beard once in a while, as she delivered speeches in as low a timbre as she could produce.

She was excellent at memorising her lines and it was with awe that I'd listen to her say things like, 'My services which I have done the signiory shall out-tongue his complaints,' and 'Do, with like timorous accent and dire yell as when, by night and negligence, the fire is spied in populous cities.' The play Othello rambled on and on in this obscure vein, losing the average schoolgirl's attention (most certainly mine) with each passing word, but not Rue's.

She not only learned her own lines by heart, but everyone else's too. Her brain was a bubbling cauldron of Shakespearean nonsense and her grasp of gibberish was second only to her grasp of Marathi, her mother tongue.

Rue had come to New York to seek her fame in the theatre. Her plan was to work her way up. First off-off, then off, then on Broadway itself, where it was common knowledge that Hollywood movie scouts lay in wait for promising actresses. That was Rue's road map.

Many, many stars had been born in the vicinity of 42nd Street (Shirley MacLaine, Anthony Hopkins and even recent stars like Mathew Morrison) and Rue was certain she was next in line.

The Broadway theatre scene was much, much, much harder to break into than the jazz scene because there were thousands of actresses from all over the world with exactly the same idea as Rue. The rewards of an acting career far outweighed a life in jazz.

Rue was in a play and she wanted me to see her in action. Not just any play but one she was starring in that very evening.

I recoiled.

I still had Shakespearean nightmares about, 'And thus the native hue of resolution is sicklied o'er with the pale cast of thought.' I had no wish to inflict such pain on myself, happy as I was to bump into Rue.

I didn't like the theatre at all. I felt it was overrated and over dramatised. Broadway expected its audiences to suspend way too much disbelief while charging an awful lot for the privilege.

If I was going to a live show, I much preferred the circus. Or Cirque-Du-Soleil. Or break dancing. I didn't like ballet and opera either, for pretty much the same reason. Or modern dance. No other performing art came close to jazz, in my book at least.

'I'm coming down with something,' I mumbled. 'Maybe another time, Rue.'

'Don't be silly!' she said happily. 'You look as healthy as an ox. Are you worried it's Shakespeare? No fear. I've left him far behind. And I'm no longer playing men's roles anymore either. In fact this time I'm an Indian goddess. The star of the show! It's an avant-garde, improvised adaptation of The Ramayana!'

'Wow!' I said. The Ramayana. Who knew people were still churning out that old chestnut? I knew the ending. But it was better than Shakespeare.

'So no more tights, eh Rue?' I teased.

'Nope. No tights. No hat. No bloomers. Nothing. Literally. I'm not wearing any clothes at all. I'll be clad only in the warmth of the audience.'

This I had to see.

♦

The play took place in a dingy, somewhat desolate, off-off-Broadway theatre in the East Village, a venue renowned for birthing a handful of now-famous stage and screen stars, but equally reputed for the debris that got left behind.

This particular version of The Ramayana featured a cross-cultural cast of players from all over the globe. In the East Village, that meant mainly from the East, Africa, the Pacific and Orient. I didn't spot any Swedes and Danes and Germans in the cast.

There were Indonesians, Malays, Thais, Filipinos, Koreans, people from Madagascar, Mauritius, Somalia, Sri Lanka and many other nations whose existence I was unaware of until that evening.

Bloody hell, the world was filled with nations.

Everyone except Rue was clothed, and I understood from the little photocopied synopsis left on each chair that her nakedness was a sign, a tribute, an homage if you will, to the vulnerability of the heroine Sita, a pious and long-suffering character around whom the whole story was based.

I am sure the BJP, the RSS and other Indian political parties would have burned the theatre down along with the actors and the director, a lady who was well known both for her brilliance in the theatrical arts as well as her bouts of mental illness, but mercifully for everyone in New York, those right-wing Indian political parties were safely back home in India.

No one knew that a naked Sita would be parading up and down the stage as the story unfolded.

I was given a seat right up front; after all I was friends with the star. And I settled down.

At first as I listened, the language of the play sounded familiar. I didn't quite catch the meaning of the words, but I put it down to the acoustics in the room, not the most top-notch. But the more I lip-read, the more I came to the realisation that what I thought was Shakespearean mumbo-jumbo was in fact, nothing of the sort.

It was frustrating. I listened carefully, because it seemed like if I focussed, I'd get it. But each time I thought I got closer, comprehension rushed right out of my head. I thought I was going insane.

Then I caught on. Every word was a nonsense syllable. The vowels and consonants followed each other in a bizarre language-like fashion. It was called 'Grammelot,' and it was like eavesdropping at a colony of chimps.

The director had made up the entire language, just for the play. It must have taken her ages to write it out and I couldn't imagine how long it would have taken the cast to learn their parts. It wasn't random rubbish that the cast could just improvise on, like scatting (a jazz doo-bee-doo-bee-doo thing).

It was specific gibberish that had to be memorized.

It was definitely theatre of the absurd.

Topping it off was a spectacular entrance made by my friend Rue, from stage left, reclining languorously on a large copper plate, held aloft by four strapping men from Haiti. They were gorgeous. Their oiled bodies gleamed in the stage lights and their gold, barely-covering-the-loin cloths were tantalizing.

I hoped they didn't drop Rue. She'd fall almost ten feet and I didn't think she'd survive unscathed with no clothes on. Mercifully, they set her down gently in the centre of the stage, to be bathed by the spot light, from where she delivered a passionate speech in jabberwocky.

It was an evening I never will forget.

Not only because of Rue and her startlingly realistic performance, but also because of one Augustus Fabio, from the group of islands in the Pacific Ocean known as the Philippines.

He played the role of Rama, the troubled, leading character in the play. I will admit, that after a while I had to stuff the pamphlet in my mouth to keep from laughing. The dialogue, which they delivered passionately, emotionally and sincerely, sounded lame and pretty stupid. Sometimes they sounded like chickens. Sometimes like ducks. That is, when they didn't sound like apes.

Luckily for Auggie, Rama's role called for dramatic, pensive pauses. Kind of manly. He wasn't naked, although I wished he was, but his clothing didn't leave much to the imagination.

Rama/Auggie was blessed with sexy, six-pack abs (maybe he worked out, I didn't know yet) and a hairless chest. The hair on his head was long, Tarzan-like. Black and straight. He was clean-shaven, and the colour of a Pacific sunset.

About an hour and a half later, (including intermission) followed by resounding applause and three curtain calls, Rue slipped into something more concealing and introduced me to the cast.

Most of them had day jobs. The theatre was a passion, a dream. In the daytime, they were accountants, waiters, taxi drivers, shop assistants, advertising executives, plumbers, travel agents and so on. Regular jobs.

Rue worked as a layout artist for a magazine directed at gay men, she told me. Of course, I thought to myself. If there's one thing a convent education will do to you, it's to send you hurtling to the opposite end of the spectrum.

The men and women in the theatre group were very close to one another. After all they spent many, many hours together, eating, sleeping, rehearsing, reviewing, performing.

It looked like so much fun. I wondered how I could inveigle myself into their midst. I was fast changing my opinion about the theatre, now that I had an 'inside' view. Besides, it was way better than going home to my lonely apartment. Getting sloshed with Shas was becoming rare since her Klaus was making more and more demands on her time.

My musical career was unreliable and at the time, going through the hibernation phase.

'What do you do when you're not acting?' I asked Auggie,

who didn't look like he had a day job. I caught him looking at me a couple of times.

'Oh this and that,' he said vaguely. 'More this than that. But forget about me, what about you? What do you do?'

I gave him the short version.

He was cute. His tight jeans, tight T-Shirt with a packet of cigarettes folded into the sleeve, cowboy boots and the smell of expensive after-shave had an instant impact. There was the teeniest whiff of lady-boy about him and it was quite sexy.

'You seem to have had a rough day,' he said. 'You look tired.' What was he talking about? I wasn't tired at all?

'Come here,' he said masterfully. 'I'll massage your neck a little.'

'Ooookkkkay,' I said happily, and sat down, closing my eyes.

He definitely had the touch. His fingers were soft and yet strong as they moved down my spine. I could get used to this.

But it was getting late. Everyone dispersed—the cast, the audience, the stage crew. And I made to stand up. I had to go all the way uptown.

'I'll drive you home,' said Auggie, only a trace of Manila in his accent. Drive? He had a car? In Manhattan? He parked? Everyday? Wow! I thought. Who is this man? And he works at this and that? What could this be? And what was that?

I thought I saw Rue raise her eyebrows a little, but I wasn't sure. Heck, I didn't know her at all. There was a large Atlantic Ocean and several years between Panchgani and New York. For all I knew, it was just a nervous twitch.

A's bright yellow Corvette was lovingly parked in a lot where it wouldn't be bumped into or keyed by lowlifes in the East Village, he explained. He vroomed me all the way up town where I lived, and asked if I'd have dinner with him the next day.

'I'm taking you to Windows on the World,' he said in a matter-of-fact way as if it was Burger King.

Chapter 10

WHEN YOUR DAY IS DONE AND YOU WANNA RUN

New York City is like a lady. A lady with many moods. She can be happy one minute and suddenly turn nasty, for no reason. She can be playful and fun or hardheaded and unyielding. Sometime's she's malevolent. Sometimes she just doesn't care. Sometimes she's arrogant and snooty. Sometimes she's dismissive. And sometimes she's loving, caring, eager and concerned. She's both cruel and kind.

So while sometimes she can treat you like you're a motherless stepsister unworthy of a drop of water for your parched throat, on another occasion, she can rain good luck and good fortune on you.

I was just getting soaked.

The deluge this time came in the form of a handsome stage actor from the Philippines with a spectacular sports car. He seemed to have access to an endless supply of cash but no obvious means of income.

In hindsight, maybe I should have done a little bit of investigation, scratched the surface a little to find out what was going on under, but as you know by now, I've never been the one to delve too deeply into anything.

I hated 'getting to the bottom of it'.

'It' was almost always not up to expectation; so as far as possible I took off in the opposite direction of introspection, knowledge and understanding since these virtues always ruined the pursuit of pleasure.

I mentioned the unexpected series of events to Shas, who raised her blonde eyebrows pretty much the same way as Rue had (although Rue, like me, had black eyebrows). I always seemed to befriend girls who looked down on my behaviour. They always seemed to have the upper hand. They were always better than me. It was most irritating.

'A man, starring in an off-off-Broadway play along with naked women? Are you sure he isn't a porn actor?' she sneered knowingly. Shas and her boyfriend Klaus watched a lot of porn, it helped while away the time apparently, so she was very familiar with the crop of actors currently making the rounds. Apparently, 'Oriental Porn' was a genre all on its own, and quite popular even among non-Orientals.

She had once told me that for a lark, she and Klaus had rented a gay porn video, just to see what it was all about. To her horror, she discovered that gay men used a lot of unnatural objects at each other in the guise of sex. In one of the scenes in the film, a particular actor had inserted an entire telephone (not a cell phone mind you, a landline) up his orifice-of-choice, and had a conversation with someone at the other end of the line. Shas and K had turned the film off immediately, swearing never to watch gay porn again. I was sure she was making it all up, but she swore it was the truth.

'Every thing isn't porn, you know,' I said haughtily. 'This play was high theatre. Avant garde. Not touristy Broadway stuff. Rue's nakedness was integral to the plot. Very sophisticated art nouveau. That's Francaise, BTW. You wouldn't understand it.'

'Of course I wouldn't,' she cackled, the tears rolling down her face. 'It wasn't in French. It was in gibberish! You just said so.'

'I'm going out with him tomorrow Shas. And he's taking me to Windows on the World, so stuff the crap and help me find something decent to wear,' I said, cutting her jolly old guffaw short.

Her clothes were far better than mine. Swedish people have

an innate sense of class and style. They are not given to the hot pink, the turquoise, the flaming yellow and the aubergine quite so much as the average Indian. Or even gold, silver and other glitter, for that matter.

They are partial to the taupe, the tan, the buff and the beige. Also grey and black. Colours that don't conflict with the person wearing them.

Also, since she was a size smaller than me, I filled her clothes out rather sexily. At least, that was my opinion.

I had always wanted to go to the WOTW. It was New York City's most expensive restaurant at the time and the view was unparalleled. I hadn't had the privilege of being taken there before (paying for myself was out of the question since it would mean bread-and-water for a month) so I'd stuck to lip smacking and salivating at food reviews in the newspaper.

WOTW on top of the World Trade Center doesn't exist. Having survived one terrorist attack, the second one did it in completely.

◆

Auggie was dressed in a jacket and tie and looked like he had stepped out of the pages of GQ. I wasn't too shabby myself, in a strapless, basic little black dress with blood red stilettos and a silver clutch. The hair was still curly and wild, thanks to the perm a few months before, so all in all in borrowed clothes and fake hair, I looked pretty good.

Dinner was a dream. A dream in which I didn't eat too much. One, the dress was way too tight for me (I guess either I'd gained a size or Shas had lost one) and two, it didn't look good to stuff one's face, dribbling steak juice down the chin on the first date. First impressions were everything.

We started off with martinis and moved on to wine. I took care to keep the alcohol levels low. My liver, despite the daily doses of Liv 52 that Shas and I were popping, was unreliable. If you're unfamiliar with it, Liv 52 is a little red pill made by an Indian ayurvedic pharmaceutical company. It is said that they pick only the freshest herbs and shrubs from the slopes of the Himalayan mountains to ensure that people can drink themselves silly every evening, while their livers remain baby-pink through the course of their lives.

I was prone to upchucking once I'd crossed the threshold of eight drinks and if there was one thing worse than steak juice down one's chin on a first date, it was vomit. I was determined to be elegant.

Auggie kept up a steady stream of complements as he probed the depths of my shallow life with ease. In about fifteen minutes he had it all. Not that there was much to tell, I hadn't actually accomplished anything noteworthy.

I tried to ask him about his life but didn't get very far. I gathered he lived somewhere in Queens and that he woke up late but stayed up all night. That was the nature of his job. Most of it was on the phone he said.

I did notice that he got up to go to the bathroom at least four times during the course of the evening, and I tried not to think too much about it.

It also seemed like he was coming down with something. A cold perhaps. He was sniffling a lot.

'Do you have a cold?' I asked innocently.

Auggie burst out laughing. 'No I don't have a cold my naïve little Indian miss. But I definitely have something for you to try.'

'Really, what's that?' I asked. I hoped he wasn't going to suggest a threesome. It was too early in the game. I needed to know him first.

'Let's get out of here,' he said, and signalled for the check. He paid cash. Crisp new bills. We took the elevators, and he held my hand during the ride down the 106 floors, pulling me close to him.

We walked a block or two to a parking lot where he'd left the ray of yellow sunshine, otherwise known as a Corvette. He never ever parked on the street, he told me.

'The night's still young. Let's go dancing,' he suggested.

'Sure,' I said. I was dressed for it. What a cool guy.

We drove uptown to 20th Street to a hot place that was well known at the time for it's cool partygoers and late night scene. It was called The Limelight.

On the outside, it looked like an old church, which in fact it once was. It had been 'deconsecrated' (that's when god's blessing is recanted by a priest/minister) before it was turned into a thriving, pulsating den of gyrating bodies, sweating and swaying to the sound of loud music. Limelight was also known for decent quality recreational drugs. No wonder god wanted to have nothing to do with it.

Limelight doesn't exist anymore in a nightclub avatar. It's a mall, but that's got nothing to do with what happened next.

On our way from the parking lot to the club, Auggie pulled me close in what I assumed was going to be a passionate kiss. But as soon as our faces reached liplock distance, he pulled out a little brown bottle from his pocket. No ordinary brown bottle this, it had a tiny gold chain around its neck, from which hung a teeny, tiny little golden spoon. Auggie unscrewed the tiny black top of the bottle and scooped up some white stuff (oh alright, I wasn't so stupid. I knew it was cocaine) and held it up to one nostril. His own. And then repeated the procedure with the next. He inhaled deeply each time, his pinky holding the non-inhaling nostril shut for maximum pull, I suppose. For a brief second he shuddered, his eyes closed and face scrunched up. Then he beamed brightly.

'Now you,' he said.

I considered refusing him for a brief second, but it was a half-hearted consideration at best and I shoved it to the back of my annoying mind.

'Sure,' I said. I wanted to be cool. I wanted to know how it felt to be high on coke. I'd been told it was a fantastic feeling, nothing whatsoever like marijuana, which had scared me senseless many years earlier.

Back then, much like Auggie, another handsome stranger (named Calvin Cline, no jokes) had introduced me to it. I was happy enough to try it, not being a girl to say 'no' to new experiences, especially illegal ones. But within a matter of seconds, I'd had a violent reaction, throwing up viciously while my head felt like it would explode.

But that was in India, back at a time when I was still living at home, within an autorickshaw's ride of the mom. On that occasion, I had rushed home to her, bleating pitifully. She had put me to bed where I lay alternately unconscious and delirious for days.

Well, for a few hours at any rate.

It was a terrifying experience for both the mom and me, and I had sworn never to go near drugs again. But that was a long, long time ago. I was a different person now. I was no longer a babe-in-the-woods New Delhi hippie chick.

I was a mature, urbane globe circumnavigator. Besides everyone in New York was doing it. I'd be the only dimwit (besides Shas) who hadn't tried it at least once.

I smiled at Auggie, bent my head down and held a nostril down daintily with a pinky. I sucked it in. Zhwoooooop.

For a few seconds I felt the same way as I once had when I swallowed too much wasabi at a Japanese restaurant, all because the chef had artistically shaped it to look like a slice of green, raw fish. I was new at Japanese cuisine then and the stinging sensation had shot straight up to the top of my head. It felt like my skull would explode and my brain matter would projectile-eject, all over the tatami-covered floors. It took a few seconds for the wasabi sensation to settle down. And then everything felt crystal clear, like the world had been hosed down or sandblasted.

It took a few seconds for the coke to settle down too. After that, everything around me took on similar bright, crisp, crystal-clear hue. I could see better, hear better and I felt like I had so much energy, I could dance the night away.

'Let's dance the night away,' I said loudly. 'Oh, did I just say that?' I had no idea. I wanted to jump and sing.

'Shhhhhhhh,' said Auggie. It was extremely illegal to snort cocaine so boldly on Sixth Avenue. Or any other avenue. Or cross street in New York City. Or the five surrounding boroughs. As a matter of fact, you couldn't do it anywhere in America. Indoors or outside. You could go to jail.

I felt like a million bucks as we danced with abandon and vigour. Auggie handed me the little bottle a couple of times during the evening and told me to go into the bathroom for a 'top-up'.

'Be sure you flush the toilet as you inhale,' he instructed. 'You don't want people to hear you.'

But the bathrooms at The Limelight were filled with the sounds of sniffing and flushing, so I had nothing much to worry about.

It was past midnight, and despite the fact that I was wide awake with so much energy and so many as yet unexplored dance moves, I knew that I had to get up and go to work, boring old work the next morning at 9.00 a.m. I mentioned this to Auggie, my newfound gentleman drug dispenser.

He drove me home immediately and promised to call very soon.

'I have some business in Atlanta. I'll be gone a few days but I'll be back. Promise,' he said.

I stayed awake till at least 4 a.m. There was nothing I could do to calm myself down to fall asleep. I called the mom back in India and for once the time difference was perfect. I babbled to her about this and that, I must have sounded disconnected, discombobulated.

'What's happened? Why are you calling me at 4 a.m.? What's wrong with you?' she asked. 'Why are you talking so fast? Are you ok? Are you ill? Shall I come there? Have you called your aunt?' I realised I had made a big mistake calling her. She could unravel me in a second. I just hoped she hadn't heard of the New York sniffles.

'No, no mom, I'm fine,' I assured her.

I fell asleep just before sunup. It seemed like my head had barely touched the pillow when the alarm went off.

I managed to make it to work by the skin of my teeth and Shas, the eagle-eyed Swedish shrew knew instantly that something had happened.

'What did he do?' she said 'What? Tell me everything.'

But she had to wait till lunch. I was still jittery from the night before, but a couple of glasses of House Red at an Italian place nearby calmed me down, and I told her everything.

'Nothing good will come of this,' she said ominously. 'You better stop seeing this guy immediately. I will not be visiting you in jail. There's no Woody,' she reminded me pointedly.

Woody, a lawyer working on the same floor as we were, was a man with whom I'd had a brief dalliance, mainly because I thought he could get Shas and me out of legal scrapes, should we ever find ourselves in a sticky situation.

But he turned out be a dreadful perv. I discovered after I'd sacrificed myself to him, that he practiced divorce law or civil law or some other type of law that wasn't the right kind of law to spring criminals from behind bars. That was my fate.

'Don't be such a wuss,' I replied. 'It's no big deal. I'm having fun.'

Chapter 11

THE RIGHT WAY TO EAT A SOFTEE

Auggie called me a couple of days later.
'Oh you're back!' I said happily. 'How were the peaches?' Georgia, the US state of which Atlanta is the capital, is famous for its peaches. Juicy and delicious.

According to A the trip was excellent and most profitable. 'Peachy,' he said cleverly.

He wanted to see me that very evening. 'Don't bother going home after work,' he said. 'I'll pick you up outside your office. Five?'

New York wasn't a place where people picked other people up, and dropped them off. Not usually.

It was a place where people walked and walked, and counted distances in terms of blocks, not miles or kilometres. Twenty city blocks was roughly a mile, and too far to walk from my perspective, especially in high heels. The avenues were much wider than streets and if you went, for instance, from Lexington Avenue to Seventh Avenue somewhere in the fifties, before the park, you could expect to drop two pounds at least.

I liked his idea very much. I wasn't used to getting picked up from work. Or anywhere else. I had to shlep here and there on the subway mostly, or if I was really tired, I'd splurge on a taxi.

A few of my colleagues observed me drive off in his fancy car, which made me feel pretty good. Unfortunately, Shas was nowhere in sight. She had this way of disappearing just when I had something important to show off. I'd told her about the Corvette but she wasn't impressed. Swedes are a funny lot. Always Saab this and Volvo that.

We drove downtown, to the East Village and found a parking lot near St Marks Hotel.

'What are we doing here,' I asked, knowing the answer already. I was just being coy. Making conversation.

The stage had been well set at WOTW and this was Act II.

'Getting to know each other,' he answered with a twinkle in his black, heavy-lidded eyes. Oriental men were really sexy. Why hadn't I noticed that before, I wondered.

To think that I had spent so much time in China, surrounded by such potential, but had wasted the entire opportunity not once but several times. What a tragedy! But on the positive side, an entire race of people was now open to me.

'Why not your place?' I wondered. 'Or mine.'

'Nah, not as much fun,' he said. He was right. There was something sexy, sleazy, lewd and exciting about going to a hotel room for a few hours. Very New York. A big turn on.

Auggie had brought along a bottle of expensive red. He'd thought of everything.

The moment we entered the room, he whipped out both his bottles.

He uncorked the red and unscrewed the brown. I eagerly accepted the contents of both. They sat nicely with each other in my head.

Our moods went from zero-to-sixty in five seconds. Off went the clothes, dim went the lights. 'Lay back and relax. This is for you,' he said sexily.

He didn't have to ask me twice.

A majority of the men of my acquaintance wanted me on top. I hated being on top. My abs were smushy and my thighs were weak. I had no core strength to speak of and found it extremely difficult to take control of the proceedings, the way I knew I was expected to. Like the pros, the ones who slithered and slid so gracefully on dance poles.

All I could manage was to huff and puff asthmatically, sweating profusely on the chest of the poor sod under me, my face several shades of green, hoping that it was good enough to get the job done.

So, I was more than happy to lay back. It didn't take more than a few minutes for me to discover that I had struck gold.

Auggie's tongue and jaw muscles, like his six-pack abs, were extraordinarily well developed. They were capable of executing many, many, many, many, many reps. He refused to tire. It was nothing short of Olympian.

'I don't want to rush this,' he said, when he came up for air, just for a second. 'Enjoy,' he smiled as he pushed me back on the pillow.

I did.

I let the warm and sweet sensation of nilabasan ng sukdulan (the Tagalog equivalent of multiple petit mort) wash over me in warm, tidal waves of bliss.

I had never known anything like it despite my vast experience, with a multi-cultural cross section of mankind, across so many continents. Not even with Arya, the mathematical genius from India, whose bedroom antics had provided me with many a delightful fantasy after our brief but memorable encounter in China. I would never forget him. How could I? He had introduced me to sex toys, some of them small enough to carry in one's purse, in case of an emergency. I had placed Arya right at the top of my list.

But Auggie was unbelievable. A silver-tongued Energizer Bunny. Or maybe, the Timex that takes a licking but keeps on ticking.

There was no comparing him with anyone else.

Until Auggie, all I'd encountered were only perfunctory and lack-lustre attempts at osculating, mostly accompanied by a lot of whining.

'I miss your face' and 'why are women built like this' and 'surely it can't take this long' and 'my jaw hurts' and 'I wont be able to speak for a week'. (Years later the actor Michael Douglas came out declaring that his throat cancer was a result of too much such activity, but who knows?)

Pre Auggie, I had become accustomed to the indiscriminate slobber, the cobra flick, the doggie lap and even darting lizard. All in very poor taste.

If all this wasn't bad enough, men always expected the 'favour' to be returned. A totally unpleasant activity I tried to avoid at all costs, although I confess, not with too much success. But luckily for me, I didn't have to think about those dreadful moments in my life. Not just then.

At that very moment, Auggie was outclassing everyone I'd ever known. Even my most recent reject, Jerry the doctor, who had the distinction of having passed college exams on the subject of female anatomy. He, of all people ought to have known how things worked.

Auggie turned the only true way to a woman's heart, into an art.

If I were to use words to describe it, since this is a book and not a video where you can actually see the step-by-step, I'd have to say it was like eating an ice cream swirl. You know, the ones that come in a cone? A delicious double scoop of chocolate-vanilla with sprinkles. No nuts.

Even more delightful was that he had no interest in the quid pro quo.

It was beyond belief.

I wanted to call Shas then and there, right in the middle of it, I was sure she wouldn't believe me.

'You are amazing,' I said gratefully. I was getting tired on his behalf. I was up to my eighth NS. 'No more Auggie,' I begged. Too much of a good thing is bad. It ceases to feel good. 'Come back up here,' I said dragging him up by the hair.

He finally did.

If his tongue scored a perfect ten, his 'titi' (that's what they called the man-muscle back in Manila) was a twelve. He was super human.

No harm in telling him so.

'My superman,' I said lovingly, stroking his hair, after his third NS.

'That's sweet,' he said kissing my fingers. 'It's not just me, you know. I had a little help.' And with that he had another toke from his bottle of coke, and offered me some.

I declined. I remembered how difficult it was to fall asleep and how dreadful I felt the next day, trying to stay awake.

Why was it illegal, I wondered? It made people so loving and giving.

'Unfortunately we have to go,' said Auggie. It was way past midnight. 'But this is only the beginning. We've only just met. We're going to have lots of fun, you and me.'

It sounded great even though I was worn and felt like I'd had enough sex to last me a month. A part of me worried that I'd wake up the next morning and feel like death had come back to pay me a visit, the way it had after my encounter at the hospital with Jerry.

Luckily, all I had the next morning was a tiny hangover.

◆

That formed the pattern of our relationship. Auggie would call me out of the blue, we'd meet at some motel, do some coke, have fabulous sex, and then he'd go off zooming in his car. He never asked to come up to my apartment when he dropped me off, which according to Shas was a very good thing since the police were most certainly following his every move.

She also told me that he sounded very much like a castrated eunuch from the Middle Ages. According to her, these men were excellent at pleasing women, since they couldn't do much else anyway so they served the ladies of the harem with their tongues all day and night, while their men were off at war.

She had an overblown imagination, that girl, and was getting her information from questionable sources, mixing up her history, her geography and her facts.

Mostly, she said things to try and upset my plans.

I assured her that Auggie was no Castrati. For one thing, he had a nice deep, voice, and for another, he was certainly in possession of all his appendages, which he used to superb effect.

But common wisdom told me that Auggie was hiding something from me. At least there, Shas could have been right.

Chapter 12

THIRD WORLD COLLISION

While I was holding nothing back, revealing myself unabashedly to Auggie so that he could get to know me almost as well as I did, I got a call from Rue, my recently re-discovered Indian girlfriend. The one who had shown no qualm or coyness as she was presented naked before New York's off-off-Broadway theatre audiences, held aloft on a copper platter by four gleaming ebony men from Haiti.

'Hey! Ever had them carry you like that out on the street? I mean like around the block? In your birthday suit.' I asked her playfully. That would have caused a New Yorker or two to stop and stare. Especially on Christopher Street where gleaming men of any colour were very sought after.

'Stop being a donkey, and listen up,' she replied. I suppose she felt she could take liberties with me because she knew me from way back.

She cut into my thoughts just as I was preparing to take umbrage at her tone. I thought it was unwarranted even if my question was a little silly. What had happened to humour of off-off-Broadway? Taken a dive into the river?

But I quit umbraging. She had an exciting proposition, so she said.

'We're doing another play,' she declared joyously.

'That's fine for you,' I said peevishly. 'What's it to me?'

Rue explained how I fit in. It was to be a musical extravaganza with real words this time, an adaptation loosely based on Helen of Troy, as seen through the eyes of one Kiko, a woman who had lived all her life in Bali, before she made the move to the East Village.

As far as I knew, many people in Bali were Hindu, so it would be logical and appropriate if she had been part of the Ramayana, the play staged earlier.

I mentioned this to Rue.

'How does that even matter?' she replied. 'For all you know, Hinduism bores her to tears. I know it bores the heck out of me. I'm seriously thinking of becoming Wiccan.'

She was joking I assumed. It was a kind of witch-crafty, vampiry religion that jaded Christians took to, mostly to be cool. She didn't look the type.

'Forget about all that, you're making me lose the thread. The point is that we want you,' she said blowing air kisses into the phone.

'To do what?' I said. It didn't sound good. I didn't want to become a witch or parade around the EV naked.

'To sing, of course! Isn't that what you do?' asked Rue cheerfully.

I was delighted. I was to be the lead singer in a small group, she explained.

'Do I have to audition?' I wondered. I wasn't so keen on rejection.

'Not at all,' said Rue. 'I've recommended you. They trust me. You're in.' I learned later that she was sleeping with Tabitha, the play's director, so had access to all kinds of insider information, besides wielding considerable influence in the selection process.

'Fantasticamundo Segundo,' I said joyously. It would give me the chance to hang around Auggie some more. And who knew what else would come my way?

We set up a time to meet at the theatre so I could be introduced to everyone else to get into the swing of things.

Shas, for once, seemed happy. This was a productive turn of events that wasn't based on sex. She felt it would be good for me.

♦

Rue met me outside the theatre on the street a few days later for a heads-up ciggie before I went in. I was a little nervous but excited too. I hadn't met the other musicians yet, and I hoped they would like me. I hoped they would like my singing. I hoped we'd dovetail musically.

I was most certainly not looking for love or even sex from anyone in the band. I wasn't stupid.

Any man (except Auggie) who would agree to spend chunks of the day rehearsing, just to perform in an off-off-Broadway theatre production that no one of note would care about, almost certainly didn't have any prospects.

Stars in one's eyes wasn't money in the bank.

I didn't want my lifestyle to sink even lower than where it was. A studio walk-up on the Upper West Side, with iffy views of Riverside Park and the Hudson River beyond. You had to stand on your tippy toes and lean out of the window clutching the sill (so you wouldn't fall out and become pulp on the street) to see the lightest glimmer of water.

No siree, there would be no falling in love for me in the East Village.

'Before we go in,' said Rue, cutting into my daydreams as she stubbed out her cigarette, grinding it into the street. 'There's something I haven't told you yet. I hope it's not a problem. We have to fork out $150 bucks each to make this play happen. And before you ask—no, I can't lend it to you.'

I raised my eyebrows contemptuously. I rarely got to do that, so I hammed it up a bit.

'Isn't it the other way around usually? Don't people pay to watch performances? That's how I thought the performing arts functioned, Rue,' I said as haughtily as I could. 'At least, that's what happens in music.'

'Oh you'll get your money back. We couldn't find a sponsor and we really want to do this play. We need the money to pay for sets and this and that. But when we sell tons and tons of tickets, we'll all be rich!' she said with conviction. She had faith in the theatre.

I didn't believe it. I didn't think I'd see my money again, not even if the entire cast (and musicians) were totally naked. But it sounded like a small price to pay for a few months of fun.

'Ok,' I said. 'I'll have the cash when we meet next.'

We went inside where the third world had collided and shattered into a cacophony of voices and mother tongues. It was scary. There were about eighty people there, cast, crew and musicians, about twenty-five languages and dialects, none of them English.

It was amazing that so many people from so many parts of the world had found each other in New York, discovering a common purpose.

Of course, some forty blocks uptown by the East River stood the UN Building, where people from many nations were also dialoguing and discoursing, but I doubted very much that they fell on each other hugging and kissing as if they were long-lost friends. People's behaviour and attitudes changed as you moved further uptown in Manhattan.

◆

Tabby, the play's director and Rue's girlfriend was a wisp of a woman with closely cropped hair, combat boots and a loud voice.

'What part are you playing,' I asked Rue.

'Helen, of course!' she said indignantly. Needless to say, the casting couch was soft, fluffy and very much alive off-off-Broadway.

Tabby cleared her throat and roared. Quite suddenly. For a tiny person, she packed a wallop. She scared eighty-odd cackling, mostly mild-mannered actors (and musicians) from the TW (Third World) into immediate silence.

She and Kiko (who resembled Yoko Ono during her frizzy hair phase), the re-writer from Bali, explained that we'd be meeting three times a week, in the evenings after work, and six hours a day, Saturday and Sunday. There would be no lunch and no dinner served, we'd have to take care of all that on our own, but they would make sure the water coolers were filled and the toilets were clean.

It was a form of exploitation for sure, but no one minded. They gave their hearts and souls willingly. And the $150.

'Look at the schedule posted at the entrance to see when your scene is being rehearsed. All of you don't have to be here at all times,' Tabby explained. It was good to know. Keeping track of so many people's comings and goings was a huge task. Unless someone was coordinating with precision, I could envision everything disintegrating into anarchy.

'Is Auggie in the play?' I whispered to Rue. I hadn't spotted him.

Just then I felt someone run a finger down my spine. It was Auggie. Beaming broadly. He was to play Paris, the prince of Troy, who steals the beautiful Helen away from her ageing husband Menelaus.

'Hey,' he said.

LWG. Life Was Good. Auggie. A play. Music. Sex. Drugs. What more could a girl want?

◆

I met the members of the orchestral pit, also known as, the band. A tabla player from Oregon, a guy who called himself Krishna but spelled it 'Krsn'. He wasn't Indian, but clearly wished he was, by the way he dressed and bobbled his head. A pan flute player from Lima called Eddie, a bass player from Mexico named Jose and a koto player from Japan, a girl named Tumi. An odd yet interesting group of people, who were going to create music for a Greek classic.

We decided that we'd get together in one of the rehearsal rooms in the theatre a couple of times a week, before we were required to get into the pit, to work things out as much as we could.

Tabby and Kiko gave us some guidelines. We were expected to create new and interesting sounds, ebbing and swelling with the natural crescendos of the play itself. Original music that could not sound the same two nights in a row. Completely improvised.

We could have broad themes. Happy, sad, fearful, tense, loving and so on—but there were to be no written scores. 'In fact,' said Tabby, 'you won't be in the pit. You'll be on stage, off to the side, so you can watch the actors perform, and get your inspiration visually. It's a heroic tale, so let go, let it all go, give it your innermost soul, but let it come out through the bowels.'

That was theatre talk for, 'make some noise'. She didn't expect us to spontaneously void, of course.

At first we sounded awful. As if hungry hyenas, lions, crows and wild dogs were all attacking the same dead buffalo at once.

We were each from different schools of music. Classical, jazz, blues, Indian, folk, etc. We weren't speaking the same language.

But music, unlike English or Tamil (which is the language of quarrelling), makes it easy to be generous and friendly. We got into it. We found each other's sweet spots; rhythm and melody. Some may have said we sounded beautiful.

◆

Auggie was hugely popular. Everyone loved him. Besides his acting skills, which weren't bad, his charm, wit and endless supply of white powder made him the MVA (Most Valuable Actor) of the theatre group.

I was beginning to understand A's revenue model. He was a drug dealer. My boyfriend, the drug dealer. It was very exciting.

Life settled into a whirl of activity. Work at the travel company followed by rehearsal downtown. Auggie and I would often slip into an empty rehearsal room, or if we had time, into a nearby rent-a-bed motel for a quick couple of nilabasan ng sukdulans.

I wanted to write an ode to his prowess, but then thought the better of it. One doesn't go showing off such things unless one is willing to have one's boyfriend stolen immediately.

I'd sniffle back to rehearsal trying to appear nonchalant, straight-faced and calm.

While I might have fooled everyone else, I didn't fool Rue. As I mentioned earlier, when it came to selecting a BFF, I always found myself in the company of the nosy, the opinionated, the interfering and the eagle-eyed. Maybe it was my subconscious, missing the mom. Maybe I yearned constantly for an authority figure. Who knew? Psychology was way beyond me, I could barely spell it.

'That guy is dangerous. I hope you're not anywhere close when the cops drag him away kicking and screaming,' she said, her eyes narrowing ominously. 'What do you know about him and his life?'

'Not much,' I confessed. 'He doesn't get a chance to talk much.'

If she only knew.

'Don't say I didn't warn you,' she said with a wag of the finger and switched the subject.

She had other things on her mind.

Such as the little opening dance sequence she had choreographed in Act IV, Scene 1, when the curtains opened right after intermission.

Besides being an excellent actress with the ability to convincingly and meaningfully deliver oratory, both clothed and naked, Rue was also a pretty decent dancer.

She had been trained back home in India, in the ancient art of Bharatanatyam, a type of classical dance mostly performed by women. The movements are not so much graceful as they are scientific. B dancers move around in a half-squat position, slapping the floor with their feet, making exaggerated hand and eye movements to signify love, longing, joy, sorrow and faith. You have to grow up with both the music and the dance form to be able to enjoy its intricacies.

Perhaps to compensate for the rigid B rulebook, where no deviation, no improv, no variation is permitted (the dance has to be performed exactly as it always has been for the past five thousand years); the costumes are bright and joyous. B dancers also wear a lot of heavy make-up and even heavier jewellery.

Heavy, stone-studded ornaments adorn the dancer from head to toe.

The ears are festooned with long dangling earrings, tethered to the hair for security reasons. (The ear lobe can detach if the dancer is caught up in the mood of the moment.) Nose rings on both nostrils, also hitched to the hair to prevent the ripping of flesh.

Often there's a third nose ring, in the area called the septum from which hangs a ruby or a pearl. The dancer will wear several necklaces, each arranged so it doesn't get entangled with the one next to it.

Her head is decorated on either side and in the centre of the forehead hangs yet another jewel. The long, single, swaying braid in the back is also covered in diamonds, emeralds and pearls. The upper arms, the forearms, the wrists are covered in bangles. The waist is cinched with a golden belt. The toes have rings. And a broadish leather belt studded with several rows of brass bells is worn around each ankle, so that the thump, thump, thump sound more like ching, ching, ching.

From my perspective, it is an extremely painful way to provide entertainment. Only the most stalwart and persevering amongst Indian woman take up this ancient form of art/torture.

But despite the thumping and the weights, an unfortunate side effect is that Bharatanatyam dancers will often develop wide hips and large bottoms. Possibly because of the hours they spend squatting.

Indian art and sculpture has always glorified Indian womanhood in the image of the B dancer, so the Indian male is quite sensitised to the wide bottom. It has never been hard for a B dancer to get a date on a Saturday night on account of her large backside.

Bottom spotters in India can pick out B dancers miles away. 'There's goes a good dancer,' they'll say when a woman's bottom is extra wide. 'She's no B dancer,' they'll say if her bottom is average.

◆

After coming to New York, Rue had taken lessons in modern dance, cleverly controlling the spread of her bottom while creating her own form of Indo-western dance, something that had never been attempted before.

She was a pioneer, boldly going where no dancer had gone before.

Rue, of course, had worked out a doozy of a part and a fabulous costume for herself.

Her outfit was a blend of the east and west. Brightly coloured diaphanous material (she would not be wearing anything under it) with plenty of jewellery, but no nose rings. Her hair would not be braided tightly, held prisoner by metal and stones; it would fly freely and trail her movements gracefully.

She would twirl and whirl, the wispy fabric twisting around her B dancer's body as the bells on her feet echoed her desire, mesmerizing and hypnotizing Paris.

The idea behind the dance according to Rue was that with each spin, Paris would fall more and more in love, and finally, Helen, who would be totally dizzy with love herself by the thirteenth spin, would sink gracefully at his feet. Paris would pick her up and proceed to Greece so that the Trojan War could begin.

It was critical that I executed my part to perfection because as Rue pointed out, it was hard to count accurately while spinning thus, the brain was not to be trusted when centrifugal forces were at play.

She had to sink to her feet on cue, my cue, a little percussive phrase repeated three times at the end of the thirteenth spin.

I tried to explain to Rue that this form of dance was better suited to the whirling dervishes of the Middle East, and that it would be difficult from the half squat to get down to the full squat then jump up and turn, and repeat this even four times.

'Pffffssst, thirteen,' she said mockingly. 'I have strong thigh muscles. You just worry about your part and leave me to mine. Come up with something that's not boring. It has to be dramatic.'

That wasn't difficult. I had also studied the ancient art of singing Dhrupad. (As an aside, I found it tiresome that everything in India was ancient. Even modern day India was pretty ancient. When would we do something Guggenheimy, I wondered.)

I came up with a repetitive 'tihai' or Indian scat vocalese that went, 'Di re re, re na na' in triplets. It was a tongue twister, but I was perfectly happy to practise till I could do it thirteen times flawlessly.

'Not twelve, not fourteen but thirteen, ok?' she said menacingly. 'I hope you understand. Precision is everything.'

We rehearsed till both of us were pleased with the results. Rue was surprisingly agile and athletic for a cigarette smoker. She didn't fall down on her face once. She jumped and thumped and twisted and twirled and didn't seem to run out of breath when she took a graceful pointe (when a ballet dancer stands up on her tippy toes).

I was having much more difficulty. With both the breath and the counting. I didn't like Indian music all that much, I decided.

Where was Auggie when I needed a pick-me-up?

◆

I kept Shas, my Swedish friend abreast of the proceedings of the Third World occurring daily in downtown Manhattan, and she seemed vaguely interested.

'I'll come see you on the opening day. I hope it's not boring. It seems so old, so done. I mean Helen of Troy, really? Everyone does it. When all else fails, H of T. Why not something more interesting, like the story of Thor and Sif?'

It hadn't struck old Shas that playing Thor and his flaxen-haired 'flicka' (girl) would be a little out of place in the TW. Greece was easier to manage. It bridged the gap between east and west.

'Just buy some tickets. I need to get my money back,' I said. 'And bring Klaus.'

◆

Pretty soon it was time for dress rehearsals. The pace stepped up drastically. Tempers frayed. Tears were shed. Understudies prayed that actors would fall ill. Costumes were fitted. Lights were tested. Musicians developed the jitters.

We had a pre-opening-night pep talk, with the entire cast and crew present. T & K were certain we'd be a raving hit, a smashing success. The Village Voice had already hinted at this. Seats were booked solid for the first two days. An excellent omen according to Rue. There would be no stopping us, she said.

It was twenty-four hours till opening night.

Chapter 13

SIREN SONG

'I'll take you to a nice dinner tonight,' said Auggie, smiling his quirkily sexy smile, after the final dress rehearsal was over and everyone had spilled out onto the street, saying excited goodbyes. There was a babble of tongues, several languages being spoken in unison.

If an alien had landed there at that moment, he would have a tough time with, 'Take me to your leader.'

Which leader, would be the question.

Auggie was unburdened by the nonsense that always went on inside my head so he continued with his own train of thought, 'Steak. I'm going to fatten you up with a nice medium-rare tenderloin wrapped in crispy bacon, with buttery mashed potatoes and a salad followed by strawberries and cream. No coffee. Nothing that begins with "C". You need to sleep so you can soar like a bird when you sing tomorrow.'

He'd noticed, the observant fellow. How thoughtful.

I'd lost a little weight since I met him. Quite a lot actually since I was almost never hungry. C had that effect. It kept away the hunger. I also had large-sized bags under my eyes, since my sleep patterns had been disrupted quite significantly. But that was a small price to pay for the multiple benefits of A's company. I piled on the make-up and hid my guilty pleasures.

A was so sweet. Always concerned about me. In bed and out of it.

'Ok Auggie,' I said. Who was I to refuse a nice dinner? Suddenly, I was ravenous.

We drove up Amsterdam Avenue, somewhere in the vicinity of the upper 60s, where there were plenty of nice restaurants and shops. It was also not too terribly far from home. It was going to be an early night. There would be no nilabasan ng sukdulan that evening, we had both agreed. We needed our rest so we could sparkle and sizzle the following day, as all eyes would be on us.

I was considering a soak in the tub before I went to bed, to loosen up the knots and soften the kinks.

Suddenly, without warning, Auggie pulled over to the side. He looked like he was going to park. It was most surprising. For one thing, there was no legal parking spot there, and for another, Auggie never, ever parked on the street. According to him, people who loved their cars as much as he loved his yellow Corvette, wouldn't dare take such a foolish risk.

Hooligans were just biding their time, waiting to bump and dent, he had told me many times. New York was swarming with people of evil intent.

'I'll leave the engine running. Pay attention. Keep looking in the rear view as well, not just in front. Look to the sides. There are maniacs all over the place,' he said darkly. 'I just have to pop in there.' He pointed to a low-end men's shoe store a couple of car lengths down the street, with plate glass windows that I could see clearly through. There were a couple of worn-out shop assistants and a sleepy looking manager moving around. They looked like they were Turkish or Algerian. There were hardly any customers in the store, but that was to be expected. It was evening and approaching closing time.

'What for?' I asked, 'You need shoes? Now?'

'No shoes,' he said with a theatrical shudder and upward roll of the eyes. I got it. He didn't shop in such stores. He was most assuredly a designer shoes kind of guy.

'I have to do something. Real quick. I'll be back before you know I'm gone,' he said and swaggered over there. He never moved very fast. It was uncool. He did have a very nice behind, I noted idly.

Auggie pushed the door open and the manager welcomed him warmly, with the traditional Middle Eastern three-air-kiss routine.

I saw A hand something over to the manager who beamed and handed him a thickish manila envelope. I saw A turn away from the prying eyes of passers-by on the street. Judging from the movement of his elbows and the fact that he licked his thumb every few seconds, he appeared to be counting something.

It was quite boring.

I knew I was supposed to keep a vigilant eye out for vagrants with sharp objects, but I didn't think such people existed on the swanky Upper West Side, especially when there was so much activity all around, not to mention, I was sitting in the car, alert and awake.

I decided to do some singing exercises. It didn't hurt to have the vocal chords limber.

◆

The first exercise was to open my mouth, stick four of my fingers inside, stretching it out as widely as possible, the thumb bent. Once I couldn't open any wider, I had to say 'electraaaaaaaaaaaah,' as loudly as I could. After doing this a few times, I moved on to the second exercise, the vocal trill. Eyes closed, I wet my lips with my tongue and began blowing out air in a controlled manner. 'Brrrrrrrrrr, brrrr, brrrr, brrrr.' Do, Re, Mi, Fa and so on, up and down the scale, moving up a half step each time I'd completed the octave.

I was up to 'Ti' when all hell broke loose.

Police sirens started wailing. Cars everywhere started honking. People everywhere started yelling, including me. I was startled out of my wits.

And before my eyes, as seen on TV, six black-and-whites screeched to a frightening halt, one after the other, in front of the shoe store, missing Auggie's beautifully maintained yellow Corvette in which I sat, by a smidgen. A hair's breadth. A whisker.

A posse of uniforms leapt out of the car and charged into the store yelling for Auggie and his pals to drop it and hit the floor. They had guns drawn and were wearing Kevlar vests. Very serious business.

First I saw the Algerians (or Turks) bite the dust (gangsta talk for, 'get down on the floor'), their recent purchases whooshing across the room in a cloud of white dust.

Then I saw Auggie fall to the floor, the contents of his manila envelope, many, many crisp green C notes flying around the store. The letter C. Again.

That did it. I snapped out of my shock.

Shiiiiiiiiiiiiiite, I said to myself. I was sitting in Auggie's car. The perp's vehicle. It didn't take a sharp cookie like me too long to put two and two together. I had to take a powder. That's more gangsta for, 'get the hell out of there.'

I carefully opened the door, and trying to draw as little attention to myself as possible, slithered out from the low-slung seat.

By then the cops had handcuffed Auggie and his buddies. I didn't wait to see them Mirandizing him, if indeed they did.

I walked in a measured way, not too fast, not too slow, blending in with non-drug peddling pedestrians minding their lawful business, and waited till I turned the corner.

Then I ran.

As fast as I could in my high heels.

Fortunately, a vacant yellow cab was hovering around the next block, and I leapt in, keeping my head down so the driver couldn't see me clearly. I didn't want him ID-ing me later. Heaven forbid. I gave him the address in a muffled, code-in-the-dode tode (cold-in-the-nose tone) and blew my nose for good measure.

♦

By the time I got home, I was shaking. Shuddering. Shivering. It was such a narrow, unbelievable shave.

This was not India, where the mom and the stepdad could call up high-level politicians to spring me from jail. (The stepdad was an important journalist with access to the Prime Minister of India and claimed that he could get anything done with one phone call. He had indeed obtained a passport for me in one day, without my having to set a foot outside our house.)

I thanked all the gods in India for sparing me and then called Rue to break the sad news. There would be no Paris to kidnap Helen. He'd been kidnapped himself, by the police.

She shrieked and wailed and accused me of sabotaging the play, but soon quit that line of talk when she realised that:

(a) I could also do the bunk and where would that leave the play? And,
(b) While drinking joyously from Auggie's never ending cup, everyone directing or performing in H of T knew that Auggie was a ticking time bomb only waiting to explode.

An emergency pow-wow of the entire cast and crew was called that very night.

'The show must go on,' said Tabby, firmly. 'And we must be ready. Jeren, here's your chance to show us what you've got,' she said to Auggie's understudy, an olive-skinned, cool-looking eighteen-year old from Trinidad. He had the tuneful accent of people of the Caribbean. Bob Marleyesque. He had beautiful rust-coloured cornrows with little colourful beads at the end.

I thought it was adorable, but I knew Rue didn't think it was becoming for a Paris, who had to look and sound heroic, not adorable or cute or cool. But she had no choice. It was Jeren or curtains for the show.

'Would you consider cutting off all that hair? Paris would look so hot bald, like Yul Brynner in the *King and I*, don't you think?'

Rue asked him half-heartedly, not expecting a positive reply.

'Oooooo,' he wailed, tears welling up in his eyes.

'Ok, ok, that's alright,' Tabby cut in. She didn't want him upset. Besides, it wasn't his hair she was concerned about. It was his knowledge of the lines. As I mentioned, this was not a play in gibberish where he may have been able to fudge it. It was in actual English.

Jeren, perhaps not believing that he'd ever rise up from understudy, hadn't memorized all of Paris's lines as he was expected to. He was patchy at best in his delivery. He kept looking hopefully into the wings for the prompter to help him along.

But on the plus side, his thick, islandy singsong prevented anyone from understanding what he was saying, even when he said his lines properly.

Maybe the show wasn't totally doomed. It would certainly be interesting.

◆

Before the emergency rehearsal could come to an end (this took about three hours with all the stopping and starting), there was a commotion at the door and someone came rushing in to the front row, where Tabby and Kiko were sitting, making copious notes, shaking their heads, whispering to each other, nervously observing the play from hell.

It was a thin, red-haired woman, not from the Third World, probably only from Queens, with sunken eyes and a windy look about her. She was yelling at the top of her lungs at Tabby. Her hands were flailing and she was incoherent. She had a prominent bulge around the middle and it was way too big to be just a large meal. She was very, very pregnant.

I noticed that she was dressed very expensively and the keys of a BMW were dangling from her hand, the ring finger of which sported a wedding band and a large diamond ring.

'You encouraged him. You and your snivelling Third World theatre group. I begged him to stop. I begged him to join my father's grocery business. But he wouldn't listen. And now he's gone. What am I going to do with this?' she pointed at the stomach. 'I'm due any day now. Auggie, oh my poor Auggie,' she wailed and the tears flowed freely down her cheeks.

Tabby and Kiko put their arms around the woman, trying their best to console her, more importantly, to get her away from the front row, where she was making such a racket that the actors couldn't hear themselves speak.

'Julia, calm down. This is terrible, I know. But we're going to have to deal with it. There's no use in spreading the blame around,' said Kiko. 'We all know that Auggie is a drug dealer and we love him for it. But the cops feel differently. Let's see how to find a way out of this mess.'

But Julia was unstoppable, she refused to listen to reason, accusing, pointing, blaming and screaming. It's a miracle that the baby didn't pop right out, there and then in the front row, which may have been poetic for the child of an actor, but perhaps not so much for the cleaning crew.

It was only because Kiko and Tabby each grabbed an elbow and physically carried her out of the theatre that we were able to get back to the play.

'Who is she?' I mouthed the words at Rue.

'Wife,' she mouthed back. 'And baby.'

The lousy rat, I thought to myself. He hadn't breathed a word about his marital status to me. Not that it mattered; he wasn't the 'here's a nice guy to settle down with' type anyhow. Too dangerous. But still, it stung to discover I'd been conned.

Serves him right if he's locked away for good, I said to myself. GRTBR (Good Riddance To Bad Rubbish).

I'd get back to eating as much as I wanted and sleeping normally again. I'd forget all about Augustus and his wife Julia.

A dumb combo if I ever heard one. Would they call their child June? September?

◆

I struggled home in the early hours of the AM and somehow managed to get a few hours of sleep. I thought of Auggie briefly. He must have been climbing the walls up there in jail. Poor guy. He may have been a slimy con artist and a despicable louse, but he was excellent at the Ice Cream Swirl, and I would miss that. I wondered if I'd ever meet anyone else who would be as good.

◆

The morning dawned the same as every other day, with the din of traffic from the streets below rising up through my window in a warm buzz, reminding me that I was a free woman, living in New York, the greatest city on earth.

I was not in jail.

I'd had more excitement the previous night than most people probably had in their entire lifetime. Not a good kind of excitement, like winning a ten million dollar Lotto jackpot, but a pit-in-the-stomach kind excitement that had me running to the loo at least five times before I felt comfortable enough to take the subway down to the Lower East Side, for opening night.

I spoke to my therapist, my catholic priest, my Hindu goddess with the many arms, all rolled into one a.k.a., my best friend, 'Shas' as she preferred to be called, for a good half-an-hour in the morning, bubbling over with the events of the night.

Her Swedish shrieks punctuated my narrative. It struck me that talking on the phone wasn't such a good idea, because everyone knew that the cops had bugs planted everywhere. But somehow, I didn't care. I had to get it off my chest, despite the, 'I told you so, I told you so, I told you so.'

Shas may have been stern and judgmental but she always

absolved me of my sins, and gave me another chance.

A new lease on crime.

◆

The play got off to a pretty good start. Despite everyone's nerves and a missing Paris. Mostly because Paris (now Jeren) didn't make his entrance until after intermission. We had a little breathing room before the tentative Trinidadian twang made its presence felt on stage.

It was not my most inspired singing, I'll admit. I was still pretty rattled by the events of the previous night. I felt that of all the cast of characters in Auggie's life, I had been wronged the most.

Maybe the theatre group had lost a leading man. Maybe Julia had lost a husband and her rotten baby would never feel a father's love. But I had almost been arrested by the police. I almost got sent away for life, all because of a few (well many) nilabasan ng sukdulan.

It was far more serious for me.

I tried to put such thoughts out of my mind so I could focus on my singing. I was hoping Tumi, the koto player, and Eddie, the pan flute player, would pick up the slack. They did. They were such gems.

We received fairly enthusiastic response from the crowd at the end of the first half, and everyone breathed a huge sigh of relief. Auggie's absence hadn't yet been felt.

My big moment, Rue's big moment and Jeren's big moment came immediately following the end of intermission, with the curtain going up on the spinning scene.

We took our places. The curtains rose up slowly. I took a deep breath and looked across at Helen, who was already in character, tapping her feet as if she was about to break into dance. She shone and sparkled as the stage lights caught the glittering stones around her neck. The ching-ching of her ankle bells was my cue to begin humming a little, a build up to the choreographed routine we had practised so many times.

It was also the moment Jeren, the eighteen year-old would make his off-off-Broadway debut. And he did. Bursting in through the door with a bunch of soldiers trailing him. He looked around here and there on stage, as if he couldn't see Helen, standing right there in front of him, shimmering. One had to suspend reality quite a bit if one was to enjoy theatre.

But something happened to me when I saw Jeren. A sort of out-of-body experience.

I didn't see Jeren's character, Paris. All I saw was a chained and shackled Auggie. Auggie with the velvet tongue. I hadn't properly grieved for him yet, and waves of sorrow overcame me as I recalled the waves of bliss he had slathered on me, it seemed like only yesterday.

It took all my resolve to keep myself from bursting into tears.

I began singing, but bright and vivid visions of Auggie overwhelmed me. I choked a few times, forgetting where I was in the count, almost as soon as the sequence began.

Helen (Rue) was not to know that all these thoughts were going through my head. She confidently began her complex twirls, jumping up from the squat position, standing up to full height, spinning gracefully and then squatting again. She was relying on me to bring her 'home' so to speak, on the thirteenth spin, with my clever clue.

But I was hell and gone from thirteen. I was possibly on twenty or twenty-one. I only came to my senses when I heard Krsn, the tabla player, roll insistently on his skins and Eddie, the bass player play, loud and suggestive accents. I realised that I had no idea where I was, so enveloped was I in my sorrow.

Rue, who had been squatting and jumping up, squatting and jumping up some twenty-three times by now, was furious. With a dramatic leap across the stage, gracefully of course, because that's the kind of actress and dancer she was, she landed a few feet in front of me.

'Change cue! You bitchhhhhhh,' she hissed at me, flames shooting out of her eyes. 'Change now! I'm going to kill you.'

I did. Immediately.

The band members held back their smiles. We were on stage after all, even if it was off to the side. Somehow, we got through the end of the play, with no other major mishaps.

Jeren's adorable island twang won over audiences as much as his bare, hairless chest and his cornrows. So what if people couldn't really understand him? Everyone already knew the ending, and for those who didn't, there was a photocopied synopsis on each seat.

We got a rousing ovation, two encores and everyone was happy. Especially, Tabby and Kiko. Rue pretended to be very upset with me. It took much cajoling and pleading for her to forgive me. She claimed she had pulled a muscle in her groin and didn't know how she could possibly make it through the next several shows.

But the next morning's newspaper described Rue as a, 'Lovely lady of Indian origin with the ability to emote and leap across the width of a large stage like an Olympic athlete, without missing a beat.' And they described me as a, 'Vocal warrior with hidden depths in her arsenal.' I think they had sent their sports writer to cover us, by mistake.

Anyhow, Rue's groin pull disappeared miraculously after the public praise, and we kissed and made up.

Chapter 14

DIPLOMATIC IMMUNITY

The next two weeks went by in a blur of activity.

I was grateful for that. I'd had boyfriends before that I'd dumped or had dumped me, but no one had been wrenched out of my arms and soul so absolutely, so finally. In jail.

Things weren't going my way at all. It was unimaginable that so much misfortune could befall one girl in the course of one life.

If not for Helen and Troy and the huge distraction they provided, who knew what depths of depression I might have sunk into?

But we performed H of T every evening except Monday, and had two shows on Saturday and Sunday. It was gruelling, tiring, exhilarating and exhausting. But it was also great fun.

Even Jeren had managed to memorize his lines to perfection by Day Five, delivering them in a passable Brooklyn accent that the audiences understood.

Rue, Tabby, Kiko and everyone in the cast and crew were pleased with the way things were turning out.

After a few wild panic attacks, my mind stayed on track. Once or twice I found myself being awakened by the ominous wail of police sirens, and loud banging on the door, causing me to sit up bolt, upright in my lonely bed only to realise that I was dreaming.

I always fervently thanked my many gods for saving me. They never let me down. I'd have to do something for them, more than just lip service one of these days, I felt. Something grand, memorable. Like maybe a sacrifice. A goat? A chicken? A black crow? Nah that was cruel.

I wondered about penance. (The influence of the convent never goes away from one's life, no matter how hard one tries to bury it in random, degenerate behaviour.) Should I give up cigarettes? Quit booze? I pushed those wicked thoughts right out of my head quickly before someone up there heard me. I didn't want to be held accountable.

The last time I had felt as frightened was at international arrivals section of Chicago's lovely O'Hare airport, when for a couple of hours I was certain Shas and I would be locked up for life (in separate cells) for committing currency fraud. But it ended up being just a misunderstanding. Something about currency conversions and exchange rates. We were eventually allowed to proceed without incident, but not before we had been forced into some serious self-doubt and introspection.

I swore never to touch the stuff again.

The C.

The cocaine, not the currency.

I did wonder about Auggie though. I was half expecting to get heartbroken letters from his jail cell, but that didn't happen.

He had probably shoved me right out of his head the moment the cuffs clamped down on his wrists. I didn't know if they allowed prisoners access to newspapers, especially *The Village Voice*. Had Auggie seen the reviews?

Rue was plugged into everything that happened to members of the theatre group even if they found themselves in jail, on account of much pillow talk with Tabby.

She told me that Auggie was in excellent shape, in a cell of his own at Rikers. His wife had visited him several times already. No conjugal visits apparently, since she was so pregnant, and neither one of them wanted their baby to be born in jail.

Bits and pieces of information about Auggie's life; his past, present and now his future came tumbling out from various sources. There was certainly a lot I didn't know about him. And owing to the nature of our relationship, as I've explained in the preceding pages, I hadn't given him much time for conversation.

I learned that he was the son of a very important minister in the Philippine government. Diplomatic entreaties had begun to take place in the dead of night, between the government of the P and the US government, barely a few hours after his capture. The G of the P did all it could to get him out of Rikers and on a plane back to Manila that very night, trying desperately to extricate him while he was still unscathed.

Auggie being a most pretty boy, with a very nice behind as I have already stipulated, they knew the danger he was in. Sadly, the Philippine government was only able to ensure that he was placed in solitary. For the time being at least while negotiations were going on.

According to Rue, the P government official had assured the US officials that they wouldn't let Auggie off lightly. 'We'll deal with him in Manila,' the officials had said, swearing there would be serious punishment.

After much back and forth and certain guarantees (Rue was unable to tell me what kind of guarantee the G of the P could possibly offer up in exchange for Auggie's safe passage back to Manila), the US had agreed to deport him, rather than toss him in with the general population at Rikers for a dozen years.

But all this did not happen overnight.

Rue smiled when she said, 'Time? Auggie's not doing any time in Manila. Most likely there will be a grand celebration, complete with roast suckling pig with an apple stuffed in its mouth to greet him.'

She had been to such a feast in New York, at the home of one of the cast members, and said it made her sick to the stomach. 'Can you imagine snatching away a suckling pig from its mother and roasting it on a spit? With the head, eyes, legs and everything still intact. It's their national dish. Litsón,' she said shuddering as if she was saying, 'Gutter rat.'

I could very well imagine that a rat like Auggie could eat a disgusting national dish like Litsón, probably staring shamelessly back at the pig's eyes as he ate it methodically, one mouthful at a time.

How could one sleep after such a meal, I wondered.

His American wife Julia was going to join him there with their little girl, who had ultimately made an exit from her mother's womb, into a house filled with boxes and packing crates and no daddy. She was named June, of course.

How stupid could people get? Not that I cared. Auggie was a filthy monster. Even if he had a silken tongue.

I hoped the island would erupt into civil war or something.

Shas told me to take a deep breath. She felt my rage was unproductive. 'Why don't you try yoga?' she suggested. 'I hear that it has helped many Indian people stay calm and sane.'

'What do you mean, I replied indignantly. 'What's wrong with me?'

◆

But I did calm down. And I resumed my work at the Department of Conventions and Exhibitions with renewed vengeance. I was beginning to hate international travellers. Foreigners. (I no longer considered myself anything but a New Yorker, and I barely had the hint of an Indian accent, except when I wanted to be cute.)

My singing skills, as fabulous as they were both on the jazz stage and now on off-off-Broadway as I'd demonstrated to reviewers in the NYT and VV, didn't fetch me more than the price of a meal. A cheap one at that. So I had no choice but to lump it until something better came along.

I decided I'd walk to work every morning instead of riding the subway, for the exercise. It was a good forty blocks, two miles, and cleared my head of its many cobwebs.

The sights and sounds of NYC soothed my soul to no end. I'd pick different avenues to walk down so I wouldn't be bored.

◆

Out of the blue, huge waves of homesickness hit me. It had been several years since I'd said goodbye to the dusty streets of New Delhi where the mom, the brother and the stepdad still lived. Where my friends (well former friends, since I hadn't kept in touch with anyone) like Leena, Jasmine, Fleur and assorted boyfriends lived.

One of the perks of working at the travel company was that I could get free airline tickets to go back home. 'Subject to load,' which meant that the airline had to be absolutely, 100 per cent sure that a paying passenger didn't want the seat. It was bit nerve-wracking, because you never knew if you were getting a seat or not. Pesky paying passengers often showed up at the airport at the last minute.

Shas had gone back and forth to Sweden a few times. For her it was a mere hop and skip of six or seven hours compared to the eighteen hours each way that I'd have to kiss off my vacation, because I wanted a little TLC from the mommy.

I was overcome with loneliness and longing for the mom. My heart, still raw from Auggie's betrayal, felt like it would crumble into powder.

Finally, I couldn't take it anymore and called the mom.

She was beside herself with delight and happiness. Screeches and whoops confirmed she still loved me as much as she always did. Nothing had changed in that arena. The brother hadn't carved out a larger chunk of her heart for himself, neither had my girlfriends won over her affection.

I planned my first trip back home.

It was just a short two-week vacation and even though I'd be spending most of my time in the air, I didn't care.

Suddenly there was nothing more important in the entire world than the mom. Her fresh, lemony-lime perfume, her very soft skin, her hair that always smelled of shampoo, her voice, her laugh, even her handwriting and finally, the way it felt to be squeezed in her great, big bear hug.

I had a good long cry in my bathtub with no one to watch me, and felt much better.

Chapter 15

WHERE HAVE ALL THE VIRGINS GONE?

The mom, the brother (whom I did not recognise at first, because he'd grown so much and was now sprouting facial hair) and the stepdad were all at the airport to greet me. We talked non-stop all the way home, the mom and me mainly, with the brother and the stepdad interjecting, mainly to tell the cabbie to slow down.

Delhi taxi drivers hadn't learned anything in my absence and if anything, drove faster and more recklessly than I remembered. It was a good thing the plane had landed in the middle of the night, there was almost no traffic around. No people to kill.

I had presents for everyone. It was wonderful to see the family again and bask in the warm glow of unconditional love. For about three days, there was only hugging, kissing and catching up.

After a few days, I was restless again. It was time to prowl the streets, to revisit my favourite haunts to see what action I could find.

But Delhi had changed.

The club Touch where I had spent much of my formative years had shut down. In its place was a swank French restaurant. Very chic and very expensive. Not my style. I had sworn off French food anyhow, so the thought of Coq Au Vin made me angry.

I hadn't yet contacted Vikram who was the DJ at Touch, and also my boyfriend, sort of. I hadn't kept in touch with him all the while I was in America, so I had no idea where to begin. Touch was such a popular nightclub back then and filled with so many wealthy patrons that I wondered why it had shut down.

'Government raid,' explained my mom. 'They didn't pay their taxes. And one New Year's Eve, when the joint was jumpin', the tax man cameth.' She was so funny, the mom. I had inherited my sense of humour from her.

Ah taxes. Not paying them got Al Capone. And it got the owners of Touch. I made a note to self: Always pay your taxes. But first, I'd have to earn enough money to qualify.

'What happened to Vikram?' I asked her. He had gifted the mom a leather-bound copy of Omar Khayyam's *Rubaiyat* and spoke of aged malts with the stepdad most knowledgeably. They liked him a lot and couldn't understand why I had tossed him aside. They didn't know that he was probably gay.

'Oh he's off somewhere in the Middle East,' she told me. 'That's what I heard.'

I called Leena, my dearest and bestest friend while I was still living at home, in Delhi. With whom I'd caroused many a night and had much fun. Who'd taught me that the colour pink can be worn as eye shadow if that's what you want.

I was looking forward to meeting her and picking up where we'd left off. My last memory of her was as I left for the airport to go off to America when the mom, caught up in the emotion of the moment perhaps, offered her my bedroom, my clothes and even the special spot in her heart meant for me.

I was furious back then. How was it possible that best friend and mothers could forget so quickly? But that was a long time ago. I'd forgiven everyone.

Leena sounded weak on the phone, but said she'd come over that afternoon.

'What's the matter with her?' I asked the mom.

'Oh she's a junkie,' said the mom, as if it was the most natural thing in the world. 'And she has three little babies. All little girls. To follow in their mother's footsteps.'

'Whaaaaaat,' I wailed. It wasn't possible. What could have possessed Leena to give up on life in this manner? I didn't believe her.

But the mom spoke verily, if sarcastically.

Leena waddled in, having gained almost her entire previous body weight. In her wake were two very little, shabbily dressed girls, tugging at her clothes. There was a tiny baby in her arms.

I was delighted to see her, through the layers of fat and offspring I could see a faint hint of former friend. But I hardly got a chance to hear her say even a few complete sentences.

The two little girls, who could walk perfectly well, chose instead to run. And yell and scream. It was awful. They tore across the mom's beautifully decorated apartment with her Lalique this and Lladro that scattered here and there for effect. She was a big one for home décor, the mom.

The girls would have flung the little glass and porcelain objects at each other, and made a puddle of blood and guts in the living room if the brother hadn't leaped up like lightning and placed them out of harm's way.

The mom, generous and cordial always, had served snacks on the polished coffee table, which was placed at the centre of her prized Bibi Baf, a Persian floor rug with a name, like a pet chimpanzee. I had never met anyone else who had a carpet with a name. It smelled freshly shampooed, no doubt in my honour, because I noticed such things.

The girls spilled crumbs and juice on the rug and then ground it in by jumping up and down. I told myself that the Persians had used these carpets on the desert sand and in dusty tents for centuries before Leena's little monsters had made their appearance. Camels had probably plopped bucketfuls of dung on them when a distracted Persian wasn't paying attention. How bad could a few cookie crumbs be?

'What happened Leena? What went wrong?' I asked this once beautiful creature I had first seen at Touch, with rainbow coloured eye-shadow over mischievous eyes and a ballet dancer's body, her dialogue sparkling with wit and her future bright with promise.

'I don't know,' she said sadly, her eyes half closed. Talking to me seemed like an effort. She didn't make any move to control her little monsters that behaved like they were the result of grafting between human and feral rodent. She let them pounce on her and screech at will. Meanwhile the little baby in her arms cried incessantly. It could have been hungry or wet. Leena didn't seem to care. She had lost control and willpower.

'Where's their father?' I asked her. But I knew the answer even before she replied.

'I don't know who the fathers are. It's a bit of a blur,' she said. 'Can I borrow five thousand bucks?'

I gave her five thousand rupees and told her it was a gift. She didn't have to give it back to me. I also scratched her off my friend's list. There was nothing I could do for her, I was barely surviving myself, and it was too painful to see her this way. The little girls, well even though I never wanted to see them again, I hoped they'd be ok.

'I've given her money before,' said the mom. 'Many times. But I've stopped. There's no end to it. And it doesn't help. She keeps having babies.'

'Horrors,' I remarked to the mom, after they'd left. I had forgotten how little Indian children were almost never disciplined. Even when their parents weren't junkies. They were encouraged to run riot through restaurants, planes, movies and other public places as their beaming parents smiled proudly.

Kids like me, shoved off to boarding school to learn manners and etiquette before we could say, 'I wanna go to the bathroom,' were rare.

'No children for me Ma,' I told her just in case she heard the pitter-patter of grandchildren in her future.

'Never say never,' she said, she was a big James Bond fan. 'Oh and before I forget, I want you to wear a saree tonight,' she said ever so casually.

My ears perked up. Something was afoot. 'Why, Ma? Do you

want me to trip over and smash my face so I won't have to go back to America? Why on earth would I wear a saree? And what's so special about tonight anyway?'

◆

The saree is made up of six unnecessary yards of fabric, wrapped around a woman's body a few times, pleated, tucked into her petticoat and then flung over the shoulder. Under the saree a woman wears her B & Ps (optional) and a blouse.

One would imagine that in a hot country like India the national garment could be a little less cumbersome, a little airier. But not the saree. There's nothing cool and breezy about it at all.

It covers a woman supposedly from head to foot, but the midriff, the back and the boobs are always available for display, if the 'palloo' or the part that goes over the shoulder falls off. Women deliberately let it slide off their bosoms all the time, depending on who's looking.

It is not an easy garment to get used to, say like a pair of jeans. To be comfortable in a saree when you're rushing to catch a plane takes at least three months of regular practise.

The beauty and elegance of its drape, the sexiness of its cling and so on is also very subjective. Very much an eye-of-the-beholder type of thing.

The mom always wore a saree. She could dash the one hundred metres in it. I'd seen her wash the car wearing a saree. Even climb up a ladder. She once beat up a thief who had snatched her gold chain and was trying to get away, in a saree.

What I mean is the thief was in pants, the mom was in the saree.

She looked good in it no matter what she was doing. She was my mom. She'd look good in sackcloth.

But I had no intention of wearing a saree that night or any other night.

'Why? Why? Why? Why? Whyyyyyyyyyyyy?' I asked her. Ever since I was a little kid, I always annoyed the mom by asking the same question over and over again. She'd get all riled up and annoyed and that would give me perverse joy.

She didn't take the bait.

'Because someone's coming to dinner. Especially to meet you. And I want you to look sweet and nice. Pretty and elegant. I want you to look perfect,' she said.

'Who is this person that can't see me the way I am, Ma?' I asked. 'Who is this person we are about to lie to? A ninety year old millionaire?' I was joking.

I assumed it was an aunt or a grand uncle or some friend who hadn't seen me in years, someone whose opinion mattered to the mom. She obviously wanted to showcase me in a good light so they wouldn't carry tales back to the other members of the family, so they could sit around a table, thumping and guffawing at my expense. At least, that's what I thought she was worried about.

'I'm not asking you to lie. I just want you to look your best. And no it's not a ninety year old millionaire. It's a young man. A very nice young man from a very, I mean very wealthy family,' she said, taking in a deep breath, expecting me to erupt hysterically into an uncontrollable frenzy.

I hadn't anticipated this turn of events when I'd booked my tickets to come home to mamma. But I suppose I should have, it's fairly common in India to arrange marriages for your children. No big deal. Everyone did it.

As a means of finding a decent spouse, all vetted and cleared for take-off, the arranged marriage was far more reliable than speed dating or the I-met-him-in-a-bar-last-night method.

'Hmmm,' I said. 'Cute?'

'Very. If only I was twenty-five years younger,' she sighed half-real, half-jest. The stepdad had been trying her patience, I had observed.

He had become more demanding and increasingly dogmatic as

he grew older. He conducted monologues that he called conversation and looked puzzled and angry if people replied. Especially, the mom.

He'd taken to giving lengthy explanations for the simplest of things, repeating himself often. He'd also begun to speak in metaphor and analogy and by the time he got to the point, she could have done the shopping, cooked a meal and washed up the dishes. Or grown a beard if she was a he.

But he did provide a lovely home, car, driver, three maids, a shopping account and also took care of the brother (her son, not his), who wasn't showing any signs of moving out to start a life of his own.

She had to make some sacrifices.

'What else?' I asked.

'His father's an industrialist. One of these days he'll inherit an enormous fortune in copper wires. He's very well educated. Yale. He lived in San Francisco for a while. He's back in India now, learning the ropes so he can move into the chairman's seat soon. His father wants to retire.'

I had no intention of marrying some industrialist's son and moving back to India. Not even if he was as rich as the Sultan of Brunei, or as handsome as Chet Baker. I never, ever wanted to come back to live in India. For one thing, I couldn't drive a stick shift. And for the other, I was having just too much fun in the old Big Apple.

But I didn't say anything. Not even, 'How d'you think he'll feel about a one night stand, just to kick in the tyres, if you know what I mean.'

Instead, we got down to the business of getting ready for the evening. Dressing up. Something that has always made my heart soar with delight, even if this time it involved being all tied down in a saree.

♦

The mom, as it turned out, had prepared for the evening even before my arrival. She'd bought a beautiful saree in a shade of pale onion in some sort of gossamer fabric with a dull copper, leafy motif embroidered all over. She'd also found a copper coloured stretchy blouse with a plunging neckline and low back that would accommodate my 38Ds. If we were in New York, one might have accused her of pimping me out, but this was India. Such events were called matchmaking and took on a pious and orthodox tone.

'Ma, are you sure you've told him about me? I mean, the truth?' I said, as I gelled my hair, the blouse and petticoat already in place. I was no shy, innocent bride. Neither had I accomplished anything worthwhile in America, except a halfway decent understanding of the male anatomy.

'Oh don't be stupid,' she responded. 'There are no virgins anymore. Everyone knows that.' Yikes. Was she reading my mind?

She draped the saree around me, pinning it here and there so there wouldn't be any wardrobe malfunctions.

Then she opened her safe and took out her very expensive diamond jewellery, to be worn only on very important occasions. She clasped the necklace around my neck and asked me to put on the earrings and bracelet.

We were definitely going overboard. I could have paid the queen (of England, of course, since we didn't have queens in India any more) a visit, the way I sparkled.

'So much dressing up for one guy?' I remarked. I looked fabulous, if one liked the Indian princess look.

'His parents are coming too,' she said quietly.

There was a long silence in the room as I digested this information. She didn't say anything while the wheels in my head whirred and clicked. After what seemed like five minutes of silence, I asked hopefully, 'Can I keep the jewellery, Ma? After tonight, I mean.'

'We'll see,' she said. 'Depends entirely on how the evening ends.'

◆

'Anything else you'd care to tell me about tonight?' I asked her, as I patted on the under-eye concealer. She was letting out the info stream in dribs and drabs. Maybe she thought I couldn't process all of it at once.

K. Aditya. That was his name.

That meant he was from South India. But of course.

She, who was au courant with the times when it came to drinking Beaujolais Nouveau exactly at the right moment, who knew with certainty if pink was indeed the new black and other trivia that made the difference between the twentieth century and the stone age, went right back to her curds-and-rice roots (a bland but popular comfort food from my youth) when it came to a husband for me.

She couldn't bring herself to introduce me to a man from the Punjab or maybe Bengal or even Maharashtra. He had to be from Chennai, where they shunned last names, but could be easily identified by ancestor, caste and bank balance.

I carefully painted on the eyeliner.

What did I have to lose? One evening, a few drinks, and I'd have plenty to talk about when I got back to America. Both Shas and now Rue would be eager to hear what happened as I was paraded before prospective in-laws like a prized cow.

I put on the lipstick and pressed my lips down on a tissue. The mom was supervising each move. We didn't speak, because it's hard to talk when you're slathering on the make-up. Defining lips takes precision. Eyeliner looks hideous if it's crooked.

Besides, my thoughts were on overdrive.

I'd never had sex with someone who could speak Tamil. My memoirs would be incomplete if I didn't give a Tamil-speaker at least one shot.

I knew quite well that sex could not be had with a prospective groom before the wedding, but we were not living in the dark ages. Maybe I could talk him into it. He had lived in SFO so maybe he'd picked up a thing or two about the importance of pre-marital sex.

I knew what petit morts were in several languages, Tagalog being the most recent (nilabasan ng sukdulan in case you've forgotten). Also Swedish, 'multipel orgasm', a slight spelling difference, but very clear in meaning. And in German where it could be, 'ich komme und komme und komme...' or 'multiple orgasmen', depending on who you were with at the moment. I didn't know how to say it in Tamil. It would be nice to ask someone who wouldn't slap me across the face, like the mom or the aunt.

Briefly, the thoughts of orgasm made me feel sad. I was still hurting from the abrupt way in which Auggie had been snatched away from me.

But I snapped out of it. I was meeting a man tonight. A man and his parents. I smiled at the mom, who was looking pretty sharp in midnight blue. She was wearing pearls.

'Let's do this Ma,' I said.

The doorbell rang.

Chapter 16

WINDOW DRESSING?

K Aditya, the son of one R. Krishnan.

South Indian children take on the first initial of their father's first name and add it to the front of their given name. It's a half-hearted attempt at identification. Maybe just to make it easier for nurses in the hospital to differentiate between one baby and the next, right after they're born.

There's never been any need for last names in the old S of I.

As a result, when someone in Tamil Nadu wants to find out who you are, to determine if you're worthy of:

a. lunch, or

b. just a polite nod before hurrying away.

c. Maybe their son's hand in marriage, or

d. none of the above,

they'll ask you a series of probing questions about your father, grandfather, town, village, street and door number to properly place you. This could take ten minutes and it's not very efficient, but that's the way it is.

The last name hasn't caught on in South India, where long conversations mean everything.

Maybe I exaggerate a bit, but only very slightly.

Aditya was about six feet tall and his skin a lovely golden brown. He wore rimless eyeglasses that gave him an air of accomplishment and control. He had short hair, no gel, no tats, nothing that could be construed as frivolous. He was dressed formally, suit but no tie. He looked like he worked out. I could see the biceps bulge under his jacket. He had a twinkle in his eye and a lock of hair that kept falling across his forehead.

He was a fine specimen of humanity and I was delighted.

I had a few fleeting moments of self-doubt. Had I wasted my time bed-hopping around the globe in the pursuit of Mr Right, when a phone call to the mom may have served the purpose? Could I have avoided trich? Who knew? Life was certainly filled with twists and turns.

'Shhh,' I said to my thoughts and returned to the present, where I was being introduced, possibly to the rest of my life in the form of Krishnan, party of three, who had made reservations at our house for dinner.

Everyone stared at everyone else for a few minutes. I tried to think of something clever to say, but my brain had become strangely silent. Before I could say, 'nuclear physics', old man K cleared his throat.

'You are liking this yoss music?' asked Mr Krishnan, the father of the delectable Aditya, imperiously waving a stubby finger at me. He said 'yoss' with an echoey lisp, spitting slightly.

He was a chubby, short gentleman with tufts of white hair festooning his ears. His nose followed the same theme. I could see the top of his head. It gleamed. Hair was the damndest thing. It grew where you didn't want it to, and stayed dormant where it ought to have been lush. Very perverse.

I knew the South Indian accent very well, so I knew his supposedly innocuous question was pregnant with scorn, derision and a lot of ignorance. He was saying, 'you're not a scientist or a doctor or even a well-known Bharatanatyam dancer. If only you were a Bharatanatyam dancer, how happy we'd be. You're lucky you have good pedigree or I wouldn't let you anywhere near my son's sperm. So tell me about this jazz-shmazz you call music. I thought jazz musicians were all heroin addicts.'

I have the ability to read minds, as you know by now.

'You could say that,' I replied, maintaining my dignity and

trying hard to respect his, despite all his rude thoughts. 'I like jazz. A lot actually.'

I casually turned to find my pack of cigarettes that usually lay on the side table. A deep drag would calm me down. Nicotine, the narcotic for the nervous soul.

The mom coughed loudly. I looked up to see her glare at me. 'No smoking,' her eyes yelled at me, 'have you lost your mind?' they added for good measure.

I took it that she would not be elegantly smoking through her carved, ivory cigarette holder either, which according to her, trapped all the tar and nicotine, sending only sweet, harmless smoke into her lungs.

I giggled each time she lit it up, it was so pretentious.

'No I will not use a cigarette holder,' I told her firmly each time we smoked a mother-and-daughter ciggie together. 'I am not a gay man.'

'You arrre yaay ticketing yaygent?' K senior cut into my thoughts loudly with his thick Tamilian accent. Tamilians added a 'y' sound to most vowels, except the 'Y' itself, which already comes pre-packaged with the sound.

They also named their businesses 'YemmYess Enterprises' (MS Enterprises) and 'ArrKayYell Holdings' which stood for RKL Holdings. RKL were also the initials of a very famous and funny newspaper cartoonist named R.K. Laxman who made me laugh every morning, but there was no humour at our house just then.

Mr K peered at me through his eyeglasses with pity. I may as well have been a seller of loose cigarettes.

You can stop at a roadside stall pretty much anywhere across the length and breadth of India to pick up one or two cigarettes of any brand, instead of buying the whole pack. It's a good plan if you're trying to quit, or if you don't have enough money.

It's a terrific deal from the consumer's point of view. Possibly even the vendor's, because he most certainly was jacking up the price per loose cigarette. Business works like that. The less you buy of something, the more you pay for it.

But from a potential father-in-law's perspective, it's not the most promising of careers. Little children definitely didn't grow up aspiring to be loose cigarette vendors.

'Not really,' I smiled cheerfully, I wasn't a ticketing agent at all. He was not going to unsettle my equilibrium or embarrass me. 'I work for the Department of Conventions and Exhibitions and we organise the travel arrangements for people attending trade shows around the Pacific and Orient. I travel all over the world for my company.' I thought that sounded quite impressive.

The mom and stepdad beamed. They'd never heard me say such a long and complicated sentence before. The brother stifled a snort. He knew what's bullshit when he heard it. I'd given him a sanitised but hilarious version of what actually happened on our trips.

'Hrmmmmmph,' said Mr K loudly, not quite convinced. Most of the South Indians of my acquaintance are very loud, without realising it. People will come right up to you and yell in your ear. I think deafness runs rampant through the land.

Mrs K piped in, the timbre of her voice surprisingly low, almost mannish, but she was just as loud, 'Do you like cooking? Aditya loves my home-made sambar and rasam,' she admitted candidly, referring to two watery South Indian must-haves on the daily lunch menu. I loathed the spicy stuff. It got you coming and going. Bad breath followed by the runs.

'I have to confess I don't,' I admitted. 'I always order in. Sushi. Chinese. You know…'

Mrs K looked at me pensively. 'Ayoooo. Have we made a big mistake? She will starve my Adi! What is this sushi? Ayooooyooooyoooo.' I could read her mind just as easily as I could read her husband's.

Aditya's, now that was the mind I really wanted to read, but that book was shut.

Fortunately, the mom announced dinner and we trooped in to the dining room where she, in deference to the Krishnan family sensibilities, had orchestrated an all-vegetarian meal, entirely ordered from a restaurant. We were not a 'home-cooked' kind of family. We've always preferred restaurant food to the slop we would otherwise churn out.

I could see Mrs K heave a sigh of relief. One that smelled a little of perungayam, a vile spice that South Indians use a lot, and one that I have spoken of at length in an earlier communiqué. I won't delve into the wheres and the whys, but suffice it to say that it is one of the main reasons I don't like the food of my ancestors. Its Latin name is 'asafoetida', and no great prizes for guessing why. In Swedish, it's called, 'dyvelsträck' which means devil's dung. I used it as an affectionate nickname for Shas from time to time, when she was being annoying.

The brother rolled his eyes heavenward. I wanted to do the same, but my fake eyelashes may have fallen into the payasam. That's a kind of dessert that one eats before the meal, rather than at the end. It's pretty delish. Filled with sugar, raisins, nuts and milk.

The culture of South India is vast, deep, mysterious and frustrating. But once in a while, it's good.

Aditya was seated next to me.

'Forgive me, my trespasses,' he whispered in my ear, 'FYI, I hate sambar. And if there's anything I hate more than sambar, it's rasam. Haven't had the heart to tell her.'

What a doll, I thought. 'Don't worry about it,' I whispered back.

'You want to go out somewhere tonight after I drop them back?' he asked me, again in a whisper.

'Yup. I do. But I have to change. I-can't-move-I-can't-breathe-and-I-definitely-can't-pee,' I confessed all in one breath, pointing to my lovely saree.

He laughed aloud, a deep and manly guffaw.

The assorted parents seated across the table looked pleased. Things were working out for all parties. I thought I saw a sad look cross the mom's face. It could have been about losing a daughter or losing her diamonds.

I got through dinner with the future in-laws asking me probing questions here, casting aspersions there and tossing innuendo around like chum in the sea.

I wondered why the mom and stepdad were feeding me to the sharks in little bite-sized pieces. Why didn't they stick up for me? Why were they beaming so happily?

I remembered that when I was little, my grandmother, would cuddle me in her lap and say in Tamil, 'I'm going to cut you up into little pieces, spread you thinly on my hot cross buns with butter and jam and eat you all up,' and 'I'm going to whack you with a broomstick, first to the left and then to the right.' And the best one of all, 'If you drop dead and turn to ashes, I'm going to be so, so, so happy.' I loved listening to her as a kid because the tone was soothing. 'More, more, more,' I'd say and nuzzle up into her ample bosom, the one she'd genetically passed down to me through the mom.

That's the way Tamilians expressed love. Through insult. By threatening. By being rude. By feeding you to the fish.

One tends to forget these cultural anomalies when one is far from home. America had erased all these subtleties from my reckoning.

Part 1 of the evening came to an end as the Ks said farewell. I smiled sweetly at my future in-laws and 'namaskaramed' docilely. I would be seeing plenty of them soon enough, so there was no harm in kicking off on a pleasant note. There was no shaking of hands. There was no kissing, not even air kissing, as I handed each of them the traditional gift of a coconut and betel leaves.

Mrs K's parting shot to me was, 'You do not put aayyeell yin your hair I see. No wonder yit yis so dry. Like coconut coir.

Female Sai Baba,' ho ho ho ho she laughed, holding her stomach. Her husband hadn't heard her, so no one joined in her cackle.

I knew what she meant. Back then Sai Baba was a very popular Indian religious figure with followers in the millions all over the world (not counting me of course). He was well known for his acts of charity and miraculous cures. He wore saffron robes, standard-issue guru stuff, and sported an enormous, wild 'fro. It was nothing like my perm, which was curly, not frizzy. But she couldn't tell the difference.

Aditya winked at me behind his mother's back. Maybe we could move to a different city once we were married, I thought. Or country.

Yes, I was seriously considering him my last stop on the Man Train.

'I'll be back for you in an hour,' he said. 'Casual?'

◆

As soon as their car pulled out of the driveway, the mom wagged her finger at me. The stepdad had already lost interest and gone in.

'No funny stuff. Please. I mean it,' said the mom. She knew me well.

'What? What? What? What did I do?' I said, feigning deep insult.

She could see through me.

'This is India. And I know you know what I mean by that. You need to hold it back. Play the game properly. I could see the two of you making cow eyes at each other.' Of course she'd noticed. Nothing escaped her. I wasn't living half way across the world without reason.

I changed into a skirt, short of course, and a tight T-Shirt, revealing all that the saree had concealed, and slipped into a pair of heels. The mom took back all the diamond jewellery that had tantalized Aditya so eloquently from my ears and wrist and neck just a short while ago. She locked it up carefully in her safe.

'What's the combination? Why won't you tell me? I mean it's mostly mine anyway, isn't it? At least half of it?' I tried for the hundredth time.

She kissed me in reply.

◆

Aditya showed up a short while later, in a large BMW. A man's car. He didn't have a driver.

'Don't be out too late,' said the mom, out of sheer habit. It's not like I needed to get up early. I was on holiday.

'Let's go,' said Aditya, and off we went.

He took me to a nice bar, I can't remember the name now, and I had a few shots of tequila while he stuck to club soda. 'I'm driving,' he explained.

We talked of this and that. He was quite nice. Interested in martial arts, boxing and working out when he wasn't working his way through the many facets of his father's copper wire business. He didn't know a thing about jazz. Music wasn't high on his list of priorities.

'What does one do with copper wire?' I asked him seriously. 'I've been racking my brains to think of one single use for it and I can't. Except melting it down to make pennies, but that's only of any use in America.'

He smiled at me indulgently and pulled his bar stool close to mine. He took my face in his hands. 'It's used in telecommunications, electronics and electricity. But I don't need copper wire to conduct the sparks I'm feeling right now, you know what I mean?'

I knew, I knew, I knew. He was so hot. I felt the sparks sizzle up and down my arm. And elsewhere.

'Shall we get out of here?' he said. Those six sweet words. They meant only one thing. Sex. He didn't have to ask me twice.

We got back into his beautiful car and drove off. It was late.

Past ten. And I wondered where we were going. Probably a nice hotel, I figured. Good, I could wash-up and get myself together before getting back home so the mom wouldn't know I was like bird-feed, there for the taking.

But we kept driving past all the swank hotels and by-the-hour places until we came to a spot I knew quite well. It was called Lodhi Gardens. A lush, green mausoleum of Mughals gone by. The tombs were mostly in decay but the trees were fine and provided good cover for druggies, lovers and other lowlifes, who didn't have a room to call their own.

Oh no, not again, I thought to myself. What's with me and déjà vu? Every time the mom set me up with a date, why did we end up at Lodhi Gardens?

Several years ago, I had been lured to these very gardens on the promise of fame and glamour. A photographer friend of the parents had claimed he wanted to create an annual calendar featuring a different looking me each month. It seemed pretty good to both the mom and me, and I'd gone along with him, alone in his Mercedes Benz, with the mom waving a cheery goodbye at the door.

But JD, that's the name he went by, only wanted a little extramarital, under-age sex. I'd gotten out of that one by kneeing him in his man-parts after which I'd dashed out of the park, in search of an auto to take me back home. Delhi was still a safe place back then, and I got home without further ado and didn't tell the mom what happened. Somethings were best not shared with the parent.

Was this another such calamity? Of course not, I told myself firmly. Aditya was a cool hunk. Not an ancient perv.

Even if the mom had also set us up and had waved an eerily similar see-you-soon at the door not too long ago.

Aditya found a deserted spot outside the garden. He seemed to know his way around the outskirts of Lodhi Gardens in the dark. He knew exactly where to park, under a broken streetlight.

There was no one around.

It had been a while since I did it in the back seat of a car. Never in a BMW. Was this going to be fun?

'No need for the A/C,' he said and turned it off lowering the windows.

I was a little nervous because I'd heard from the mom that Delhi had become a pretty dangerous place at night. According to her, knife and gun toting criminals roamed about freely looking for a quick buck, and they didn't mind slicing the odd jugular to get at people's handbags and wallets.

The driver's side door opened and Aditya got out. I didn't follow him. Maybe he needed to pee, I thought. I averted my eyes to give him a sense of privacy and busied myself getting ready for him. I popped some breath mints into my mouth, sprayed on a little perfume, slipped off the panties and stuffed them in my bag.

First impressions were everything.

Since I was an old hand at car sex and I knew how to scoot over the gears if the need arose.

I felt someone tap me on the elbow through the window. I jumped out of my skin. I looked up expecting to find a fiendish criminal with a Walther PPK or switchblade stiletto waiting to slice me into ribbons while Aditya was watering the bushes.

But no, it was Aditya himself.

Smiling fiendishly. He deliberately and slowly unzipped his trousers. The chirping of the crickets masked the sound of the zipper coming down.

He reached into his pants and pulled out his gun.

The K. Aditya Night-time Special.

I noticed that it was especially large and snub-nosed, .44 calibre? More? There was no silencer. How had he become so fully loaded, ready to fire as it were, without the slightest help from me?

While I was drawing parallels and perfecting my metaphors (instead of scooting out across the driver's seat and running out of Lodhi Gardens as fast as my high heels would carry me once more), he reached in the car and grabbed me by the head, which was perfectly aligned with his crotch, since he was standing at the window. He used both his hands and gripped me tightly, so I couldn't move either this way or that. He shoved his pistol into my mouth.

I couldn't scream. It's hard to, when your mouth is full.

There was nothing I could do except choke.

Chapter 17

EEEEEEK, A MOUSE!

Judging by the time it took for Aditya to get his happy ending, I gathered that he wasn't a man who arrived at hasty conclusions.

While debating, pondering, thinking over and ruminating may have been a good way to conduct business at the copper wire factory, if he had continued his gun boring for even one second longer, there would have been blood on the streets. I would have chomped, hard.

◆

No one heard me get back in the house, except the brother who popped his head out to find out who was clanging about so late at night. I had gone straight to the stepdad's stylish bar, in one corner of our living room, searching around blindly for a glass to pour myself a very, very large shot of whiskey. I didn't want to turn the lights on, so I was relying on the moonlight.

He smirked at me as if to say, 'Alcoholic.'

What did he know?

I had to get the foul taste first, out of my mouth and then, the rest of my alimentary canal. I downed it in one gulp like a thirsty nomad in a desert. I poured out some more.

I held my fingers up to my lips in a 'shhh' hoping that the years had put some sense of propriety into the brother. Fortunately, he had lost interest in me and taken off.

I felt much better in seconds.

◆

I can bet you a million dollars that you can look high and you can look low. You can look in any corner of this big, bad world but you're never going to find a girl who will say, 'Oh I love how it tastes, yummmmmm,' unless she's getting paid to lie.

There is no redeeming quality about the way it looks, smells or tastes. It is utterly disgusting. In fact, it's astonishing that the entire human race originates from a source so foul.

'Nuff said, I thought to myself. A good night's sleep would help me dream up a way to tell the parents that wedding bells would not be a-ringing in New Delhi any time soon.

I was certain that the moment she'd shut the door behind me earlier that evening, the mom would have whipped out her old address book to make a list of invitees for the wedding of the season. She may have already shortlisted the caterers. I was hoping she hadn't called the aunt up in New York.

We're a family of chicken counters, all of us. It's a trait. Before the hatching of the egg and all, I mean.

She would be most disappointed, the poor thing. But nothing, not even millions of dollars extracted from copper wire would make me agree to such a diet for the rest of my life.

The day dawned for me around 11 a.m. The scotch had done its job well. No one woke me up. They let me get my beauty sleep. Almost-to-be brides couldn't be disturbed.

The mom came to my room as soon as she heard me moving around. She had with her a tray of toast, butter, jam and tea. I never drank coffee, the official drink of South Indians. She was beaming with happiness and seemed very excited.

'We're going to dinner at the Krishnan's tonight,' she said gaily. Apparently, Mrs K had called her at about six in the morning, waking her up, gushing about how pretty I was, how smart, even without a proper education. (South Indians are very early risers. My grandfather used to get up at 4 a.m., have breakfast at 6 a.m. and lunch at 10 a.m. His day was done by 8 p.m. I always wondered why he was in such a rush to get through life.)

According to the mom, Mrs K had said, 'It's a good thing you didn't waste money on her college tuition. You can give all of it to the young couple. They can start off their new lives in style. The babies will start coming soon.'

'Babies?' I sputtered and some of the toast in my mouth landed on the pretty bed sheet. 'I'm not going to any dinner Ma,' I declared. 'I'm coming down with something. I think the mixed nuts at the bar last night didn't agree with me.'

'Nonsense,' she said. 'I've already picked out the saree for you. And tonight you will wear my emeralds.'

'Ma, I'm not sure I really like Aditya,' I tried. 'There's something…'

'Why? Don't you think he's handsome?' she asked in surprise.

'No it's not that…' I was trying to find a plausible explanation for my overnight change of heart.

'Oh, he's unintelligent, is he? And short. And poor. And smells bad. Oh no, I get it. He's not a drug addict! That must be it,' she said sarcastically.

I shook my head sadly. While it was true he was none of the above. Not even a drug addict, the real reason was hardly a subject one could reveal candidly to one's mother, even if the said mother was a modern woman of the times who knew her chardonnay from her Chablis.

I missed having an understanding girlfriend around, like Shas. She'd have found a way out, after laughing her head off first, of course. I briefly thought of calling up Leena, my cohort in the days of yore. But she wasn't the same person anymore. Three kids and a bad habit. She'd have hit me up for more money.

'Why, what happened?' asked the mother not willing to let things be. 'You liked him at dinner. You liked him when you left to go out. Now all of a sudden you don't like him? You must have done something. What? What did you do?' she demanded, jumping to conclusions as she always did when it came to me. She hadn't changed. It was always my fault.

'Nothing!' I yelled at her. 'Why is it always me? Why couldn't he have done something?'

'Calm down, calm down,' she said hastily. 'He likes you a lot. He spoke glowingly of you to his mother and father. Apparently, he thinks you'll be the perfect wife. He really likes your style. That's why they've pulled a quick dinner party for you. They know you're going back to New York in a few days.'

The perfect wife! He likes my style! I was shocked.

My version of the events of the night before were somewhat different. It was with utmost self-control and a fear of jail that I had kept myself from chomping down on him with my nutcrackers, separating him from his pistol, permanently.

Instead, I had choked, gagged, coughed and spluttered all over the expensive car onto the door, on the plush seats, on the dashboard, over the gears, on the fancy sound system and even in the little nook where you keep your glasses. Not to mention on Aditya himself.

Aditya had just laughed, handing me a few tissues and a bottle of water.

He had kept up a merry chatter on the drive back home while I had maintained a stony silence, hoping to convey volumes about my opinion of him.

I couldn't figure out how he took that to mean, 'I do.'

'No Ma, I don't want to go to this dinner. I hate vegetarian food and I can't spend another evening without a cigarette. I'm serious.' I tried again. 'Maybe another time. I'll be back in India before I'm fifty. I promise.'

'Nonsense,' she said fluffing the pillows. She wasn't paying the slightest bit of attention to me, or my entreaties. 'We're going to the beauty parlour. A massage, a steam, a long shower. A mani-pedi while the girls do up your hair. Then we'll come home and dress for dinner.'

She had me at beauty parlour.

What the heck, I thought to myself. What was one more evening in my life? I had nothing better to do. Aditya couldn't, very well, wag his pistol at me in front of family and friends. And I wouldn't be going anywhere with him after dinner, for sure.

Maybe I could drag him to some bedroom in his miserable house, maybe his mother's, and get him to return the favour, Auggie-style. I wouldn't wear panties under my saree, I decided nastily. Tit for tat.

The thought cheered me up a bit.

'Ok Ma,' I said, managing to look a little pained. It wouldn't do for her to think she'd won the round.

She smiled at me indulgently. I could hear her thinking, 'Ah the stubborn tantrums haven't gone away, but I know how to manipulate my little lovely. Will she ever grow up?'

♦

It was a pleasant afternoon at the parlour. A decidedly bridal glow was coaxed out of my body. I didn't resist. It was so nice to have five women massage me, one for each limb and one for the head. The mani-pedi and hair styling done, we went back home, feeling relaxed and pampered.

The mom had laid out an off-white silk saree with scattered green embroidery. And her set of fabulous emeralds. Necklace, earrings, bracelets, ring. Where did the mom get the stuff from I wondered. It looked mighty expensive.

'It's from your grandmother, silly,' she said. 'And she got it from her mother.' Heirlooms. It all seemed mighty fancy, way too ostentatious for an evening at the Krishnan's. I told her so.

'Rubbish,' she said. 'Everyone dresses like this in Delhi these days. What's the use of having all this stuff if you don't wear it?'

And off we went, the mom, the brother (grumpily) and the stepdad.

The Krishnan's lived in a large two-storey bungalow in Golf Links, which is a ritzy neighbourhood in Delhi. The parents, even the brother, were impressed.

It left me cold. What's a nice house if it produced a selfish boor like Aditya, who felt the way to a woman's heart was through her mouth? The very thought of it made me want to throw up. I hastily popped a mint in my mouth.

There were many cars parked on the street. Expensive cars. If the K's were rich, their relatives weren't far behind. Copper wire was a good racket, apparently. I wondered if one could make an effective garrotte with it. Snap, pull and voila.

We were welcomed by Mrs K who was all honey and sugar. 'How pretty you look,' she said to me with love, 'Come in, come in, everyone's waiting to meet you.' I wonder if they knew that her son couldn't produce any heirs, not the way he was going about things.

There were about twenty-five or thirty people in the room. They fell silent as we walked in. The women were dressed in shimmering silks with expensive brocade shawls, the diamonds and the pearls out in full force. The men were more sober, in suits and ties. All of it was in my honour.

The mom stood by my side for the most part as people came up, asking questions, greeting us and making polite conversation. It was a charade. It was all very boring.

I looked around. The room was filled with ornate carvings and idols from South India, dark clunky stuff that looked scary enough to be authentic. The music of M.S. Subbalakshmi (a famous classical South Indian singer) was playing, and the scent of incense mixed with the smells of cooking sent me into a downward spiral, rapidly.

I'll get a drink, I decided, scanning the room for a bar. I'll feel a lot better once I've had a few under the petticoat, I said to myself. But I couldn't find one. Maybe the bar was in a different room.

Aditya ambled over, smiling possessively, 'Hey,' he said as if nothing had happened the night before. 'You look beautiful,' he said.

'Where's the booze?' I replied rudely.

'Ha, ha, you're joking,' he said. 'My parents don't serve alcohol or meat in their house.'

I glared at the mom, who was watching this little back and forth. Her eyes glowered in her best 'you'd-better-behave-or-there-will-be-hell-to-pay,' face. She shrugged her shoulders and disappeared, leaving me in Aditya's tender care.

She had known there would be no liquor, but had chosen to keep it to herself. Evil woman. No wonder she and the stepdad had frontloaded with at least three large whiskeys each before we left. I hadn't thought anything of the way they were bottoms-upping at home. We were a family that liked our alcohol. It was normal.

A bunch of Aditya's nosy relatives kept me busy with questions about America and jazz. It was tiresome, but I answered patiently, making up things as I went along when I didn't know the answer.

I didn't really know everything there was to know either about America or jazz. I had restricted myself to the bare essentials as far as knowledge of the country was concerned, so I didn't know how many senators there were in congress, why there was a civil war, and what went on in New Orleans and why jazz musicians needed to flatten or sharpen notes. Maybe it was because you could strike people in the heart better, I figured. I made a mental note to pay more attention to things besides sex and make-up.

We'll have dinner soon and leave, I told myself. This nightmare will soon be over. It will be just another tale to embellish while I regale Shas. We can roar about it over one or six *Caipirinhas*. (A deceptively lethal cocktail from Brazil, made with lime, sugar and white sugarcane rum, very delicious.)

With no chance of getting a drink in my hands, I had been reduced to daydreaming wistfully about booze.

Thankfully, Mrs K signalled dinner by ringing a large temple bell. Meaning the bell had likely come from an ancient temple somewhere in South India, and acquired illegally. It was a brass objet d'art with an ornate handle. It looked very heavy. I could see her strain her flabby arms as she rang it. I wondered what Aditya would look like after I'd dropped the bell on his head from a height of say, eight feet.

Unaware of my murderous thoughts (the bugger was so unobservant, it was a reason in itself to refuse his hand in marriage), he shepherded me towards the dining room, his hand on the small of my bare back.

The dining room could be loosely described as a cross between a frilly army mess and an ancient South Indian choultry—a place where poor people went to be fed.

There were four long rows of tables, seating five people each on plastic chairs. The tables had been dressed in flouncy white satin skirts with pink and blue bows.

There were no plates on the table.

Instead, the Krishnan's had decided to go the way of our ancestors, pre Iron Age. There were large banana leaves on the table. No forks and knives or even spoons. Of course. This was India. We ate with our hands.

The nuns in school back in Panchgani had frowned on this way of eating, making it a point to teach us how to eat properly, British-style. We were taught the difference between a soup spoon and a tablespoon. A steak knife and a butter knife. A fish fork and a dessert spoon.

The Krishnan's didn't confuse anyone with unnecessary cutlery.

Oh I knew how to eat with my fingers of course, but I didn't like it at all. It was going to ruin my manicure and would most likely spill all over the mom's expensive off-white silk saree with the emerald accents. But there was nothing I could do.

The tables were placed far apart enough from each other so that the people serving the guests could stomp past, slopping various items of food from large steel buckets onto the leaves. It was not an elegant sight.

These servers (they were not waiters) wore the 'veshti', a garment most traditional South Indian men are rather fond of, because of the way it keeps things cool and airy, I've been told. The veshti is nothing more than a flimsy white cloth, wrapped around the waist, folded up in half whenever there's work to be done, such as when food has to be served. The leg's equivalent of rolling up one's sleeves.

Since there were almost forty people waiting to eat, they would have to take turns.

This is a common way to treat one's guests at weddings and other family functions. The concept of a buffet hasn't caught on down in South India. It's not possible to walk around holding a banana leaf in one's hand filled with watery food, searching for clever conversation. So people are quite used to standing in line, jostling, pushing and shoving each other in a rush to get to a spot at a table, or the floor at more traditional functions.

Aditya propelled me towards a table, where our backs would be toward the wall. I went along meekly. In my head I was checking off the sequence of events. Dinner, dessert, goodbye. Forty-five more minutes at the K's, tops. That's what I was counting on.

There were two people already seated at our table. I scooted in next to a lady with gems glowing on either side of her nose. She was quite old and Aditya introduced her as a distant relative. She began interrogating me immediately in Tamil and I answered her questions as politely as I could. Her husband, seated next to her, would whisper in her ear and she in turn would repeat the questions to me. 'Have you smoked marrywanna?' I just smiled coyly, not wanting to commit this way or that.

While she got to know me (I never got to ask a single question in return), the tables began filling up and there was a general buzz in the room in a variety of tongues. English, Tamil, a smattering of Hindi and Punjabi. Mr K had invited some of the people from his office.

Pretty soon the food service began. The men in their veshtis folded up to reveal hairy calves, knees and in some cases even thighs, began pounding the aisles bearing their buckets, keeping up a steady stream of piping hot items. All vegetarian of course. I got into the spirit of it.

You weren't supposed to begin eating until all the courses had been piled onto the banana leaf, little blobs of food around the leaf, ranging in colour from reds to rusts, browns to beiges and ochres to yellows all offset by gleaming white rice. You always began with the sweet, the payasam.

There were no napkins on any of the tables. These were seasoned banana leaf diners who obviously didn't spill on themselves or make any kind of mess. They would arise from their meals, their hands mostly as fresh and clean as they were before the meal and proceed to a hand-washing area, where they'd jostle and push to get to the taps, the soap and the towels.

All part of the traditional South Indian experience.

But that was later. We still had to get through the meal. I pushed my saree all the way up my shoulder and tucked it into my waist as tightly as I could, so it wouldn't fall into the sambar or the cabbage kootu. I pushed my emerald bangles up my forearm so they wouldn't jangle into the eggplant and got ready to eat, as delicately as I could with my right hand.

I was far more comfortable with the other one (being left handed) but alas, that's the hand one uses to wash one's bum. Using it to eat was not only a marriage deal-breaker (which might have been one way to get knocked out of the nuptials), but it would have irrevocably destroyed the mom and the stepdad's reputation. I couldn't be so selfish.

While my right hand snaked towards the banana leaf, in search of the payasam, I felt Aditya seize my left hand with his right hand, and pull it under the table, surreptitiously, but very firmly.

Hmm, he's trying to be nice, I thought to myself. Making

up for being such a pig last night. But this isn't going to cut it. A little hand holding is ok on a first date, but a little late in the game when you've already gone and shoved your ding-dong past said date's honey-sweet lips, without so much as a by-your-leave.

I tried to extricate my hand gently. I didn't want to hold hands with him. I was mad at him.

But he wouldn't let go. He clutched my hand a little firmer. And each time I tried to pull it back, he yanked a little more. There was a tug of war going on under the table.

'What are you doing?' I hissed at him under my breath. 'Stop it.'

'Shhhhh,' he said back under his. 'Don't draw attention to us. Just eat normally and relax your left hand.'

'Stop it, Stop it,' I said as the biddy next to me asked if she could have my 'vadai' (a doughnut shaped, salty and oily snack) if I wasn't planning on eating it.

'Yes, yes, go ahead,' I said hastily.

She reached out across my leaf and snatched it up.

I don't know if Aditya took this comment of mine to mean carte blanche with my left arm (he may not have heard the biddy, as the noise levels in the room were quite deafening), but in a moment my arm was stretched to the maximum, and it was now half way across his thighs.

All of a sudden I felt my fingers forcibly wrapped around something warm, rubbery and squishy. It felt like what can best be described as a pulsating, long, water balloon.

Aditya's right hand closed down on my left hand and squeezed it hard over the balloon. He began moving it up and down. Rhythmically. The great-grandmother's priceless heirloom emerald bracelets began jangling roughly against each other and I was terrified that the stones would come flying off.

I struggled to get my hand free. But it was trapped like a canary in a coalmine, unable to find the exit.

The more I resisted and the more I yanked, the larger the

thing grew in my hand. The more I let my hand grow limp, hoping to snatch it away when he wasn't expecting it, the more tightly he squeezed.

It was unbearable.

I thought about it for a moment. There was only one thing I could do.

I took in a deep breath, sucking in as much air as I could and screamed at the top of my lungs, 'What is that furry thing running under the table. Eeeeeeeeeeeeeeek! It's a mouse.'

And with that I stood up abruptly, yanking my hand away from his water balloon, making sure to grab the corner of his banana leaf while I did so, the one onto which just moments ago, steaming hot sambar and rasam had been poured over a bed of equally steaming hot, fluffy, white rice.

The sambar, rasam, cabbage kootu, vadai, payasam and other South Indian delicacies splattered all over his lap and clothes and wee wee.

He stood up in a shot, yelling at the top of his lungs, the food flying all over the place, a little of it on me and the beautiful saree.

The banana leaf provided him a little dignity, like Adam in the Garden of Eden, I thought fleetingly. I wondered if he'd pulled such a stunt on Eve.

Aditya ran to the bathroom, screeching in a most unseemly, unmanly manner, clutching the banana leaf to his groin, while his mother and father ran behind their son. Their family's jewels were at stake.

The servers fell in a mad scramble to the floor, hunting for the furry thing that was rumoured to have been running under the tables.

The dinner guests abandoned their food and rushed out of the room.

Finally, just the mom and I were left in the room. The stepdad and the brother had rushed solicitously along with Aditya's parents to see if they could be of help. How much assistance could one little appendage need, I wondered.

The mom glared at me, a volcano about to erupt, 'This is definitely one of your stunts. Was there really a mouse? Do you swear you saw a mouse? I just don't believe you,' she said spewing molten lava.

I shrugged.

'It sure felt like it,' I replied.

Chapter 18

DOES KARMA WEAR A TURBAN?

'Apples don't fall far from trees,' the mom said the next morning, 'I think we've had a close shave. A stitch in time and all.'

I knew that the disconnected metaphors meant she'd forgiven me and still loved me. Considering I was leaving to get back to America in two days, there was no time to waste in being mad at each other.

'Are you going to tell me what really happened?' she tried.

'Ma, you're right about the apples and the needles and the shaving and all. You're always right. Why don't we forget about it?' I knew how to be as vague as the next person when I chose to. It was easy when you weren't burdened unnecessarily with things like a conscience.

But still, I noticed that the emeralds and the diamonds had gone back into the safe, the combination of which was still being kept from me, although as I tried to point out to her repeatedly, I was the rightful inheritor of half her legacy.

'This and more will be bequeathed to you one day soon, when your destiny isn't quite so murky,' she said sagely.

I shuddered involuntarily, shaking off memories of the disagreeable Aditya and his unhealthy obsession with his wingle-wangle. I had never met anyone like him before. Thrusting it into my mouth, my hands, and god-knows-where-else, given half a chance. I'd gladly forswear the mom's jewels as long as I never had to see his again.

'Shopping?' I asked brightly.

We renewed our shopping expeditions with gusto. I had gifts

to buy, friends to gratify, money to blow.

We went to one of my favourite areas in Delhi at the time, CP (Connaught Place). It was filled with nice stores and nice restaurants. We were going to a shop that the mom had discovered in the past few years, when I was in America. It was called Potato Print and it was a sunny, cheerful, large, airy store with wooden floors and shelves. The lighting was subdued and there was the air of New York about it.

It wasn't far from the infamous night club/disco/restaurant Touch where I had spent so many hours learning how to sing, break hearts and have a marvellous time, all the while pretending to the mom and the stepdad that I was attending college. Of course, as I've already mentioned the place was now a dull French restaurant, and not one that I had any interest in. I'd had my fill of the French, merci beaucoup.

Potato Print was filled with modern, friendly, bright looking Indian objet d'art including fabrics, linen, rugs and the like. A larger, more contemporary version of the aunt's store Aditi, back in Huntington on Long Island.

The shop was run by a friend of the mom's, a charming and very sophisticated Sikh gentleman. 'He's loaded to the gills,' she muttered under her breath to me. 'He's thinking of opening up a shop in New York. I thought he should meet you.'

I wasn't surprised by the mom's abrupt shift in approach. Palming me off to a pecker-obsessed pervert one day and acting as if nothing had happened the next. I operated the same way. A genetic thing I am certain. We'd be thick in the midst of a particular topic of conversation one moment when, without warning, without preamble, we'd transition to a tangentially different topic very smoothly, without a blip, understanding each other as if we were synchronised swimmers. Of course, it confounded the people around us, folks whom we had to talk and interact with, but between us (and the aunt too, come to think of it) it was seamless.

'Married?' I asked.

'Yes, lovely wife. Does all the designing for the store,' she said. 'Very talented.'

'Kids?' I asked. Not that I cared.

'Four,' she said.

I rolled my eyes heavenward. What sort of bumblehead would have four kids? No wonder he wanted to run away to New York.

♦

'Hello, hello,' said Harpreet, tall and tan. His wife Manpreet looked slightly wilted. The four kids and the designing career had evidently taken its toll.

The Sikhs are an equal opportunity community that believes in unisex names. A bit like the French. Although the French think that by adding an 'e' to the end of Michel or Christian or Jean, they've got the gender covered. The truth is, when you say the name out loud, there's no telling if it's a man or a woman. The 'e' is silent.

The Sikhs have no such distinction. Manpreet can be a man or a woman and you're not going to know until the very last minute, when you're standing face to face.

A passing thought struck me. It could be most disconcerting, terrifying even, for a man to find a coarsely bearded Gurpreet nuzzling up against his chin when he was expecting a Gurpreete.

I burst out laughing at the image in my mind where the Gurpreets, with the 'e' and without the 'e' had just punched each other's lights out. The mother glared poison-tipped kirpans at me. (A ceremonial dagger that true Sikh men are supposed to carry on them at all times, now made somewhat difficult especially at airports, on account of terrorist threats.)

I checked my thoughts and zipped it up.

Manpreet(e) took me on a guided tour of the store and I ooohed convincingly at this and aaahed sincerely at that. I remembered that the aunt had always taken a shine to customers who appeared appreciative, even shaving off a few dollars, as she was ringing up the sale, if the customer was particularly convincing. Anyone can be swayed by a little flattery.

I selected a handful of items and carried them back to the cash counter where the mom and Harpreet (no 'e') were laughing about something.

The conversation got round to what I did in New York, and I was about to give them a breezy account but the mom cut me off before I blurted out that I knew zip about shop-keeping, fabric weaving and sales tax. That my skills lay in wasting time in the Orient, sampling the local cuisine (I was now a whiz with the chopsticks, holding them elegantly at the fat end, and not like a crude peasant, right at the bottom) and washing it down with copious amounts of local liquor. That another of my skills was singing for peanuts at a handful of jazz clubs in New York.

'She has learned everything there is to know about running a store in New York,' the mom beamed at the Singhs. 'My sister tells me that each time she manages the store for her, her sales triple. She has the knack. She is a born sales person.'

This was as blatant a lie as I'd ever heard, but as I have mentioned somewhere, I learned very early on in life that you do not contradict one's relatives as they perjure themselves in public. You could expect stinging slaps and scalding tongue-lashings if you made that mistake. Sometimes instantly, right in public and sometimes later, when the time was right. We were a family that believed that the lie was a tool to be used in the course of one's life, for the betterment of others. So you were expected to be nimble and dexterous, bobbing and weaving, agreeing and backing up the whopper du jour. No matter how big the tale.

'Yes,' I said sadly. 'And yet, despite my amazing skills, it's the aunt who drives the Porsche. I take the subway.' This was a partial lie. The aunt only drove a Peugeot.

Everyone laughed and Harpreet's eyes crinkled. 'Call me Harry,' he said.

He was getting ready for America. 'I'm almost done with all the permissions and licenses to open up a shop in NYC, and it would be great if you'd agree to run it,' he said astonishingly. I'd only just met him and he knew nothing about me at all.

'Oh no,' I said before it went any further. 'I can shop there though,' I offered as consolation. 'And I'll tell all my friends…'

But he was not going to take no for an answer. He continued smoothly, quietly. 'Not even if I pay you fifty thousand dollars plus a bonus if you exceed targets?' he stopped me dead in my tracks with that.

'Really!' I was pretty shocked. That was a large sum back then for someone without a college degree.

The mom looked very happy.

She was a schemer beyond par. I didn't know how many other plans she had set up for me. Plan A was out and the very next day she was presenting me with a fait accompli Plan B. She had been a busy bee. Husbands, jobs, they were pouring out of her bottomless cornucopia of delights.

Manpreet stood by expectantly, waiting for me to say something. Her future, and the future of the four snotty brats also hung in the balance.

'Well, it sounds pretty good. Let me know when your plans fall in place so I can rearrange my life,' I said breezily. No need to get into an argument. I was sure he didn't mean it. People didn't offer you fifty thousand big ones just for walking through the door. Even if your mother produced miracles like a god-woman.

'It's going to be very soon,' he said to me. 'Very soon,' he repeated. 'I will be going to New York of course to sign the lease and get the place ready. It's on Amsterdam Avenue, by the way,' said Harry. 'Upper Seventies.'

I stopped short. The mom must have told him where I lived.

Less than a mile away. Walking distance. My eyes widened. Was this what good fortune looked like? Six foot one, black beard, blue and yellow turban, deep voice and a pocketful of cash?

◆

For the balance of my stay in India, the mom walked around dripping self-congratulations, making puddles all over the house. She talked non-stop about my new job, even though I hadn't accepted it yet. Even though I was getting ready to go back to China again, on yet anther expedition.

'You can find a bigger apartment. I can come over and visit often. Maybe now you'll find a nice husband…' she was so happy counting the chickens that would run around in the castles she was building in the air. I let her be.

◆

It was sad to say goodbye again to the mom. I would miss her dreadfully. That was the bad part about being an adult. You had to leave your mother behind.

But fortified by several mini bottles on the plane, I made it back to New York, ready to be swallowed up by the hustle and bustle of Manhattan. I loved that city. I loved the smell. The sounds. The surly people who'd look away if you tried catching their eye. The people who'd push and shove you rudely on the subway. Everyone. Everything.

My apartment was still standing, the plants were still alive and Shas came over right away to hear all about my trip. So did Rue. The three of us sat down to a good old yakkety-yak with moo-shoo pork and Tsingtao (pronounced 'chingdow') beer. We were very classy when it came to our beer. We had Kingfisher with Indian food and Asahi with Japanese (along with the sake) and so on. Except French. I'd never heard of a French beer.

The girls roared with laughter as I described Aditya and his wandering wee wee. They wept hysterically as I described the banana leaf with the hot sambar and kootu that I dragged deliberately onto his offending body part. They quickly wiped up their tears of mirth when I said a total stranger had offered me fifty thou, all because the mom was a talented fibber.

'You really have the strangest things happen to you, don't you?' asked Shas, rhetorically. She and her boring boyfriend Klaus, both from Sweden, lived predictable lives that ran on precision Swiss timing, never mind that the countries had nothing to do with each other. Karma, at least the kind that kept clobbering me on the head, never came near either of them.

Meanwhile, my friend Rue, also from India, she of the theatrical bent and the distaste for costumes, had been plagued with problems of her own. Her ladylove, Tabitha, the director who specialised in off-off-Broadway plays as long as they were unorthodox, preferably with a naked cast that spoke earnestly in gibberish, had dumped her for a pair of identical twins from Holland.

Rue was depressed. Crushed. 'I mean, I'd understand if they were from Senegal or Thailand or even Kazakhstan. But Holland? That's the unkindest cut of all,' she bleated pitifully. I didn't know why she didn't like the Dutch. Their Heineken beer was pretty good.

Shas patted Rue's head as if she was a little Chihuahua. 'Someone else will come along. Maybe you'll find triplets from Tanzania.' she said comfortingly.

Must have been the jet lag and the Tsingtao, but all I remember is that I fell asleep mid-sentence.

Chapter 19

ONE NIGHT IN BANGKOK

It was back to the daily. Getting up at half past dawn (not really, but close enough when you consider when I went to sleep), trudging along to the Department of Conventions and Exhibitions, wondering how to snatch excitement from the jaws of boredom, which at the time was yawning very wide.

Shas and I were finalising the last dribs and drabs of a small, but deluxe, mucho expensive four-day expedition for twenty Mental Health Professionals (shrinks, as you and I know them) to Bangkok. Their gig was called, 'It's All in the Mind: Mental Health Today'. Cute.

A part of me was excited about travelling on the job again, especially to Bangkok for the first time, which from all accounts was an excellent place to succumb to one's senses.

The other part of me was getting a little tired, bored of all this globetrotting. The world was the same pretty much, no matter where you went. People were the same even if they looked different and spoke funny.

Another airport, another surly customs official. Another hair-raising taxi ride to another hotel. More packing and unpacking. Jet lag. All the while slavishly catering to the whims and whatnots of whiny tourists.

That part made me want to pull out my hair and stuff it into Shas's mouth.

I dreamed of the crisply painted white picket fence surrounding the freshly cut grass. The pretty window boxes with geraniums. The kitchen garden. The over-sized refrigerator, the washing machine and dishwasher. I dreamed of hanging clothes out to dry on a line, while fluffy white clouds flitted about in the clear blue sky. The garage. The driveway. The sound of utter silence. No traffic, no raucous marauders in the middle of the night outside my window playing salsa music through extra loud boom boxes. The 2.2 kids. The golden retriever. Life in the 'burbs. You get the pic.

I sighed sadly as I pulled the curtains down on my fanciful dreams, but brightened up immediately when I took stock of the brighter side of reality facing me in Bangkok.

Tips.

Usually hefty, all-cash and therefore IRS-proof.

In addition, there was the slight possibility (although it was beginning to look more and more unlikely) that the man of my dreams could be twiddling his thumbs, waiting for me to show up, say by the bar at Cabbages and Condoms, a famous restaurant in Bangkok. Serendipity has been known to fall before, like a coconut from a tree, on the heads of a few lucky people.

Despite the mom's earnest protestations that I should hold on to my horses and brush up on shop-keeping, Indian artefacts and sales talk because she knew with certainty that Harry, Potato Print and their fifty thou were about to make their New York debut, I didn't believe her. It seemed too good to be true. There were no coconut trees in New York.

But taking a chance that my karma could have been wearing a turban, I asked Shas and Rue to meet me for a drink on the Upper West Side, in the vicinity of where PP was supposedly being birthed.

I always said, 'let's meet for a drink,' as if we'd stop at one drink. Rue, a girl with a bladder like a man, knew that for both Shas and me, 'a' drink always meant at least six. A few pre-dinner cocktails, followed by wine with the meal and finally, the après dessert cognac. She had no objection to weaving back home drunkenly as we routinely did. That's what cabs were for. New York cabbies always took excellent care of drunken girls.

To my delight, there were signs of massive renovation on Amsterdam between 78th and 79th, in the middle of the block. The hardwood floors and shelves were unmistakeably PP.

I stared wide-eyed at the construction crew banging, hammering, drilling and painting. Through the plate-glass windows, I saw a sign laying for now on the floor, just waiting to be fixed on the outside of the store, that said Potato Print in elegantly hand-carved, very expensive gold leaf.

My mind whirred like a reel of film. I could sleep an extra twenty minutes in the morning. No more smelly, underground snake pit, a.k.a. the New York City subway, where they hadn't fully cottoned on to the concept of escalators. I could saunter to work in ten minutes. Five, if I was snappy. I could go back home for lunch and catch a few soaps on TV. Maybe even take a little afternoon siesta. Or nookie, if I found someone to canoodle with.

I'd been going through a very dry spell in that department after Auggie. As for Aditya, the less said the better. The Upper West Side was rich with banker, lawyer, doctor, and businessman potential.

I beamed and I gleamed as things fell into place, a perfect row of Tetris blocks. Boing, boing, boing, zwooooop.

Shas was quick to understand what it meant when my eyes glazed over and I got a certain faraway look. She brought me back to earth. 'He probably meant five thou a year, at the most fifteen. Not fifty,' she said cleaving through my happiness like a butcher attacking a leg of lamb. 'Just in case you're thinking of quitting your job, I will not be giving you couch space in my apartment, so you can forget about that.'

She always threatened me with homelessness, as if she had the power.

Rue chimed in, 'I don't see why anyone would pay you that much money to stand around all day. I mean, where's the skill in that? They're probably better off hiring a guard with a gun so people pay up before they leave the shop with merchandise.'

A radical approach to shop keeping for sure.

It was plain to see that Shas and Rue were horribly jealous. Neither one of them had seen fifty thousand of anything at one go, not even M&Ms, let alone money.

'Let's drink,' I said wisely changing the subject. We found a bar serving oversized Margaritas, keeping us pleasantly occupied for several hours. I'd save my daydreams for later, when I was back at work.

◆

A few weeks later, Shas and I found ourselves aboard a Thai Airways flight, en route to Bangkok along with twenty shrinks and their wives. Handling these tourists was going to be a piece of cake, Shas and I knew already.

When men travelled with their wives, their itineraries were already plotted, charted and etched in stone. There would be no need for us to helpfully suggest that they did this or that. That was the job of a wife.

So we'd have plenty of time for the extracurricular. This was not a 'convention' in the traditional sense. It was just a short, laid-back medical seminar, which according to one Dr Lieberman who had confided in Shas, was a complete waste of time. It had been pretty much forced on them by the ACCME (Accreditation Council for Continuing Medical Education).

'As if mental health is the latest Milan or Madison Avenue fashion,' sneered Shas dismissively. 'I mean, everyone knows that "mental health" is only about how you feel about your parents. What's to learn? Anyone can be a shrink.'

CME (Continuing Medical Education) was the US government's way of ensuring that doctors kept abreast of ever-changing medical advancements, new drugs and modern techniques of health care so doctors wouldn't walk around saying, 'Thalidomide. You're kidding!

When did they stop prescribing that?'

If doctors refused to attend these seminars, their license to practice medicine could get revoked.

Lieberman and the other reluctant shrinks were treating the trip more as a tax-deductible vacation than the serious ongoing study of brain matter. Ergo the wives.

Shas and I hoped we'd never, ever lose our marbles.

We were staying at the Shangri-La, a beautiful luxury hotel on the Chao Phraya River. Since the seminars were also being conducted in the same hotel, Shas and I didn't have to worry about angry men who missed their buses and got left behind in the rain. (This happened to us in China a few years ago, and it was very unpleasant.)

'Patpong ho,' we said in unison as soon as the last of the delegates and their spouses were accounted for. We hopped into a cab. It would be fun to check out the sex bars. We'd already done extensive homework on the after-dusk delights of Bangkok.

The atmosphere in Patpong was happy, warm and buzzing with urgency.

Sidewalk hawkers offered genuine faux everything. Bags, shoes, cameras, watches, antiques, jewellery. There were people everywhere. Mostly foreigners, tourists, like Shas and me. You could tell them by the wide-eyed, wondrous smiles on their faces. The look the locals sported was more, ok-let's-hurry-up-and-get-on-with-it-I-haven't-got-all-day.

Time was money if you were a hawker in Bangkok.

There were neon lights blazing in multi colours all over the many restaurants and bars located cheek-by-jowl on the stretch. Most of the establishments had placed large sandwich boards on the street, proclaiming the menu and daily specials.

Pussy Shoot Balloon

Pussy Smoke Cigarette

Pussy Shoot Banana

Pussy Shoot Ping Pong
Pussy Magic Razorblade
Pussy Shoot Fish
Pussy Write Letter

It was hard to pick a pussy. 'Oh ping-pong, ping-pong, ping-pong,' I said to Shas, jumping up and down like a little kid. I was pretty good at ping-pong, although back in India, they took the game seriously, calling it table tennis.

It was the only game I had even moderate success in. I am not a sportsperson, by any stretch. Even TT terrorized me. I was in mortal fear that the ball would fly across the net and land right in my eye, so I'd close both of them, tightly and stick out the paddle in the general direction of the ball's whoosh, hoping for the best. I'd connect about three times out of ten. I thought that made me an expert.

Shas dug her nails into my side, her way of keeping me focussed. We were on the seedy, dangerous streets of Bangkok where hustlers and other scam artists were waiting to pick our pockets or drag us off to dark alleys to be dismembered and left to writhe and bleed to death while they stood around laughing.

I snapped out of it.

We followed a cheerful, mostly toothless old lady into a large bar, dark all around except for a brightly lit stage with floor to ceiling dance poles at intervals. Behind the stage were curtains, like a real theatre. Strobe lights flickered, lighting up the room in spurts and the music was loud. There was a sense of anticipation.

Once our eyes got used to the dark, we could see that we weren't alone. There were people from all over the world sitting at the tightly packed tables that surrounded the stage. I even saw ladies in abayas, the head-to-foot black covering worn by orthodox women of the Middle East.

It was vaguely comforting.

'I come back liitahh,' said the old lady after she was sure we were seated. 'I take you for happy ending, okayyyyy?'

'No, no, not tonight. Already finished. Thank you. Maybe some other time,' I said sweetly, as Shas stifled a giggle.

We had no intention of paying for happy endings from any boy, girl or lady boy in Bangkok.

As far as Shas and I were concerned, it was the other way around. People wined, dined, fawned and bought us expensive dinners prior to the privilege of providing us with happy endings. But I didn't know how to say all of that in Thai.

Every table had a TT paddle on it.

We sat down and ordered our drinks. I launched into an explanation of the rules of table tennis to Shas, mostly to while away the time till the show began, but she motioned for me to shut up. For one thing it was too loud to hear anything, for another she already knew the rules. So we idly fiddled with the paddles and sipped our drinks.

In a few minutes, as soon as all the tables were full, there was an electronic drum roll followed by a crash of canned cymbals. It sounded very real. The stage curtains parted and in entered a middle-aged woman with a fairly well preserved body, covered only barely by shiny, tasselled pasties and a teeny G-String. She was carrying a red swivel chair with casters. The kind you find in offices.

When she arrived at her spot, marked with an 'X', she set her chair down and with a snaky slither, she slipped off her G-String and tossed it on the floor, as her come-hither tasselled breasts jiggled tantalisingly. The music grew louder.

The curtains on the side of the stage parted again, and this time a younger girl, also barely dressed, walked in. She was carrying a pink toy plastic bucket filled with standard issue, white TT balls.

The music reached a minor crescendo as the older woman sat down on the chair, now clad only in the tassels. She spun around rapidly, waving to the audience, encouraging them to applaud. The audience obliged.

Then she put both her feet up on the chair's arms, her knees apart and legs splayed, offering visitors from all parts of the world unfettered visual access to her smooth, baby-like unmentionables.

She smiled coyly at the audience, her face and eyes soft and innocent as she spun around slowly on the wheels this time, so that no corner of the room was denied a view.

The younger woman with the plastic bucket knelt quietly by her side until the woman on the chair had finished the unhurried, deliberate 360 degree rotation, then she held the bucket up to her pal and laughing loudly she yelled, 'Go Nancy go.'

Nancy smiled back at her. She bent down and picked up about ten balls and one after the other rapidly inserted them inside her magic portal.

Sakoooop, sakoop, sssssakooop.

Each time she 'swallowed' a ball, the crowed went, 'ooooh'. Finally, she'd reached her limit, a frightening ten balls inside her canal of love. The crowd was roaring in disbelief.

But before we could say, 'Table Tennis Tournament,' there was a loud 'poppppppp' and a ball came flying out of Nancy's nether regions in the direction of a table of young soldiers, probably US Army. It was obvious they had been there before, it wasn't their first time, because one of the boys picked up the TT paddle and thwacked the ball right back at Nancy.

She ducked, laughing loudly and popped again. This time she aimed the ball at the Arab lady who cowered under the table screaming, 'No, no, no, not here.' Her husband, unafraid of a mere ping-pong ball coated with a strange Thai woman's bodily fluids, picked up his paddle and smacked the ball. Unfortunately it landed into his wife's drink.

The crowd erupted with laughter. The woman punched her husband in the arm. Playfully of course. Nancy knew what she was doing. The Arab lady was forced to order another drink.

By now Shas and I were ready for our turn. 'Here, here. This way,' we yelled. Nancy obligingly shot us a ball. I fielded it cleverly with my eyes closed and it went right back into the bucket on stage.

I got a huge round of applause for that. I stood up and bowed regally, shaking my palm from side to side like Queen Victoria acknowledging her subjects on a ride through the dusty roads of some third world country. Not Thailand though, the British had never made it part of their empire.

I was having such fun. I liked this combo of sex and dexterity.

After about five minutes of ping-pong, when all the balls in the bucket had been shot all across the room, Nancy took a final bow and made way for someone else.

Tiffany carried her own clear bucket filled with wriggling fish. She treated the fish like they were lowly ping-pong balls. Slop, slop, she shot them across the room, but they didn't make it as far as the balls. And no one thwacked them back at her. I felt a little sorry for the fish. They were alive before Tiff wrapped herself around them.

After her came Jessica, the banana popper, a big hit with the soldiers. She kapowed the plantains (which I believe are larger than bananas) here and there across the room with great accuracy. A particularly boisterous soldier even peeled and ate one, to a loud, 'Eeeeeeeeewwwww,' from the crowd. Jessica just laughed uproariously.

She made way for Jezebel, a chain smoker who opened my eyes (and everyone else's) to the incredible, unbelievable and miraculous potential of the human body. Until that moment, I did not know that women could inhale cigarette smoke from the business end of their reproductive tracts.

Jez put the cigarette in her mouth first, lit up and inhaled deeply. She blew the smoke suggestively out of her mouth and reached down to insert the unlit part into the above-mentioned tract. Then in a show of mighty ab and Kegel control, she 'inhaled' again. And then 'blew' out the smoke. Inhale. Exhale. Glow. Dim. All the while keeping up a merry chatter about the sights and sounds of Bangkok.

The ash grew long at the fire end of the cigarette, keeping its perfect cigarette shape. I was reminded of an Eric Clapton concert where he had stuck a cigarette into the guitar strings, near the keys while he played Layla soulfully. The ash never broke off.

In Thailand, the ash from Jez's cigarette also grew all the way to the end, down to the filter and never broke off.

It took superior smoking skills to be able to do that. I wondered if Jez was into Clapton.

The show ended with a calligraphist.

A woman who wrote, 'Welcome to Thailand. Bangkok loves you!' in cursive writing, dotting the 'i' and the exclamation point perfectly. Her pen, wrapped in a bit of tissue (for better grip, I guess) was clenched tightly in her aperture, providing her the perfect 'hand.' It was sheer poetry.

After everyone applauded wildly, before she departed from the spotlight, she offered to paint portraits in watercolours. It would be a private session, about an hour or so, she explained, and would cost extra. She held up a portrait of John F. Kennedy that she claimed she had done. There was a resemblance, amazingly. The brush strokes were controlled and there was even a little feathering and crosshatch. I was most impressed.

Shas and I considered it for a moment. 'Naaaaah,' I said, and we left. There were far better things to do with our bahts.

Chapter 20

TOAST POINTS WITH PEPPERCORN INFUSED GOAT BRAIN

By the time we could say, 'One Night In Bangkok,' Shas, I and our coterie of head-shrinkers, found ourselves fastening our seatbelts, on the plane which was now pointing west, in the direction of New York City.

'I'm not sure how much I can take this either,' I said to Shas as we crossed over into Europe.

All the way as we flew over Asia, she'd been muttering something about quitting the travel industry. Her beloved bore Klaus was starting up an importing business, bringing in Christmas goodies (food mostly) from Sweden. He planned to sell these to homesick Swedes in New York during the holiday season. Christmas was a big deal in Sweden and people in the home country began their celebrations right in the middle of December itself (earlier if they could get away with it), adding Christmas spirit and cheer to the days leading up to C Day with various little traditions and customs, all of which involved food.

Apparently, Klaus felt this was an untapped gold mine.

It seemed to me like a lame thing to do.

There weren't enough Swedish people in New York to consume all the Pepparkakor, Glögg, Lussebullar and Knäck that Klaus would have to sell in order to maintain Shas's I-will-have-nothing-but-caviar-and-designer-wear snooty attitude.

I knew for a fact (since I spent more time with her than he did), that she was as fed up with hot dogs and Chanel knock-offs from the streets as I was. So why was she agreeing to this nonsense, I wondered.

I couldn't let the subject pass.

'What are you going to do with plum pudding on January second? Huh?' I asked, half needling her and half concerned. Usually the roles were reversed. I said the silly things and she reacted caustically.

New York was a city where tradition was everything. No one wore white after Labour Day. Those in the know would turn up their noses at you if you did.

Everyone wore a little green on St Patty's Day, even if they were Swedish. Or Spanish. Or Indian.

Everyone cooked turkey on Thanksgiving, no matter where they came from, even if they had no one to thank.

Everyone put up a Christmas tree and bought presents for each other, even if they were only Buddhist.

No one ate plum pudding after 1 Jan. (Leftovers didn't count.)

And yet, despite being fully aware of New York and its rigid rules, Shas had fairy lights in her eyes when it came to Klaus. 'I'll eat it all myself. What's it to you?' she replied defiantly. I could tell from her tone that she would not tolerate any questioning of the omniscient Klaus's decisions.

'Ok, ok, you have it all worked out. What do I know? I was only concerned for you,' I said hastily. I didn't want to get into an argument. We were about to land soon.

I kind of got it though.

Both of us had been working at the travel company for many years already and while it was exciting and fun in the beginning, as the bones grew brittle, neither one of us wanted to do it anymore. We were willing to give up handsome tips, strange and exciting men, the sights and sounds of the world around us, all on someone else's nickel, just so that we could walk to work, instead of flying six thousand miles to earn a living.

Just so we could come back to the familiar scent of our own pillows at night.

So as far as Shas was concerned, if that meant following Klaus the bore all over the USA selling plum pudding in the middle of July, then by golly, that was exactly what she would do.

Sadly, us girls hadn't come up with ideas of our own. We had briefly considered money laundering, smuggling antiques from China and other unsavoury activities that would have been very easy for us based on the amount of trans-Pacific air miles we were clocking, but those ideas didn't pan out.

We were completely worn out just trying to wrap our heads around company incorporation and tax liability so there was no question of coming up with a killer idea to make us millions.

It was far easier to hang our hopes on our menfolk. She on Klaus and me, well I didn't have a 'men folk' yet. Harry was it. I clung hopefully to the memory of his turban.

But would he come through for me?

◆

As luck would have it, he did.

True to his word (and the mom's relentless hounding no doubt), Harry made my job official with a letter of appointment on which he'd affixed the company seal, a potato stamp.

My duties were catalogued in the pretty document.

I was to see to the daily operations of Potato Print, keeping things crispy fried and fresh. My key responsibility was to ensure that PP's merchandise moved out of the store quickly, so we could sell more. I had to charmingly coerce customers to buy things they may not have wanted and probably didn't need.

I was also to keep an eagle eye out for shoplifters. Tell-tale signs were 'pregnant' women, women with infants carrying diaper bags, teenagers with large tote bags and people who spent inordinately long amounts of time in the dressing room.

Manhattan was definitely chocka with thieves, so the old monocles had to be on the eye at all times.

Other responsibilities included:

- Opening and closing the store on time
- Keeping the store clean
- Making sure the merchandise was hanging nicely
- Making bank deposits daily
- Ensuring that stocks didn't run out so that we'd be left with bare shelves.

I recalled all the little tricks of trade I'd picked up from the aunt at her store when I'd first arrived in America. Back then I had nothing to do except follow her around all day asking inane questions.

I knew I would need a 'Back In A Few' sign to hang on the door when I took a loo or cigarette break. The aunt had wagged her finger at me explaining that one hung the sign out only in the most dire of circumstances because above all else, business meant that the doors had to be open for customers to walk through. She didn't smoke and didn't seem to pee much either so the sign almost never got hung on the door of her store, Aditi, unless she had gone to make a bank deposit.

I remembered how she'd make fabulous window displays with slow moving merchandise, giving passers-by the false notion that they were oohing and aahing over the latest fashions. Who had time to read Vogue and Elle from cover to cover? No one knew for sure what was hot and what wasn't, anyway, so the aunt counted on her clever window tableaus to draw in the passer-by.

She had taught me how to complement overweight women. How to fawn over ugly ones. She had made it clear that as a responsible merchant, I would have to pay extra attention to single men, who were always unsure of what to buy in a store geared mostly towards women.

I knew I was supposed to chitchat with wealthy-looking people.

I learned how to identify window-shoppers and time-wasters. And I also knew the cardinal rule of the shopkeeper. If a couple walked in, my focus was to remain on the woman, nodding only in passing at the man, no matter how dishy he was. Money was at stake here, not sex.

Oh, I was an old hack. I was a master. I had seen the aunt in action. I even knew how to spin a plausible yarn when merchandise was defective.

Most handmade things from India had something wrong with them, despite the umpteen quality checks they were supposedly put through before they were crated and sent off to foreign shores.

Eagle-eyed, picky New Yorkers could spot these defects in a minute. So if you sold merchandise from Ye Olde Bharat, unless you had a convincing tale to tell, you'd end up having to put a lot of expensive merchandise on sale, eating into your profits.

'They're all one of a kind,' I had heard the aunt tell Corey, one of her wealthy customers, who was dismayed that a $2500 area rug was ruined by an ugly weaving error.

'That's not a mistake, sweetie. It's deliberate. It's the "flaw" all master weavers deliberately include to ward off the evil eye,' the aunt had said glibly when she saw Corey's face fall.

'Indian artisans believe that if something is too perfect others will covet it and something bad will happen. So they put a disfiguring mark on it to "disguise" its perfection. In fact, Corey, they even do it to kids! You'll see cute little Indian babies all over the place, with a black dot on the cheek—lovingly disfigured by their own mothers.'

The aunt was so convincing that Corey went away delighted, believing she was the proud owner of a one-of-a-kind collector's item, and not something that was a result of a weaver falling asleep on the job, somewhere in Madhya Pradesh.

Over the years, the aunt had managed to palm off several defective, disfigured, faulty items on to Corey. Despite that, they remained the best of friends for years.

♦

Harry and his wife Manpreete (I had taken to adding the 'e' in my mind, just so I wouldn't mix-up the many male and female Sikhs I was sure to meet in the course of my new job) would be making periodic visits to ensure that things went according to plan. They were hoping to expand all across America, a Potato Print in every state.

I was a key part of that starchy dream.

The aunt was sceptical. 'I hope Harry knows what he is doing with you,' she said to me bitingly, when I'd gone to visit one weekend, after serving two weeks' notice at the travel company. 'Call me before you run into problems. I don't want you to lose this job. I wish you'd stay in the travel agency. Shopkeeping isn't all fun and games like you're used to. And you're going to be all alone. No office full of friends.'

'Too late, I quit!' I told her gaily.

My employers were equally sceptical about my career shift. 'Well, the door is open if shopkeeping doesn't work out,' said my boss, expecting me to be back in a week. 'But you'll have to start from the bottom all over again. You and Shas.'

Shas had also put in her papers.

♦

The first week at PP went by in a blur. Harry arrived from Delhi and we spent hours stocking the store, doing the window decorations and getting used to where everything was. It was great fun. Harry was kind, gentle and patient. We would break for lunch; grab a sandwich from the gourmet deli next door, run by Fabio and Luigi Ricci. They were from Italy and mouth-wateringly handsome. Their sandwiches weren't too bad either.

We had a store-opening deadline and worked against the clock so we wouldn't be late. Everything had to be perfect.

Finally, it was the opening day.

Harry had sent invitations out to many of New York's wealthiest, most influential and discerning patrons. We were nervous. Word of mouth meant everything in the retail business. So we served champagne, three types of expensive wine and specially formulated nouvelle-Indian canapés. Curried shrimp vol-au-vent. Tandoori quail with pineapple glace. Dried, salted shark shavings on rice pancakes. Toast points with peppercorn infused goat brain. Harry knew an Indian chef who was unafraid to experiment.

And the combination of ingredients somehow seemed appropriate. It wasn't as if a bunch of traditional Indians were expected to come crashing through the doors, hunting for kababs and curry or dosas and idlis. In fact, I was worried that people would talk more about the food than the clothes and furnishings.

As it turned out my worries were unwarranted.

Potato Print's grand opening was a glittering, elegant, social affair. There were even a few press photographers.

We sold a ton of merchandise and I spent most of the evening ringing up sales, fortified by plenty of bubbly, which I absolutely needed in order to coruscate and effervesce.

The aunt was a no-show. She was very busy at her own store. It was my first inkling that we were now in competition with each other.

Harry entertained his guests with élan and pizzazz, a glass in his hand and a tale on his tongue all evening long. He made sure the customers were fed, and their glasses were filled. He spun romantic yarns about the villages of India. He spoke of the way Indian art, industry and originality had developed over centuries. He painted a picture of bliss. He made it all sound so colourful and happy, so charming and harmless that you almost forgot the reality of the dirt and grime, the dust and heat, the poverty and inequality, the power cuts and the lack of amenities in the average Indian village.

You don't get to be a hotshot businessman with global expansion in your heart by speaking the truth.

People were delighted. Everyone seemed to love Potato Print and promised to come back again and again. Bringing their friends with them.

The champagne and wine had worked. We were so happy.

Finally, the last of the guests had left with their purchases. The cleaners had mopped up the little bits and pieces of gourmet goop from the floor. Even the sophisticated can be slobs, I noted dryly.

Harry and I were the last ones to leave.

♦

He turned off the lights. I stood poised, ready to make the dash to the door as soon as I heard the beep-beep-beep-beep-beep-beep of the burglar alarm being set. We had ten seconds from the time he armed it to get out of the store and lock the doors behind us.

I waited.

There was no beep.

I waited some more.

Still no beep.

It was dark in the store, faintly lit only by the streetlights outside. I turned to see what was going on and felt someone's arms grab me, spinning me around.

A bearded face and hairy mouth fell on my face. A tongue was trying to make its way past my lips. I smelled champagne tinged with goat's brain. Not a tantalising combo as I am sure you will agree.

'Oh stop Harry,' I said playfully and pushed him away.

'I've been waiting to do thishhhhhh,' he slurred.

'You are so sweet, I really appreciate all that you're doing. You and Manpreete,' I slipped in hastily, hoping to shock him back to reality with the mention of his wilting wife's name.

'Shessssss nottt here. Shesssss in Indiaaaa,' he continued, slurping at me happily. Indeed, the Atlantic Ocean never loomed larger and more impassable than at that very moment.

'The alarm. The alarm,' I cried, jabbing at the buttons. I grabbed him by the hand and pulled him out of the store onto the street, and forced the door shut and locked it before the silent alarm triggered the police.

I gave him a kiss on the cheek. 'I'll see you in the morning,' I said gaily and dashed off before he could say any more.

◆

The telephone rang on the morning of the first day of the rest of my life. The day I would ride the train to work, not the plane.

I groped groggily.

'Hello,' I said. My head ached a bit. I looked outside, the sun was barely up.

'Your eyes are filled with sleep, my heart is filled so deep
I ache—I long—I weep. My love is yours to keep.'

It was said in Urdu, the language of North Indian poetry. The native tongue of love-trash. The voice belonged to Harry.

I burst out laughing. It was funny. Not the voice. The poetry.

'What are you doing up so early?' I asked him. 'I'm not supposed to meet you at the store till nine, right? It's only six. Whassamatter, jet lag?'

He'd been in New York for over a week. Jet lag didn't last that long.

'No, it's my heart,' he said, also in Urdu. He sounded breathless.

'Oh noooooooo,' I wailed. 'Call 911. Now. They'll be over immediately.'

'What? What 911? What are you talking about,' said a puzzled Harry, in English now.

'Your heart of course,' I said, trying to sound equally puzzled.

'Foolish girl,' he said without the hint of myocardial infarction or coronary thrombosis.

'I missed you. I couldn't wait to see you. I couldn't sleep. I haven't thought about a single other person since the day I met you back in Delhi, with your mother. I've been holding my tongue. Holding back my love. My heart is heavy. It can bear no more. We must be one.'

I held my head in my hands to stop it from banging into the wall. Again and again.

Chapter 21

BIG HOUSE, LITTLE HOUSE

I tried to focus on the glass half full.

The positive.

The fifty thou.

In some quarters, like back in the Punjab, Harry may have been considered extremely desirable. Certainly Manpreete had fallen for his charms.

I knew he came from a family of renowned writers. Always elegantly dressed, he spoke with the cultured 'public' school accent preferred by all Indian men who'd gone to Doon or Mayo or similar educational institutions, where polo and tennis were commonplace and 'bearers' served lunch.

Although they are called 'public schools', they have never been accessible to the general public in India. They are the most private and elite of learning institutions that required not only a large bank balance but also connections in the right places and excellent marks. So unless you can meet all the criteria above, it's more than likely you've never been allowed past the gates of one of these hallowed institutions, India's equivalent of the Ivy League.

Harry was tall, well over six feet and his colouring was a blend of pale onion and new potato. Pinkish-brown.

He oozed confidence, privilege and intellectual superiority.

You had to visualise the rest.

Whether his features were a perfectly symmetrical 1.618, I couldn't say. There was so much facial hair and lengths of fabric (seven metres of turban) camouflaging the truth, that you needed a little trust and faith. You could also get a measure by looking at his offspring I suppose, to see what the genes were capable of producing, but (happily) those brats were far away in India.

Which brought me to the negative.

The glass half empty.

The deal breaker.

He was married. To a wilting wife who had so far produced four children.

What was he thinking? He didn't behave like a man in search of a one-night stand. I was certain of that. You didn't hire someone to take care of your business, pay them double the market rate and then follow them half way around the world for an ONS.

You could get plenty of that locally for a fraction of the cost.

My radar went up, tickling my nose.

Then I got it.

He was looking for something semi-permanent. He was looking to make me the 'Lady of the Chinna Veedu' (that's what they called it down in Tamil Nadu) a.k.a. Madame of the Little House.

Although I was unfamiliar with the intimate details of North Indian extramarital culture, I knew everything that went on down south, from whence I sprang. The concept of 'Peria Veedu/ Chinna Veedu' (Big House/Little House) was a fairly commonplace tradition.

While polygamy (unless you were Muslim) was against the law in India, it was accepted without murmur in the streets and by-lanes of Chennai and many a movie star, politician and industrialist had multiple squabbling wives and children. I personally knew several men supporting two households, without the slightest furrow of the brow.

Here's how it worked:

In the Big House lived Wife Number One. The one whose stars aligned perfectly with the man's, so that the union would safeguard the sanctity of caste, property, inheritance, business interests, blood lines and so on. Children of this coalition stood to inherit the big man's fortune without a fuss. No long and bitter court cases with DNA evidence and so on. Being in the Big House was a definite advantage.

Then there was the Small House, where Wife Number Two, the illegal one, lived. She was usually young, pretty, poor, caste-no-bar. She was selected on the basis of her other skills, the ones that unfortunately, often produced progeny as well.

These children had to hire lawyers and forensic experts to fight for their rightful share of daddy's fortune upon his passing. It was tough being the M of the LH, but there were plenty of women who wouldn't turn up their noses at the chance because it beat having to punch the calculator in an accountant's office or have the fingers bleed in a garment factory.

Mistress of the Little House? Me?

Following our ancient family tradition of counting chickens, I'd been too busy blowing up money I would soon be earning, to anticipate this conundrum sticking its smelly tongue into my mouth and distasteful poetry in my ears.

I had already put tons of very expensive stuff on layaway all over town. New furniture. New kitchen equipment. New clothes. Even a vacation to Baja. With Shas and Rue.

All based on Harry's solemn promise of fifty thousand big ones a year.

Bloody hell, it was a crisis.

Not the moral dilemma of having my rent and expenses paid up in exchange for services provided, but the real problem which was that the man who held my future in his hands, the one who was offering me his heart, a few other organs and some money wasn't really the boss of the manor.

He was not the fairy prince of Potato Print and the spuds weren't his to dish out freely.

The mom had told me very clearly that it was Manpreete, his wife, who held the family's finances in her hands and that came to her via her father, one Maninder Singh, a trucking billionaire from the Punjab. By his side was Manpreete's older brother, Sukhminder, an up-and-coming politician with questionable morals.

Legend had it that S'minder had once viciously mowed down some poor sod on the highway because he'd cut him off without signalling properly. There were no charges filed against S, even though the unfortunate victim, a struggling father with a family of six, was paralysed permanently from the waist down.

A paltry sum of money had been paid to the victim and his family to shut them up and a warning was issued to the paraplegic: 'Make sure your children don't drive the way you do. There's much more where that came from.' That was the kind of clout the family wielded.

It didn't take rocket science to figure out that one could benefit hugely by the patronage of such people, if one played one's cards right.

But one could just as easily find one's self tossed into a stinking sewer, blindfolded, still breathing, with concrete shoes, if one wasn't smart.

I needed to think about my next move.

◆

I was a terrible poker player. I couldn't remember the rules of bridge. I made mistakes in Solitaire. I had no idea how to play my cards, as it were.

'What's to think?' my ego asked rhetorically. 'You can't play cards, but you can play this game. You've had practise. Damn, but you're perfect at this kind of subterfuge.' My ego and alter ego stepped in to provide me with clarity on this problem.

The M Ego continued: 'It's not like you haven't ladled yourself out like free chicken soup at a homeless shelter before, so why would you think twice when the benefits are excellent?'

A Ego: Benefits? Oh really? And what happens when Manpreete

comes a callin', the machete a swingin'? With Sukhminder, the bloodthirsty brother behind her, the pistols loaded? (It sounded liked the AE was watching too much Quentin Tarantino.) Mixing work and pleasure. Disaster.

M Ego: Pleasure? Who said anything about pleasure? I call this working. Overtime. Thankfully, he's not going to be around 24/7. Two or three times a year tops. I can handle it.

A Ego: And what if he's a sexual degenerate. What are you going to do?

M Ego: I'll think of something. I've put down more than half on most of my layaways. There's no refund.

♦

The A Ego was right about one thing at least. In matters of the boudoir, Harry was a boor.

He could barely find his way around a woman's body. He poked where he ought to have stroked. He prodded where he ought to have massaged. He bit when he ought to have kissed. And he took ten times longer than the average man to achieve 'balle balle' which is a term the Sikhs use when they refer to happy concatenation of circumstance.

It was clearly difficult for him. I couldn't see much happiness. If I were to describe the top half of his face, which was all I could see anyhow, I'd say it looked disconsolate. Who knew what thoughts and distractions kept him from getting on with the job? And I wasn't much help either.

Maybe the children weren't his at all. In the dark of night, one bearded, turbaned man looks much the same as another, so perhaps some other lusty Sardar had pleasured Manpreete four times.

Almost as if he heard me think, 'I want to keep all the lights on,' he said. 'I never get to have the lights on. I never get to see anything. Manpreete insists on turning off all the lights and playing loud bhangra music. It's torture.'

Of course. As the M of the LH, I had to do all the dirty work.

Well, Manpreete and I had two things in common: Harry and the need for the dark. It wasn't so much that I was embarrassed by my expanding waistline (although I had every reason to be) it was more that I didn't want to look at Harry in the flesh.

With the turban on his head and the beard neatly tucked under a net, he looked dashing, even swashbuckling. It was easy to picture him on a horse, brandishing a sword, slicing off heads heroically. Stuff that turns women on.

But free of net-and-turban, his hair all over the place, he looked like a Sasquatch. It took all my concentration to keep things going.

But on the plus, for the privilege of his hard-fought BBs, he showered me with gifts and took me to expensive dinners. He even agreed to a raise, although I'd only been working at PP for two weeks. I would now be earning seventy-five thou a year.

◆

It was no fun at all.

This is not how I'd seen my future pan out. Servicing a hairy man with a wife and four children. But I was stuck. Caught between the Scylla and Charybdis.

I thought about calling Manpreete. But that was a bad idea. She'd sack me in a minute. I considered calling the mom, but that was worse than a bad idea. She would most definitely call up both Harry and Manpreete to scream at them for destroying her daughter's life, resulting in my getting sacked.

I considered refusing Harry access. But I didn't think I'd last longer than ten days in my job with that kind of attitude.

All roads led to the sack, one way or another.

Time crept. Was the clock broken? I didn't know what to do. Harry wasn't going to stay in New York forever, I knew, which was a sort of bright light at the end of the dank and gloomy tunnel. In the next two weeks, I feigned monthly troubles, stomach flu and a host of other excuses to get out of overtime duty as much as I could.

Any normal man would have seen through the charade but not Harry. He was most understanding and solicitous, the gentleman that he was, and not a little blinded by his own sophistication and charms. He never forced himself on me.

It was annoyingly, irritatingly unsexy behaviour. I am certain if he'd clobbered me on the head and dragged me off to bed, I'd have felt a lot better.

I was saved by the bell. Manpreete's fifth frantic phone call that the weavers were about to go on strike and the tailors had already stopped sewing, woke Harry up from his lust-laden sloth. He called Air India and made a booking back for New Delhi. First Class of course.

'Six months will go by in a flash,' he assured me lovingly and left for the airport. 'I'll be back,' he said.

I simpered alluringly and shuddered at his retreating back.

◆

The nice thing about pain is that once it's over, you can't remember it. I soon forgot all about Harry and his return. I turned instead to Fabio and Luigi Ricci, the Italian brothers who ran the gourmet deli named 'La Rive Gauche' next door to PP.

'Why do you have a French name for your store when both of you are Italian?' I wondered as I paid for my prosciutto and warm Brie with sun dried tomatoes and pesto sauce on a buttery baguette. They made what tasted to me like the world's most delicious sandwiches. The brother's were pretty delectable too, especially Fabio.

'Italian names suggest pizzas and spaghetti. Cheap stuff. Can't make any money on that. Now give a place a French name and you can get away with meurtre (murder),' said Fabio with a dimpled grin. They gave me huge discounts, so I didn't care a croissant's crumb if they were ripping off the average Upper West Sider.

Every afternoon, instead of walking home to eat as I had planned, I'd hang the 'Be Back Soon' sign on my door and shoot the breeze at Rive Gauche for half an hour, flirting with Fabio and stuffing my face.

'Where is your husband?' asked Fabio one afternoon.

'What husband?' I replied puzzled. 'I don't have a husband. I'd like one, but I haven't found one yet. Know any? Good price?'

He ignored my humour. 'The tall guy with the beard. The one who owns the store? Isn't he your husband? The burino (which could be either lout or bumpkin or boor or peasant or all of the above in Italian) who got McDonalds to cater the store's opening? I heard many of your guests were food poisoned and died on their way home,' he said cheerfully exaggerating. 'Nouvelle Indian cuisine! It sounds frightening. Curry makes you hurry to the bathroom.'

Oh he was hilarious, that Fabio.

We hadn't invited the Ricci's to our elite, grand opening as either guests or caterers. They were well beneath the calibre of Harry the burino's invitee list.

'Hahahaha,' I said laughing. 'He's too hairy to be my husband.' Just then I caught site of Fabio's fairly hairy chest, festooned with a gold chain. Being Italian and all, it was to be expected. Quite sexy. I felt the stirrings of passion. In my toes. I quickly changed the subject of body hair. It's funny how Harry's hair grossed me out and Fabio's made me all tingly. Physical attraction is a strange bird.

'He's married and has four children back in India. He's a friend of my mother's, that's how I got the job,' I explained. 'Indian connections.'

'But I thought I saw both of you, ahem…' he continued, not wanting to say it out loud, out of European politeness, I suppose. But he rolled his eyes theatrically and clasped his hands to his chest. It is a well-known fact that Italians speak with their hands and accentuate words with the roll of their eyes.

An American would have just come out and said it: 'I heard the bearded guy's been bangin' you like there's no damarra.'

'Ahem? Ahem? What do you mean ahem?' I said as indignantly, as I could fake. 'There's no "ahem" going on here. He's my boss and that's that. Indians are like Italians. We hug and kiss a lot. It doesn't mean much.'

That was a big lie, since Indian men and women said the chastest of hellos and goodbyes to each other (even brothers and sisters and fathers and daughters) with 'namastes' (palms held together under one's own chin) at least three feet apart from the other person.

There was no kissing. Not even air kissing. In fact, once, the Hollywood heart-throb, Richard Gere, made the mistake of kissing an Indian actress on the lips in public (in a chummy sort of way, not in the least bit romantic) and almost set the whole country aflame. Gere had to beat a hasty retreat before India could get back to being normal.

Men and women never touched each other unless they were in the privacy of their own bedrooms. Anything else was too shameful.

The only handholding that would pass public decency norms was between buddies of the same sex, as they walked down the street hand in hand or arm in arm as if deeply in love. Gay, to the average Western bystander, but harmless, non-sexual palsywalsyness in India.

'Oh,' said Fabio. 'My mistake. So you are single, eh?'

'My single days are numbered,' I informed him haughtily.

'You know, if you lost fifteen pounds, you'd be quite beautiful. I may even ask you out on a date,' he said.

I had just licked my fingers after wolfing down a large Smoked Salmon and Camembert with honey mustard on a croissant drenched in butter while I eyed a large slice of strawberry cheesecake under the glass. It was almost better than sex.

'Really? Are you serious?' I said, looking up from the food display.

It was intriguing. I wondered if he was joking. Not about the weight. There Fabio spoke the truth. I'd gained two whole sizes in the past few years. I could no longer fit easily into Extra Larges and I was secretly scouting out Plus Size stores. I had even planned to buy myself a wig and huge sunglasses so I could walk into a Lane Bryant, maybe even Eileen Fisher, one day without being recognised. I knew I needed to drop fifteen pounds before they turned into twenty and thirty and one hundred. Pretty soon they'd need a forklift to move me here and there.

The putting on of pounds happened very quickly in my case.

I blamed it on my less-than-perfect love life. It had propelled me towards food, since cigarettes and booze could no longer do a good job by themselves to fill up the void.

'What if I lose twenty pounds?' I asked. 'What do I get?'

'Why then I will have sex with you! Most definitely,' he replied. 'And celebrate the day with champagne. Maybe some sugar-free chocolate.'

Luigi (Fabio's brother) roared with laughter at this ridiculous conversation. But I didn't care if he did. Fabio drove an old Alfa Romeo Spider with a soft top that came up and down. He treated the car with humble love and heartfelt compassion. It would be nice to roar off in it to a champagne-and-sex date.

◆

Fabio, classy, handsome and owner of half a business, was an intellectual too. He talked with reverence of Voltaire and Rabelais and Balzac. The French had made a profound impression on him. He hummed from Verdi's *Rigoletto* (to keep in touch with his Italian roots, I suppose) and pretended to conduct an orchestra with a baton when he was trying to amuse me.

Once we'd agreed to the bet officially, he'd pop into Potato Print all the time to see if I was cheating on him. With a little chocolate or perhaps French fries.

In the short while that he had come to know me, he had figured out that I wasn't to be trusted. But I wasn't two-timing him. I controlled my appetite.

♦

PP was doing pretty well at the time.

I'd built-up a steady stream of regulars. But there were long hours with no customers and no activity. Hours that I used to fill up with peanuts and chocolate and cheese and Oreos. But all that was in the past, après Fabio's wager, I took to reading.

I'd hunted all over the place for Mills & Boon (my favourite form of literature) and no one had ever heard of either an M or B. 'Is that a brand of ice-cream,' someone asked me at the book store.

They were called Harlequin Romances in America and they were a little raunchier than the tame stuff we were used to back at the nunnery, where pale breasts never quivered under someone's touch, only heaved with sorrow or desire all on their own.

I bought myself a pile of HRs and hid them under the cash register so Fabio wouldn't discover how lowbrow I really was.

I didn't know which was more embarrassing. Being caught eating Reese's Pieces or reading Harlequins.

'The fastest way to lose weight is on a high protein, low carb diet,' he said. 'I will make it my mission to feed you properly so I can have the pleasure of taking off your clothes soon.' A pact to get down to the act.

'Yes indeed,' I said. 'Thy will be done.' There was a part of me that didn't believe he was serious, but losing weight was a good thing in itself.

I spoke to Rue and Shas about my life's new target. They thought it was fantastic. Rue bought me a large calendar to hang up in the stock room, where I would cross off the pounds day by day, as I whittled my body down till it was good enough for Fabio.

I showed him the calendar. He thought it was a great idea and made me write down every morsel I put in my mouth each day. That was an eye opener. It was embarrassing to see how much I had actually been consuming. I hoped he wouldn't ask me to weigh my daily discharges or something equally disgusting.

Shas brought over an old stationary exercise bike that Klaus had discarded because he'd taken to running all over the Lower East Side, whatever the weather. She also bought me a set of noisy cowbells to hang over the front door, so I'd know if someone came in while I was in the back, pedalling off the pudge.

It was exciting. I had a new goal.

◆

While I chatted with the customers and rang-up the cash register joyfully each time I made a sale, cycled away my excesses and flirted with Fabio, I also got to know some of the other merchants on the street. A friendly bunch of people who became like family very soon.

There was a hosiery and lingerie store called 'Stop the Runs' owned by Aileen and Sherry, whose husbands were both in the construction business. They didn't really need the money, the store was just a hobby. So they'd hang up their 'Be Back Soon' sign all the time and go off to lunch, out shopping at Bloomingdales, or hit the beauty parlour on the slightest whim. Very lucky ladies.

Corcovado was an upscale woman's clothing store run by a woman from Brazil named Dona. I loved her clothes although nothing she sold fit me. 'Breve, breve (soon, soon),' she would say in Portuguese.

All of them got wind of the bet between me and Fabio, and it became a street secret. A street mission. To get me down to a Size Twelve. To ensure that I was at the larger side of normal, rather than the smaller side of fat.

They encouraged me with smiles and tempted me with gifts. Sherry even bought me a baby-pink, egg-shaped buzzing toy for the day Fabio and I would fulfil our oath.

It was top-of-the-line; she assured me, and not the discounted fare you'd normally see in sex stores. But she was holding on to it until she felt I deserved it. She'd give it to me with pomp and celebration when the time came.

Fabio began making me lunches. Crispy grilled salmon skin and tossed multi-leaf salad. No Caesar's dressing, only cold-pressed, virgin olive oil and balsamic vinegar. Tomato and mozzarella salad drizzled with pesto. Roast beef with cauliflower rice. I was allowed strawberries and blueberries with heavy cream for dessert. Salami and hard cheese cubes when I needed a snack. Egg salad and tuna salad were ok too.

Once in a while, he'd make me posset, which is a dessert from fourteenth or fifteenth century England made with heavy cream and lemon. The lemon curdles the cream and if you add sugar, you get a delicious moment in heaven, similar to condensed milk. Of course, Fabio used sugar substitute. I felt as if I was at the Pearly Gates.

It wasn't a bad diet, but it was very expensive. If not for Fabio's ulterior obsession with my weight, I'd have given up after paying five dollars for an avocado. It was one of the few low-carb-high-protein veggies you could eat.

◆

Finally, five weeks and three days into the diet, I stood on the scale in Fabio's store and I was down to 138 pounds. The bra size was down to a 38C. Not exactly a Size Zero, but a respectable Twelve Plus. The jeans zipped all the way up over the belly and not much of me flopped over the belt. The white shirt could be finally tucked in, the buttons across the chest weren't threatening to pop, the view from the side was not that of a pregnant woman.

I felt pretty good. I took a deep breath and looked at Fabio. It was the moment of reckoning.

All the while, on my odyssey from porky down to almost petite, a part of me couldn't believe that the bet was more than a joke between friends. The deal and its implementation were so matter-of-fact, that I didn't quite give it serious thought. Not that I didn't think he was sexy or anything, I most certainly did.

Fabio must have heard me thinking. 'You're not backing out, you chicken, are you? A bet's a bet. We are leaving right now.'

It was only eleven in the a.m. I had a store to run and he did too.

'Where are we going?' I asked Fabio. I noticed he didn't pick up his car keys.

'Next door,' he said. That was where my store was. Potato Print. 'Let's get out the sign,' he said, reaching for it under the cash register. He knew his whereabouts in my store.

I hung 'Be Back Soon' up (I didn't know how soon), locked the door and led Fabio to the back room. He had a bottle of champagne in one hand and two glasses in the other. He poured for both of us. 'Cheers! Here's to a long and happy sex life for us,' he said gaily and glugged. I knocked back three.

'Off with the clothes,' he said bossily, waving a finger at my pants. I stripped. So did he. There was a huge mirror on the back wall of the storeroom into which I had stared at myself every day, as I pedalled away, visualising the pounds melting into little blobs of fat on the floor.

I had spent many a stationary mile fantasising about this very moment, although in my plan, there was a bed, flowers, music and a few rose petals.

Things in my head almost never became reality.

My storeroom was small. There was a small bathroom off to the side, crammed with inventory waiting to be sold. There was no place to lay down. Or sit, for that matter. Besides the mirror and the bike, there were boxes of merchandise everywhere.

'The bike,' ordered Fabio masterfully. I grabbed the seat and leaned forward. He was behind me.

♦

I learned a few things during this fairly pleasant encounter.

Exercise bikes are made to withstand lots of pressure and pounding. They don't collapse like beds. Especially, the kind they make in France.

Enjoying a mirror depends very much on your sex partner and how firm and un-floppy you are.

Sex in the standing position is a great way to exercise one's thigh muscles.

All in all, it was a capital experience and we finished off feeling accomplished, satisfied and very, very sweaty.

And quite smelly.

I cleaned off as best as I could in the bathroom while Fabio pulled on his clothes to go back to his store.

'Salad tonight?' he asked, like we were an old married couple.

'Sure,' I said.

I unlocked the store again, flipped the 'Be Back Soon' sign which read, 'Open: Come On In' on the other side and waited eagerly for the customers to come pouring in. I was in a great mood. I'd make a few good sales for sure, I was confident.

One of my regulars, a German lady named Greta, walked in first. Her husband, a pilot in Lufthansa, had recently dumped her for a newer, fresher, firmer blonde-and-blue: a flight attendant.

Greta was getting over the heartache by shopping at PP almost every week, dropping several hundred each time.

I liked her a lot.

'What's that funny smell,' she asked sniffing the air. I hastily lit a few incense sticks and sprayed air freshener around the room.

'Must be from the air conditioning vent next door,' I said blithely. 'You know the deli? They're always cooking fish. There's nothing I can do about it.'

'I don't know. It doesn't smell like food,' she said unconvinced. Germans can't be fooled very easily.

I distracted her with a new shipment of cashmere shawls.

I knew I'd have to find a way to hide the smell of good sex if Fabio and I were going to have any encores in the store.

Chapter 22

SITAR SHANKAR

Fabio and I settled into an easy, casual and fun relationship based on low-carbs, high levels of sex and several bottles of fine, aged wine, sipped slowly. I started saying things like, 'velvety flavour' and began to see the difference between 'short' wines and 'lively' wines. I learned when a wine was merely 'mellow' and when it was well and truly 'maderized'. I was getting to be quite the connoisseur.

Not for him the cheap Chianti and wine-in-a-box that Shas and I were perfectly satisfied with. Rue was equally comfortable with the notion that there was no need to blow one's entire pay check on expensive alcohol when the cheap stuff actually did the trick faster and better, hang the hangovers.

But it was nice to live life in the fine lane.

Being with him sort of set the tone for my future aspirations. To this day, I'm partial to fois gras, smoked salmon, caviar, truffles, escargot et al. I like anchovies too, although I think that takes me down several notches on the scale of sophistication.

Fabio and I did not plan for a life ahead with each other. There were no expectations and no demands. There would be no 'ménages' in our future, 'a deux' or 'a trois'. We were a here-and-now couple.

Since he was right next door, it was a convenient way of getting my RDA (Required Daily Allowance) of OM (Orgasmo Multiplo), which is Italian for the same thing.

Fabio liked the excitement of sex in dangerous places. The closer we came to getting caught 'in flagrante delicto' (which is

Italian, well ok Latin, for 'caught with one's pants down') the more excited he became.

So we went at it with abandon everywhere we could.

In his store during the post-lunch hour lull, in the bathroom, knowing full well that his staff and brother were loitering outside. In my store with the front door unlocked (we were interrupted once or twice by the clanging of the cowbells) which was nerve wracking. In Central Park at dusk (which brought to mind previous encounters at Delhi's Lodhi Gardens, but CP was nothing like LG. It was much cooler and there was no smell of beedis…), in the parking lots of strange supermarkets and even in an elevator once, very quickly.

But Fabio especially liked his OMs as he drove his car (stick shift of course) way past the speed limit, trying to catch green lights on the avenues. He never closed his eyes, not even at the moment of 'mort' and we never got into an accident. Luck shone on us like the floodlights from a police helicopter.

We took a trip out to Jones Beach once and in the hour-long drive I counted five OMs. One for him and four for me. Of course, it was the Long Island Expressway and there were no traffic lights so there was a certain flow to it.

'I can balance a glass of wine on the dashboard. I won't spill even one drop. I'm that good a driver,' he boasted. I believed him. He kept his car spotless.

It was a dangerous, reckless way to have sex. But it was fun too. I was getting caught up in his madness, his fantasies and I couldn't help myself.

He was a strong, controlling personality. For the first time I realised that I was quite the wishy-wash. I had no great strength of character or steely resolve of my own. I was like a leaf in the wind. Anyone with half a will could blow me this way or that.

Shas who always knew this, tried to tell me that he was taking control, reshaping my character and making me do things that were very bad for me. 'You'll end up in the hospital or dead,' she said. To which I replied with a song sung by Billie Holiday, 'Ain't no body's business if I do.'

◆

When we weren't tempting the Furies at ninety miles an hour or the cops patrolling the parks and parking lots, we frequented his beautiful apartment. Woody and masculine with gleaming steel kitchen equipment, he played opera while we tested out a few Kamasutra positions. He knew more about it than I did. Both opera and the Kamastuff.

Fabio was the second man in my life to buy me toys. I'm not talking Barbie Dolls either. The kind that make playing with one another so much more fun. He also had an extensive collection of porn from all over the world.

He took his sex very seriously.

A little too seriously for me.

I was getting older, close to the scary three-oh and felt I had paid my dues several times over. Done all my wood shedding, so to speak. I felt I was entitled to the kind of sex where I could lay back and reap the benefits of my vast experience as my partner ploughed the earth, tilled the soil and sowed the seeds. Did all the sweaty work. Wasn't sex supposed to be relaxing?

◆

Meanwhile, out on the streets of New York where things other than sex were happening, my musical career was taking a new turn, mostly because of Rue, who was into the exotic, the colourful and the weird.

The Sexy Sitas were getting the odd gig here and there, providing New Yorkers with cultural confusion. They didn't call the city 'The Melting Pot' for nothing.

If I'm being honest, most people in NY didn't have a clue

about Indian music or Indian dance, so Rue and I could get away with pretty much anything.

And we did.

Back in Delhi, I'd had an Ustad (teacher) training me for a while. He came from a long line of very well-known proponents of North Indian Classical music, and it was something of a coup that he had even agreed to teach me.

He had a navy seal-like approach to Hindustani vocal training. According to him, a singer had to be capable of powering through coughs, colds, lack of sleep, raging fevers and power failure. He smoked heavily and told me that a good singer ought to be able to smack a smoker's cough on the head and make it disappear with the sheer strength of will power. He often cleared his throat loudly and spat the contents that accumulated in his mouth right onto the street, no matter where he happened to be. It was acceptable behaviour in India, especially if you were an Ustad.

As I write this, not much has changed, although some civic-minded people have taken to painting pictures of various gods and religious icons on walls, corridors, fences, compounds and so on, hoping to appeal to some higher sense of civic responsibility in the average Hindu, Muslim or Christian Indian. We didn't have too many Jewish Indians in India, so they had no representation. And despite the fact that Buddhism originated in India, Buddhists didn't get little Buddhas painted here and there either. There weren't enough of them to make a strong case for it.

Like all traditional gurus, my teacher expected his chelas (students) to fetch, carry, fawn and follow him around slavishly, waiting to be bossed around. There was an ancient method to this madness. To allow knowledge to get inside one's head, according to the Vedas (those rigid, ready reckoners for Hindu behaviour), first, one needed to empty out the bad attitude.

I gave up learning Hindustani music after about six months. Humility did not suit me well at all. But I had learned enough for my specific needs. To toss it around the jazz idiom as I pleased, peppering my songs with little unexpected trills and wails. It was original for sure, especially in America, but I don't think it caught on.

But it's important to note that I had studied North Indian music and not South Indian music, even though I was as South Indian as vetthalai pakku (a bitter leaf with even more bitter nuts that people loved chewing). This was because there was a dearth of South Indian music teachers in Delhi at the time.

I make a point here since there's a massive sinkhole between North and South India, literally and figuratively. It's miles and miles from New Delhi down to Tamil Nadu. And everything's different. The food. The scripts. The holidays. Language. Body shape. Mind shape. And of course, the music.

So while the kind of singing I'd learned really didn't go with the kind of dancing Rue was fond of—Bharatanatyam—this was New York, home of the avant-garde, the bizarre, the experimental and the spectacular.

My fear was that anyone who knew sambar was not just an animal but also a popular staple in the South Indian diet; would know immediately that the kind of 'fusion' we were creating was pretty awful.

If I'm being honest, we were more into our costumes and make-up and general sexiness than the substance of it. Our performances would take care of themselves, we felt.

One of our most memorable shows was at the Asia Plaza Stage at the Bronx Zoo. The guest of honour was a former first lady of the USA, known for her iconic style and grace, now deceased.

Rue and I were rightfully nervous. It was an event organized by the Asia Society, a very hoity-toity organization that didn't invite you to perform without a lengthy background check. At the last minute, I decided to rope in Stu Woodcock, an upright bass player with a percussive streak.

The bells on Rue's feet matched the boom-boom of Stu's bass

while I sang little trills up and down the scale. Set amidst the shrieks of peacocks, elephants and other exotic animals from far away, there was something fabulous and unforgettable about the evening.

Since all things experimental have always been welcomed into New York City's tolerant, benevolent bosom, Rue and I never got terrible reviews. It was hard for critics, even New York's harshest, to decide whether what we were doing was good or bad. So they wrote things like, 'From the underbelly of India's dark side, two young Indian women make modern history'.

Once we performed in a coffee shop and the reviewer wrote, 'In a refreshing change from the classical tradition, here is a modern take on the raga and the muffin'. It was a little humiliating.

But publicity is nothing to sneeze at, good or bad. So, brandishing a fistful of snippets from *The New York Times, The Village Voice,* even *Newsday* (Rue had lined up a gig on Long Island, at a county fair), we were able to get work here and there.

The Sexy Sitas, wore colourful, often bizarre costumes for our shows. Like the one at CBGB, where NYs most cutting-edge punk rock was being showcased at the time. Rue and I slapped on green and white Kathakali war paint on our faces and tossed purple feather boas around our necks. The pierced and tattooed audience didn't know quite what to make of us. There was pin drop silence and then a few hesitant claps when we were done. The roar never came.

I was glad for the make-up.

◆

Fabio was delighted to follow me around to these odd performances even though he hated them. According to him, only Italian opera qualified as music. What we were doing was annoying at best, he said jokingly, but I knew he was mostly serious. 'Hey, don't forget the make-up,' I reminded him. Operatic stars slathered it on almost as much as Kathakali dancers.

'Not the same thing,' he maintained.

But he quite enjoyed the many strange bathrooms and backstage areas that we popped into for quickies.

◆

It was at one of these performances that I ran into Durga, a fragile, beautiful, cheerful, red-headed, green-eyed girl with a model's figure. Her ancestors were originally from Ireland. I would have never pegged her for a Durga, which she pronounced Duh-rr-gaah and not Doorga. It's probably why I didn't make the connection at first with the invincible, ferocious, warrior-goddess with the myriad arms worshipped by many in India.

'Ohhhhh you mean Doorga,' I said smacking the side of my head like I had just discovered a V8. 'I thought you meant "Dargah" which is a terrible name to give anyone, since it's basically a Persian tombstone.'

Durga told me that her parents, both now respectable accountants, back in the sixties, were flaming hippies and faithful followers of either Rajneesh or Sri Chinmoy. Maybe even both. She didn't know. They were now part of the Rotary Club of East Orange and didn't want to dwell in the past.

Her mom especially, wasn't so sure if their fellow Rotarians would understand the concept of the orgy, which consisted of indulging in unabashed sex with multiple unknowns: armpit shaving, optional.

For those not in the know, both Rajneesh (a.k.a Osho) and Sri Chinmoy were Indian 'gurus' who had garnered much power and influence over a number of pliant American minds at the time. Those who hadn't already been gobbled up by L. Ron Hubbard and his Church of Scientology.

Whether it's Indian gurus or alien abductors, it's quite easy to get a fan following in America, provided you have the shtick.

The O'Leary's had produced a little baby girl and one of the gurus had thoughtfully named her Durga—the slayer of the buffalo devils.

In a strange twist of fate, while the parents were trying to live down their Indian hippie past, Durga couldn't get enough of it. She worked at an Indian travel agency where she booked flights for people to and from India.

She followed Indian dancers and musicians around New York to immerse herself in the sights and sounds. She was also trying to memorize the names of all the Indian gods and goddesses. She ate mostly at Indian restaurants and knew how to rip up a 'naan' (the soft bread) with one hand, and scoop up the pork vindaloo (a spicy dish from Goa) into her mouth without much fuss.

She hadn't yet been to India, but that was Number One on her list of priorities. She was preparing for her journey.

I mentioned to her that perhaps she ought to begin by pronouncing her own name correctly, but she pooh poohed the idea.

'No one's going to be able to say it in New Jersey,' she explained.

We became friends.

She came to visit me in the store once in a while. She liked the food at La Rive Gauche, but didn't think very highly of Fabio. 'Too creepy,' she said immediately. I couldn't understand why.

I pointed out his ability to keep the Alpha Romeo perfectly steady in the roaring traffic's boom, as I focused on the OMs, his and mine. Wasn't it worthy of something, I asked her.

'The multiple orgasm is by no means the yardstick by which we measure our mates,' she said sagely. She herself had plenty of experience in that department. She was, like me, also on the hunt for the happy ending.

Of the forever after kind.

◆

'One of my clients at the travel agency is the sitar god Ravi Shankar,' she told me one day. 'I've just booked his tickets from WAS to

NYC,' she said, using airline abbreviations that Shas and I once employed regularly, in another life.

'Oh,' I said, half-listening to her. I wasn't interested in Ravi Shankar. I wasn't too keen on his music, which the aunt used to play in her store, out on Long Island. Maybe it's because she'd gathered a collection of the most sorrowful, plaintive ragas that he had ever performed, and played them over and over again, that the mere mention of the words 'Ravi' and 'Shankar' made me want to stick my head under a jackhammer.

But she persisted.

'I had to book a ticket for his sitar. Seriously. Imagine that. He wouldn't check it into the cargo hold. Apparently the thing is priceless. So I wrote a ticket for Sitar Shankar and it sat next to him in First Class,' she said grinning.

It was quite funny. I wondered what he'd do if the oxygen mask fell down. I burst out laughing.

'Stop it!' she said. 'Here's the thing. He's doing a concert at Alice Tully Hall (a fabulous performance space at Lincoln Center, where only the most famous and successful musicians in the world performed) and his manager is looking for a tanpura player. I thought you could do it. In fact, I've already told her you would,' Durga informed me in a surprising twist.

I always picked the same kind of girl to befriend. One who would have only my best interests at heart, no matter whether those interests interested me or not.

'But I don't want to play tanpura for Ravi Shankar,' I wailed. Playing the tanpura was like playing the dining table with a spoon. A really lame thing to do.

◆

'Tanpura player wanted: No talent required.' That could be a want ad for a gig.

The instrument looks like an elaborate pumpkin with a long

neck. There are four strings that you sort of slide your fingers over. And over. And over. And you kept that rhythm going so that the end effect was a drone.

Indian classical music required that sort of earthing, so soloists would find their way back home after exploring the stratosphere with their improv.

But my faint protests (since a part of me liked the idea that I would be rubbing shoulders with the rich and famous) were soon smothered.

And so it was that one warm afternoon in New York City, I stood outside Alice Tully, chewing the nails of one hand while wielding a tanpura in the other. It wasn't mine. I'd borrowed it from Rue, who had an assortment of Indian instruments, mostly percussion, but also one beat-up tanpura. It looked appropriately antique at first glance. Like it had been lovingly played by legends through the passing of time, when the truth was, it had only been tossed around back and forth in the stock room of some store in the West Village, waiting for a buyer.

I'd hung the, 'Be Back Soon' sign on Potato Print. I hadn't told Fabio about this audition, just in case it fell through.

I was all by my lonesome outside ATH, and found that every ounce of my bravado had deserted me. The old heart was thumping a bit. I was nervous.

Durga had warned me to be on my best behaviour because the sitar maestro had the reputation of being moody and cantankerous. Apparently, he could bark and bite.

He strode into the entrance, a tiny man surrounded by about ten blonde goddesses. Each one with bigger breasts than the next. I looked down at mine and felt inadequate.

One of the beauties crooked a painted nail at me. I obeyed. We entered a dressing room filled with the scent of jasmine where a man sat fiddling with the tablas. I realised he was the famous Allah Rakha.

Someone shoved me in front of the master.

'Hmmm, you play the tanpura?' enquired Mr Shankar melodiously.

'Yes,' I said redundantly. As I said earlier, any moron can play a tanpura.

He looked me up and then down. 'These clothes won't do,' he declared. I was wearing blue jeans and a tee shirt. 'You have to wear a saree,' he said.

'Yes sir,' I agreed.

'Ok, let's do a little riyaz,' he commanded. Practice. Rehearsal.

I followed him up onto the stage, overflowing with history. I couldn't really believe where I was. A few steps away from fame. There was a fabulous looking carpet on the stage and some microphones, not much else.

The tabla player settled himself down.

So did Mr Shankar.

'You sit there,' he said, pointing to an area behind him. I obeyed. He nodded at me to begin the rhythm of the strings.

He began the alaap (slow introduction) to Megh Malhar. Monsoon clouds and dark skies. He soared here and flew there. I stayed rooted to the tonic, straying only briefly to the fifth.

'Give me that,' said the maestro suddenly, grabbing my instrument. The clouds disappeared.

'What? What? What's wrong?' I jumped.

'It's out of tune,' he barked and tightened the wooden knobs, listening intently to the resonating of each of the strings. He handed it back. 'It's fine now,' he said. His sense of pitch was perfect. No surprise there, the sitar can have up to twenty strings. About half a dozen of them are used to play and the rest vibrate sympathetically, filling up the room with sound.

Each one of them has to be perfectly in tune. Tuning can be nightmare if you don't have perfect pitch. These days, you have devices that turn from red to green when you're tuning a stringed instrument, but Mr Shankar didn't have anything like that, he relied only on his ears.

I'd heard of a concert where he'd spent several minutes tuning his sitar in front of a restless crowd of thousands. When he was finally satisfied it was in tune, he stopped to take a breath before getting on with the show. But the crowd erupted into thundering applause, thinking he had just played an actual piece.

American audiences can't tell a raga from ratatouille.

I reshuffled my legs and began twanging, already feeling like a household name.

'What did you just do?' he glared at me.

'Nothing!' I said hastily. 'I'm just getting comfortable.'

'No,' he said conclusively. 'No comfort. You may not budge. Not even an inch. Like a statue. A statue with fingers that move. Do you understand me? You cannot uncross your legs once they are crossed.'

'Yes sir,' I said wondering how I'd do it. How was I going to sit in one position for the length of the concert, which could last anywhere from two to three hours, depending on how inspired the maestro was.

There was no concept of the three-minute single in Indian classical music.

But I'd passed the audition. Thousands of New Yorkers would come to see Ravi Shankar. And me.

I ran back to the store filled with news of my fabulous fortune. Fabio was suitably impressed. Despite his declarations that he listened to nothing but opera, he had heard of Ravi Shankar.

◆

The day of the show arrived and I slapped on a saree I'd borrowed from Rue, who on account of her dance performances, had a vast stack of them in all colours of the rainbow. I grabbed one in red with a fancy gold border. Very glamorous.

Mr Shankar looked me up and down and nodded his approval. 'Hmm,' he said. He was a man of a few words. Or maybe, I didn't inspire him enough cough up more than a grunt.

Pretty soon we were up on stage, tanpuras tuned, sitars tuned, tablas tuned and Mr Shankar began playing. The huge audience fell silent as the maestro closed his eyes and let his soul do the talking.

He talked and talked. And talked some more. That man had a lot to say. And just when I thought he was completing a sentence, the audience would encourage him to speak some more. This went on and on. For about three and a half hours.

I could see my legs falling off like dead branches from a tree by the end of the night.

I sent up several prayers to the gods of music to make him stop. My legs had lost all sense of feeling. I was certain I'd never walk again.

Finally, the concert ended and all of us stood up to take a bow. Me with a bad case of pins and needles and Mr Shankar and Mr Rakha with joyous smiles.

I made a vow to myself.

Never again.

Chapter 23

THE MAGICAL MYSTERY TOUR

Shas, who was now no longer a flighty travel agent, ok, Convention and Exhibitioneer, had become a bona-fide business owner, fast turning into slow-moving sludge like her boyfriend.

Our afternoon three-red-wine-and-tapas lunches were a distant memory. Evening trysts that continued into the wee hours of the morning with New York City's nightlife had vanished in a blur. Gone was the under performing employee mostly pursuing her own pleasures.

In her place was a new, crisp, somewhat frazzled Shas, applying her mind to the business of selling Christmas supplies from Sweden.

She was ordering and stocktaking. Creating marketing plans, making advertising campaigns. Fulfilling orders. Delaying payments to suppliers so that collections met cash flow requirements. Calculating profits and staying clear of losses. That sort of stuff.

I was expected to know all this as well, even though I was selling merchandise from India and not Sweden. The cash register didn't care what language you spoke or which country your goods came from.

It spoke the universal language of kaching.

But there was a huge, huge difference between 'employee' and 'business owner'.

I'd barged into her rented warehouse in Queens. She'd kissed me hello in-between phone calls, handed me a glass of Glögg and pointed in the direction of an empty chair. That pretty much meant, 'Drink this and shut up. I'm busy here, can't you see?'

She tore around her little warehouse-office like a little dust bunny in the breeze. I was amazed. How on earth had she managed to cram all this into her head?

'No one's paying me on the nose every month anymore, you know. I'm responsible for what I earn and whether we'll be living in our apartment above ground or down with the Mole People in the sewer,' she informed me dramatically, when I pestered her to go out carousing with me as she used to, not so very long ago.

I took a sip of the Glögg, reluctantly. It's a drink made with red wine, brandy, port wine, cloves and other spices. It tastes exactly as it sounds. A baby's drink, like eggnog, if you're familiar with that.

'Why don't you switch to Long Island Iced Tea, Shas?' I suggested helpfully. 'It's going to get your spirits up and running much faster than this.'

'What's wrong with my spirits?' she asked with a frown.

'Oh I don't know, you haven't sat down for one second. You're bustling around like things are falling apart. Can't the centre hold?' I asked, baiting her with a Yeats quote.

She brushed me aside, 'We're doing really well you idiot. In fact, we're moving out of here soon to a larger space.'

It turned out that Klaus (the bore) actually knew something about the business of selling Swedish Christmas goodies, not only in New York, but all around America. Especially in the mid-west, where there was a large population of people of Swedish origin, Svenskamerikan, as they were known.

I didn't give a hoot one way or another about the Swedes or the Indians or the North Vietnamese for that matter, I was worried about not having a familiar face to complain to. But Shas was gone. At least for the moment. That much was clear.

Klaus had won the war.

My other girlfriend Rue and I met often enough, but only when we had a gig coming up, a performance. Rehearsal meant no personal conversation was allowed. Definitely no drinking.

Shas, out. Rue, out. It was time to expand the old horizon.

Durga became my BFF. She was a never-ending soda fountain. She gurgled. She fizzed. She bubbled. She was fun.

Like me, Durga was also on the hunt for a man who would hold her hand and fill it with expensive items till the end of days.

Her sights at the moment were trained on a car salesman in Connecticut, a fellow named Edgar from whom she was trying to wangle that famous mnemonic, the diamond ring. The one that stood for half his wealth, should their union disintegrate.

Edgar was no stereotype. He was not a car salesman with slick talk and slimy sales pitch. He came fully loaded with the entire dealership. When he spoke, his employees listened.

This turned Durga on as much as his wealth. She loved the way he bossed his staff around. Apparently, he had once punched a wayward mechanic in the jaw in a move that made Durga weak in the knees.

It is common knowledge that violence turns women on. D was just like the rest of us. She loved the cave man, the beast that would clout and clobber just for her amusement. Road rage turned her on especially.

Despite all these admirable traits, it wasn't easy for her to land someone.

Like most wealthy single men in the tri-state area, he was reluctant to share his fortunes with just anyone. He would not be committing with the 'I do,' until the last possible moment.

Till he was very, very sure.

Divorce was very, very expensive in Connecticut.

If that wasn't hard enough, other single women were also competing fiercely, ready to stab her with the nail file, given a chance.

Durga had a plan.

I decided to pay close attention. I had similar ambitions and had tried pretty much every trick (and trich) in the book to nail my, 'Woh' (which is one of the few Hindi words I know, and which means 'him' and is said with a side-long glance, the eye lids lowered, a tilt of the chin and a girlish twitter, Bollywood style) but hadn't gotten very far at all.

◆

Durga charged into PP, just as I was closing up one evening.

'No, stop, stop,' she said rushing in, clutching her coat, her purse and a small shopping bag from Victoria's Secret.

I had nothing planned for the evening. Fabio had the sniffles and was in bed. I was ready for a night out. Brandy Alexanders maybe, I was thinking. Tequila Sunrises?

But D had something else on her mind.

'I have to get undressed. Quick. Help me. I gotta get to Grand Central to catch the 6.41 to Westport,' she said, referring to the Metro North trains that ladled commuters back and forth between New York and Connecticut every day.

It was chilly outside and people were already in their winter coats. Mink, sable, white fox if you were rich. Down, wool and fleece if you were in my league.

And if you were Durga you compromised with racoon.

She'd explained to me that racoon looked very similar to sable especially in the dark, and unless one earned upwards of a ten mil a year, with a keenly developed sense of luxury, it was hard to tell the difference. 'You stand a much better chance of bagging the right guy and the right kind of fur,' she claimed. Appearances, according to her, were everything.

I nodded wisely.

I didn't like fur at all, nothing to do with any warm or fuzzy feelings towards animals, I didn't have those. Not in the least bit. I ate them with gusto. Cows, goats, pigs, chickens, snails, partridges, quail, eels, even frogs. Once I'd tried dried alligator at a friend's house, and it tasted no different from beef jerky. An animal is an animal, I suppose, once it's cooked.

I had no qualms about killing animals either (well, ordering the offing if I'm to be honest, I was too squeamish to do it myself) if they happened to be rodents or cockroaches or lizards.

But the thought of wearing fur on my body made me shudder because of something that happened at the aunt's store Aditi out in Huntington.

◆

The aunt sold seasonal merchandise from ethnic parts of the world like India, Morocco, Greece, Bali and, bringing me to the point, Afghanistan.

She had imported a bunch of Afghan coats to appease her customers who still hankered for the sixties, even though it had been years since the Beatles had released their album *Magical Mystery Tour*.

Possibly because I came from a country of clunky craftsmanship, where even little children's wooden toys had rusty nails sticking out of them, where the so-called sophisticated elite ate on leaves at family functions, I couldn't understand why anyone who had access to perfectly sewn machine-made garments would want to be seen alive in a colourfully ugly, crudely embroidered, smelly fur coat, come winter.

Made of sheep or goat skin, the coats suited the people of Afghanistan exceedingly well, what with there being no pressure on the average Afghani to posture in Prada, or even gallivant in The Gap as the snow piled up high on the Hindu Kush and the wood fires just weren't warm enough.

The furry part, or the fleece, is on the inside of the coat and the leathery part (suede as it's called once the gore is cleaned off) is what's sported on the outside. If you haven't seen an Afghan coat, visualise a goat turned inside out.

The coats originally came from the Ghazni province near Kabul and were made with love and care for the comparatively small population. Maybe they were even considered elegant, by local standards.

But one day, they caught the attention of a certain Craig Sams, a famous chocolatier from England, who was at the time paying homage to the home of hashish. Perhaps inspired by the produce of the fabled poppy fields, he decided that it was the right time for the people of London to be wrapped in swaddling Afghani goat.

He imported a few hundred of the coats and persuaded a few trendy boutiques in London to stock them.

Then one day, the unthinkable happened. A popular musical group, a band of troubadours calling themselves The Beatles, passed by a shop that carried the coats.

It isn't clear whether it was John, Paul, George or Ringo who first fell in love, but by the time the Fab Four (that's what people called them) exited the store, each of them had their very own Afghani coat.

The Beatles were an unconventional bunch of people, history will attest to this. Some of them have lain in bed for weeks to protest war, for instance. So rather than wear the coats the conventional Afghani way, they flipped them inside out.

The paparazzi in England have never been far from their celebs (nothing's changed, even today), so as J, P, G and R walked into the sunlight in their furry avatars, they were photographed, or snapped, as they might say in Ye Olde.

Fashion is born in the blink of an eye, someone said (may have been me), and the coats became overnight sensations in the city of London.

But that wasn't all.

The Afghani coat was destined to much greater fame. The Beatles wore them on the cover of their album *Magical Mystery Tour*, along with comical antler hats and walrus fangs, setting off a new fashion craze that swept England, Europe and of course America, at least in the colder states. The fad didn't catch on in Southern Asia and the Orient, possibly because of the weather. Or possibly because they were considered unpleasantly peasantly.

The public in the Occident went nuts.

Everyone wanted an Afghan coat. Women wanted Afghan coats. Men wanted Afghan coats. Little boys wanted Afghan coats. Little girls wanted Afghan coats.

There just weren't enough goats or Afghanis to keep up with the demand. The overworked, exhausted coat-stitchers of Ghazni tried as hard as they could but demand just overwhelmed supply.

So naturally, inferior imitations began to make their appearance. Knock offs from Turkey and Iran. Hastily cured, these rip-off wrappers smelled foul at the best of times. Regardless, these spurious items made their way across Europe and then the Atlantic Ocean, to America, specifically to Long Island, in New York State, to a store owned by the aunt. One she called Aditi, which means 'goddess responsible for life, boundless and free'.

The aunt sold them like McDonalds sold burgers. By the minute.

There were a pile of them in her stock room awaiting buyers when one day, the sprinklers went off. Of course this happened in the night, when we were fast asleep in our own beds.

We didn't discover the disaster until the next morning when we opened up shop, to the god-awful stench of dead dog. (As I've said, an animal is an animal. It's hard to tell dead dog from goat from cow.)

The coats, unfortunately placed directly under the fire sprinklers were drenched through and through.

Soggy and stinking, we squeezed, we wrung, we powdered, we sunned. We put then in the dryer. We sprinkled rose water on them. (A South Indian tradition.) We tried everything. But nothing worked.

We could never dry them out fully. The store smelled like an abattoir and the coats had to be tossed into the garbage.

It took several weeks of intense incense burning to get rid of the smell of dead beast from the store. It was awful.

The aunt lost a pile of money on that incident, but that was a temporary setback. She ordered a new batch and before you could say, 'I wanna take you higher,' she'd hiked up the prices and covered her losses. She was clever, that aunt.

Fur coats turned me off.

So did formaldehyde.

But Durga felt sexy and communicative in them. The coats, not the formaldehyde.

◆

'What are you up to?' I asked as she slithered out of her silky racoon coat, flinging it on the floor, as she rushed into the back room, the one I used for my extracurricular. I followed her and stood watching.

She shed all her office clothes and everything underneath. She wasn't ashamed of her body, which was quite perfect, I noticed with envy. Not the hint of a roll or wobble. No cellulite.

She slipped on a lacy red teddy, a black garter belt and fishnet stockings. Her six inch red stilettos matched her blood red nails. She fluffed up her hair and redid her make-up. She sprayed on the perfume, Obsession, on areas of her body she felt Edgar's nose was likely to visit. Finally, she slipped back into the racoon.

'Toilette à cochon' as they call it in France, meaning the bath of a pig, with no water, just perfume.

Nothing came between her and the hide.

The coat was of elegant drape with a high collar, and fell all the way past her torso and legs ending just above her ankles. It did not feature buttons, clasps, zippers or even a belt. It was meant to fall open casually, unless you clutched it shut with your fist. A sexy look favoured by movie stars.

'How are you going to get from Manhattan to Westport without hooking all of Wall Street in your fishnets?' I asked, visualising the train swaying this way and that while Durga tried valiantly to keep her coat clutched shut, straphanging for dear life.

'No silly, I'll get a seat. I'll be sitting down,' she explained. 'Edgar knows which car I'm in, so he'll be waiting exactly at that spot where the doors open. I'll be running to him, and as I get close to him, I'm going to fling my arms open wide so that the coat reveals all. Accidentally,' she winked. 'He'll get a perfect view of his special gift. Me,' she had the scene plotted to perfection.

It sounded chilly to me.

Connecticut didn't have tall buildings to protect one from the bruising winter winds.

'Have you done this before?' I asked. It seemed like a big risk to take, wearing scanty underwear, amounting to nothing really, under a coat in the dead of winter, while crossing state borders. Anything could happen.

'Nope,' she said cheerfully. 'I came up with the idea at lunch.'

Landing a man was hard work.

♦

The ploy worked for her because pretty soon, Durga became a regular commuter on the Friday evening 6.41 p.m. to Westport.

She also spent a lot of time at Victoria's cash register exploring other shades besides red. Pink. Purple. Black. Even virginal white.

Pretty soon Edgar was wobbly jello in her clever hands.

He proposed.

She agreed.

He gave her a large diamond engagement ring, which she showed me proudly.

Shortly thereafter, she switched to more formal attire, skirts, blouses, pants and jackets. She had conquered the mountain she'd set out to crest so she no longer needed to risk frostbite every time she went out to visit Edgar. She could see her future clearly now. It glistened like the morning dew.

'You'll be my bridesmaid, right?' she reminded me, although

the wedding was still a few months away.

'Mm hmmm,' I said a little unsurely. Being the BFF of someone who was getting married was an expensive affair.

I'd gotten used to enough American customs by then to know that bridesmaids wore hideous dresses in awful colours (selected by the bride-to-be, generally after she'd downed several Cosmos or Harvey Wallbangers), and had to pay for the privilege of said humiliation.

I'd have to come up with some kind of plan to get out of it.

◆

As luck would have it, I didn't have to. Fate intervened instead.

Commuters, even weekend commuters, soon develop 'train' habits. They'll sit in the same spot, talk to the same people and develop friendships. These friendships would generally last only the duration of the train ride, but sometimes, once in a while deeper bonds were created.

Durga found herself sitting every weekend next to a man who, to her smiling Irish eyes, was exceedingly exotic.

He wasn't from around Connecticut, or New York City or even New Jersey. He came from much further away. Across the ocean. In his late forties, he was quite dapper. He wore a beret sometimes, a cravat on occasion, paint-splattered overalls once in a while and wild T-shirts once or twice. He was colourful and magnetic.

Durga, in her racoon, sometimes in a very short skirt, sometimes demure in her little black dress was a delicious eyeful and he drank her in.

They became friends.

He was an artist from Turkey and lived in Norfolk (not too far from Westport) and painted in a loft down in the Meat Packing District in Manhattan, which he shared with a few other artists.

He travelled only by subway and had no money to speak of, but he had salt-and-pepper hair, a gruff voice, five-o'clock shadow and something else in his eyes.

He was into nudes, he told her. She was enthralled.

He showed her photographs of his art. To Durga, who until then had only been interested in Indian art which was mostly realistic, and Indian music which could be considered mathematical if you got past the drone, his paint splotches and jagged lines, his broad strokes and use of colour was deep and mysterious.

She couldn't understand it. She couldn't see nudity the way he saw it.

'I hope you'll paint me one day,' she said to him.

It was the beginning of the end.

◆

She went to his less-than-perfect apartment in Norfolk one day (a weekday, to throw Edgar off scent) and there, Turkey met Ireland in a sweaty, explosive burst of passion.

In the short span of two weeks, Durga shed her racoon for an artist's pea jacket and her high heels for sneakers. She stopped wearing make-up and shaving under her arms.

She was in love.

Madly in love. With Erdem Turan, struggling artist almost in his dotage.

I'd met him a few times, a man with illusions of grandeur and a snotty opinion of the other artists who were popular in the Soho art scene at the time. I couldn't understand what Durga saw in him.

She returned Edgar's fabulous diamond ring and said goodbye to the luxurious life she had worked so hard at achieving and turned around to embrace a life of poverty with Erdem.

She was happy she told me. She felt such fulfilment. In a month of knowing Erdem, she became pregnant.

◆

'Margaret Sanger ho?' I enquired cheerily when she told me she'd been careless with the condoms. I was referring to a health clinic that performed abortions. Planned Parenthood they called it.

'I'll go with you Durga, I hear it's no big deal,' I said to her. I knew several people who'd had abortions on their lunch break, and didn't look any the worse for wear.

Not for a moment did I expect that Durga would do anything but terminate the pregnancy. She wasn't even thirty. She couldn't have possibly wanted to be saddled with squalling brats and diapers.

But I guess I wasn't looking closely at her eyes. When I did, I saw that she was filled with the light of love or some other soppy emotion. She welled over with tears, 'What's the matter with you?' she said. 'I'm gonna keep my baby.'

◆

Durga and Erdem soon moved to Turkey because he knew he'd be unable to sell enough paintings to keep mother and soon-to-arrive child fed and clothed in New York. Durga used her travel agent's special discount to get them one-way tickets to Istanbul and I lost touch with her after that.

It was a sombre lesson I learned. Carry condoms. Life can change in a flash.

Chapter 24

MOSHI MOSHI

A few things happened almost at once, throwing my desultory life into a panic.

I use the word 'desultory' because although I had a job, a boyfriend (or at the very least, someone to have sex with), mother and aunt who both loved me no matter what, girl friends who were wonderful, a possible future in music and enough money from my day job to take taxis home because I hated the subway and walking didn't do a thing for me when it came to losing weight, I was still plagued by a sense that everything was haphazard, unsettled and hazy.

I was going through yet another change. Not the change of life, but a change of heart.

I didn't like Fabio anymore. He was becoming more and more unpredictable and scary, bordering on the psychopathic. Dangerous.

His hairy chest, the very physical quality that had initially made me weak in the knees, now made be break out in a cold sweat.

How was it I hadn't noticed that he shed like an unkempt animal? What sort of spell had he cast on me that I was blinded to the lint brush I needed after every bear hug? Why hadn't I been turned off by the strong smell of Parmigiano-Reggiano and Sulmona Red garlic that he exuded? The finest of ingredients but unsexy nevertheless.

And then there were his unrelenting sexual demands. 'On your knees. Bend down some more. Hold still now. Move to the left. No, not that left, the other left. (I have always been a bit dyslexic when it comes to my lefts and rights.) Faster. No teeth,' and other commands that I had originally thought were so masterful and Tarzanian.

Now I was only feeling angry and resentful.

His driving terrorised me to where I point blank refused to get into his Alfa ever again.

There comes a time in a relationship when scent and aroma become odour and stink. That's when you know that it's time to move on.

I learned that I wasn't being singled out for his bizarre outbursts.

One of La Rive Gauche's dishwashers, a Cuban immigrant named Pedro told me (in confidence, since gossiping could get him fired) that Fabio's own brother Luigi had been subjected to far more abuse and terror than I'd ever faced. I think Pedro was trying to comfort me.

According to Pedro, Fabio had recently tossed Luigi out of his moving Alfa, right in the middle of the street. Fortunately not on the avenue, where traffic whizzes at top speed, especially when the lights turn green all in one go. Lucky for L, it was in the dead of night and there wasn't much traffic around and F wasn't going all that fast.

Only by the grace of the Madonna (whom Fabio invoked freely when things went right, when things went wrong, even when they were just iffy) was Luigi still alive, and not a pile of hamburger meat in the middle of the street, recalled Pedro as if he was present at the time, which he wasn't.

However his friend, one Jose, who had applied for a job at La Rive Gauche and been rejected on account of his excessive body art, and who just happened to be passing by, saw everything clearly.

Jose waited till Fabio had taken off in an angry screech of burning rubber before rushing to Luigi's help. Luigi by then had rolled safely down to the kerb, out of harm's way. Jose had dusted L off and found him a cab, sending him home.

'Did Luigi call the police?' I asked Pedro.

'Choo kidding or what?' he laughed at me. Apparently blood being thicker than water and all, Luigi couldn't bring himself to send his brother to the slammer.

There was more.

Fabio had smashed an espresso machine at the store, stomping on it with his feet, because it refused to cooperate. Pedro, who may have been embellishing a bit, claimed that all the offending machine was guilty of, was not being plugged in.

All in all, I knew Fabio was a live grenade waiting to explode.

I had to lose him quickly, but peacefully. Who knew what frenzy I might provoke if I got him enraged?

♦

Right around then, Shas announced that she was getting married to Klaus and I was to be her maid of honour

I wasn't surprised really. I had expected things to progress in this manner. It was natural. Shas was very much the 2.2 children type. Her wild days in the Orient were over, and she was ready to settle down with Klaus, the Köttbullar (Swedish meatballs) and Janssons Frestelsse (a potato and fish dish) to have a couple of platinum blonde, blue-eyed babies. Shas told me all babies in Sweden were born looking like cherubs, and it was hard to tell them apart. Hospitals in Stockholm and Gotteborg were filled with the sound of squalling of angels.

I heaved a sigh of relief that it was Shas and not Durga whose MOH I was going to be. Durga was a wild one, and her idea of an MOH's dress could have ranged anywhere from Janis Joplin to the goddess Saraswati.

With Shas and her impeccable taste and leanings toward ecru, dove, olive, ash and dun, I knew I wouldn't be embarrassed.

'We'll go shopping soon,' she promised me. 'Don't worry, I'm keeping it simple. You'll look great. I'm in white and all of you will be in black.' A few of her cousins who were coming in from Sweden.

I couldn't wait. I had missed her a lot. The wedding would be a great opportunity to hang around her a little longer.

◆

Meanwhile, back at Potato Print, where I earned my monthly income, now up to seventy five thou a year, on account of services rendered, where till then things were going along without incident, I got a phone call.

A familiar male voice that intoned in the way I assumed Shakespeare and his buddies had, when they were casually chitchatting with each other:

'I count the days,
There are eleven
Like the stars in heaven
Rise as bread after leaven...'

It was Harry, of course. Calling me from India. All excited because in a few days he was going to be back in New York, and I would be in his arms again.

Apparently, he had spent a decent amount of time working on his English poetry, since he knew the Urdu stuff turned me off.

Unfortunately, the men of North India (influenced heavily by the poetic Arabs who had invaded and left the country several centuries ago) feel compelled to speak in rhyme and riddle, couplet and song, to get their point across romantically.

The 'point' without exception is always a variation of 'I want to nail you'.

Almost all Urdu poetry can be loosely translated thus: 'Oh, were it that she were single and nailable, but she is betrothed to another'. This is a familiar theme.

A poem could plaintively moan, 'I nailed her, felt her breath on my face and now she has left me for another', or the more tragic, 'I nailed her and loved her, but the white dove of death claimed her and now she's gone forever'.

Urdu poets of yore thought nothing of saying, 'I nailed her as a bud 'ere she was plucked away, 'fore she could bloom under my care.' The concept of sex with minors being illegal and so on did not exist, back in the day. The theme never changed no matter how obtuse the analogy and how imperfect/perfect the metre.

They called it love. And longing. And loss.

Nailing.

Harry wasn't a poet by a long shot. In English or in Urdu.

He was just a businessman. Not self-made, but in-law made. He was married to the daughter of a rich businessman and had fathered four children.

He was coming to check up on his store. And nail me. My horrible fate was wending its way toward me, like a heat-seeking missile.

◆

I wanted to kill myself.

I would now have to deal with two men, each one expecting my full and undivided attention, neither of whom I liked anymore, no matter how different things had seemed at first.

I took it one step at a time.

To start with I had to make sure Fabio and Harry (Harpreet) didn't cross paths. I had to prevent the accidental comparing of notes. It wouldn't do for either one of them to catch wind of the other.

I told Fabio that he couldn't come into my store for the duration of Harry's visit. 'I'll lose my job, if the boss finds out how often I've hung up the 'Be Back Soon' sign on the door. God knows how many millions I've already cost him.'

Fabio understood that quite well, being half a business owner himself. He knew how fortunate he was to have a brother who kept the store open all day, so his weekly income/coitus wouldn't be interrupted.

Taking advantage of the situation, I added, 'And by the way, I am also going to be busy with Shas's wedding, so it's unlikely I can spend anytime with you in the near future. Maybe you should join a gym or something.' Let him figure it out, I said to myself. I couldn't possibly be any clearer without saying it out loud. I was hoping he'd tire of waiting around for me and find someone else to boss around. That would be the simplest solution, the most painless way to break-up.

Soon enough Harry arrived.

With the dawning of day eleven.

I greeted him sadly and informed him that my best friend, the wretch, had chosen the most inopportune of times to get hitched. That there was nothing I could do. Since I was the MOH to boot, I'd be busy all the time I told him earnestly. 'Please, please forgive me if I can't spend nights with you. I'll be at work every day though,' I assured him.

He paid my bills. He deserved at least a decent lie. I blew insincere air kisses at him as I rushed out the door at closing time.

♦

Shas's wedding actually kept me very distracted. There were a ton of things to do. I was so pre-occupied that I didn't pay attention to some hints that Harry was dropping at the store. Hints that would and could affect my future.

I failed to pick up on the fact that he wasn't talking about expansion as he did in the early stages, spinning glorious tales of the Potato Print invasion of America, a store in every nook and cranny. The saffron, green and white slowly swallowing up the red, white and blue.

I didn't pay attention to the glaring fact that supplies in the store were thinning out and Harry wasn't jumping to replace them.

I was a little taken aback when he sacked the cleaning lady who came in at night, requesting me nicely to do the vacuuming myself. But I didn't mind. The aunt vacuumed, dusted, threw out the garbage and even changed the light bulbs herself. She did so proudly. This was America, there was no indignity in labour.

'Sure I will,' I said agreeably. 'I'll do it.'

I suppose deep down I felt something was up, because I mentioned to Shas that I had a funny feeling.

'Focus on my wedding,' Shas had said. 'Everything will work out.' She was a wise girl and I believed her. I had no reason not to. She had led me astray only on the rarest of occasions.

◆

Harry spent about a week in New York and abruptly informed me that it was time for him to leave.

'So soon?' I asked, all silk and satin, smiley and sweet.

'Hmm,' he nodded, thoughtfully and nervously. 'What ideas do you have to drum up more business for the store?'

'None,' I said cheerfully. I had no ideas whatsoever. I was under the impression that you rented a storefront, filled it with good stuff, hung out a pretty sign and the customers poured in. That's what I'd seen the aunt do. She never spoke of ideas. Things just happened.

'No marketing? No advertising? No flyers? No sales?' Harry persisted.

'Well we could put some old merchandise on sale if you like,' I replied dubiously, 'I do that all the time anyway.' I had no idea what he was talking about.

'Hmmm,' he said and went back to his Quicken, an accounting software program that pulled no punches. It baldly announced whether you were successful or not.

Manpreete, his wife back in India had taken to calling him on the phone at least six times during the day.

'Summer's here and business should pick up. We're all about the hot weather aren't we?' I offered gaily. He looked so gloomy

I felt the need to cheer him up a bit.

And then just as soon as he came, he was gone, leaving me to sink into Shas's wedding plans.

The venue, the caterers, the dresses, the flowers, the menu (all Swedish of course) and the myriad little details that go into making a wedding beautiful and memorable.

She prepared the guest list and ran it by me. I had to strike out Fabio's name because I didn't want to encourage him in the slightest. A wedding party was a good place to scout for fresh meat. I didn't want to be carrying old baggage.

She'd also hired a jazz band led by a famous Japanese guitar player whom I'd been dying to meet.

'You can sing one song with them after the wedding,' Shas offered generously. 'This is not an elaborate ruse to rustle up a gig for you, alright? You have responsibilities at my wedding.'

I understood. She wasn't getting married so I could enthral the audience at her expense.

◆

The night before the wedding was the rehearsal dinner, where close friends and family met to run through the sequence of events for the big day. Shas's parents would meet Klaus's parents. One hoped there would be no fireworks and only smiles all round.

Since Shas spoke fluent Chinese, she'd decided on a fancy Chinese restaurant. Her knowledge of Mandarin had always thrown the Chinese people we met in Beijing for a loop, back when we were organising exhibitions there. It was a source of great amusement for us. Maybe she'd impress a few waiters at the rehearsal dinner, I thought. It was fun to see. Although I knew most of the waiters in New York were second and third generation American and many of them couldn't speak Chinese at all.

We were about twenty-five of us, seated around a large circular table, with a Lazy Susan that was being replenished constantly.

There were at least twenty courses that came and went. Between each course there was much 'skåll-ing' (cheers) in Swedish and 'ganbei-ing' (also cheers) in Chinese. People stood up toasting the bride and groom to be, roasting them sometimes.

I had been strictly warned by Shas not to say anything except how sad I was to be losing my BF to someone who was now going to occupy her day and night, but despite my loss, how happy I was for her.

She'd actually written it all out.

She didn't have the faith that after a few ganbeis, I wouldn't blurt out all the intimate details of certain African nationals, one or two Danish persons, a Moroccan man and a few others whose nationalities were a little unclear.

Yes, both she and Klaus were Swedish and forward thinking, but as Shas pointed out, jealousy is jealousy.

So while Klaus had no objection to Shas laying on a park bench in the middle of Stockholm, no blouse and no bra, so that she wouldn't get tan lines, he would not be as forgiving if he'd known how active her sexual life had been overseas, while he pined away for her in New York.

I understood of course. I was her friend. Not her enemy. 'I'll read,' I assured her. 'I won't ad lib. No improv, I promise.'

By the time dinner was done and the dancing began, I was pretty relaxed. The inhibitions had been shed.

I went up to the band tentatively to see if I could perhaps sing one song. The guitar player, who had beautiful black hair down to his shoulders, tied up in a ponytail smiled at me. I liked men with long hair. 'Sure,' he said. 'What do you want to sing?'

I picked a song called, 'My Romance'—appropriate under the circumstances I felt. It went down well. Shas was smiling. So was Klaus. 'One more,' they hollered. I briefly considered how strange it was that no one ever yelled, 'two more', or 'six more'.

I dug through my repertoire of jazz songs to find one that was joyous, cheerful and happy. It was hard going. Most jazz songs are filled with sorrow. I suppose it's easier to write with words that rhyme with 'lie' and 'die' and 'sigh' rather than words like 'laugh'. I couldn't think of anything, except calf.

So I sang 'I've Got the World on a String' which is more of a show tune. There were feeble encores after that so I gracefully stepped off so the band could do their job.

'Pssst,' said the guitar player, as I left. 'Don't go. I want talk. Wait break.'

Sure I said. He was very cute. His name was Hiro Sato. I liked his staccato English. I understood it.

In the break, we had a few more glasses of wine (at least I did) and he got cuter by the sip. Wiry and muscular, he was dressed in black and looked like a ninja.

'What you doing after?' he wanted to know.

'After what?' I asked. It was already almost 2.00 in the a.m. and the wedding was around 5 p.m. the next day. I needed to get to sleep so I could be all pretty and fresh.

'After party. Where you going? I want show songs. You maybe like sing? I work on album for Sony Music,' he tossed in, to tempt me.

Any shot at fame and stardom always trumped my better judgement. I followed him to his third floor walk-up in Chelsea, a large room filled with all kinds of musical equipment, guitars, amplifiers, wires, microphones, a sound booth and a bed.

He was gentlemanly.

'You want sake?' he asked.

It was 3.30 a.m.

I had a little over nine hours to get to the Swedish Church. Shas wanted me there a little early so I could help her get ready.

'Sure,' I said. 'Just one.'

But one sake turned to two, and two into four and as I listened to the beautiful music Hiro had created, awaiting only the dulcet tones from my throat to turn the record selling machinery at Sony inside out in a frenzy, I fell asleep.

Right on his bed.

I remember that he was stroking my hair. I had no idea what time it was.

Chapter 25

GET ME TO THE CHURCH ON TIME

When I finally woke up, my head was throbbing, I felt it would explode. Over the years my tolerance for alcohol was deteriorating terribly. My hangovers were getting worse and I could drink less and less. I couldn't understand it. And yet I hadn't learned when to say 'no' or 'stop' or even 'go slow'.

For a few moments I didn't know where I was. I flailed around blindly and heard the crash of glass. My eyes got accustomed to being open and I saw there were sake bottles and cups strewn here and there and I stumbled on a few of them as I got up to go to the bathroom.

Waves of nausea rose up from my stomach, threatening to ruin his expensive musical instruments and equipment. I swallowed. I took deep breaths. Human beings aren't meant to drink as many champagne toasts and red wines and white sakes in one night as I had done. Even if their best friends were getting married. Even if they'd just met someone who could introduce them to Sony Music bigwigs.

I bent down to the faucet in the bathroom sink, splashed my face and then gulped down the cool, clear tap water, which New York City is famous for.

You couldn't try that in India, according to the mom. She would scare me as a child. She had said that even if one drop of unfiltered, disease-filled Indian tap water made it down to my stomach, I wouldn't make it past the week. 'You'll get some horrible infection and rot to death. There's no antidote either.'

'How come I can't drink it but it's ok to brush my teeth in

it,' I asked the mom. 'I'm sure I'm swallowing a little each time I brush. I've probably digested gallons of it by now. How come I'm still alive?'

'Do not question your mother. Ever. Do you understand?' was her reply.

I stopped reminiscing about the mom as the memories of the night before came tumbling back. What memories?

I vaguely remembered listening to a song composed by Hiro, with his own lyrics. I recalled thinking how much more meaningful it would sound after I'd had my way with it for an hour or so. The grammar and punctuation intact, the meter clever and the alliteration crisp.

After that there was a black hole. A big nothing. That's probably when I fell asleep.

I suddenly had a horrible thought. What had happened to me? Had Hiro gloriously helped himself to me while I was unconscious? Why would anyone do that, I thought fleetingly. I was so much more fun awake, participating actively.

But I needn't have worried.

I looked down at myself and heaved a huge sigh of relief. I was still fully dressed.

Except for my shoes, which had been neatly arranged by the side of the bed.

Hiro wasn't a perv, thank goodness. And I hadn't been ravished without my knowledge.

That was the bright side.

'What time is it?' I asked Hiro as the memory of Shas, her wedding, my responsibilities as MOH and other bone-chilling details she and I had worked on for so many months pierced through the fog of my stupor.

'Hello, hello,' I said a little louder. There was still no answer. There was no Hiro.

I found a note next to my handbag. 'You sleep. Like baby. I go gig. Swedish Church. Sound check. See you. Sayonara. P.S. Namaste.'

I looked at the time. It was 2.15 p.m. already. Shas would be furious. I was supposed to be there before lunch. How the hell had Hiro managed to make it? Could Japanese men drink more than Indian girls? It wasn't fair. Life wasn't fair.

I dashed out of his apartment like a possessed person, shot uptown in a cab and ran up the stairs to my apartment. I went straight to the bathroom, tossing my clothes off as I did.

I leaned over the toilet, and holding my curly locks up with one hand, I stuck two fingers down my throat with the other and threw up as much as I could of the night before. I immediately felt much better.

I brushed my teeth four times, gargled with Listerine till my throat felt sore, showered, popped three aspirins with a large glass of chocolate milk, slathered on the under eye concealer and zipped up the black dress Shas had ordered for me (but that I had paid for) and dashed back in a cab cross town and then downtown to the Swedish Church which is on East 48th Street.

I didn't like the subway at the best of times. And this counted as the worst of them.

'Faster, faster,' I yelled at the cabbie. He was from Iran I think, so although I had considered singing 'Get Me to the Church on Time', which was appropriate and very funny, I didn't. It would have likely been lost on him.

By the time we got to the church, it was 4.30 p.m. Half an hour before the nuptials.

I have mentioned before that the Swedes are a punctual bunch; respectful of the fact that time passes very quickly. As a nation, they feel it's better to be on it (time, that is) than after it, because there's no such thing as catching up with time. Once it's gone, it's gone. And no amount of 'sorry' and 'I won't do it again' and 'forgive me' is going to bring it back.

Swedish people are polite and courteous as long as thing's go according to the clock. But all hell breaks lose if someone shaves a few seconds off.

I had seen her swear at our Chinese tour bus driver once, in her crudest Mandarin, all because he'd kept a few fidgety conventioneers waiting for five minutes. The Chinese are a punctilious lot too, by and large, so it was most uncharacteristic. 'Maybe he had to take his wife to the hospital because she was having a baby,' I tried telling Shas, to make her stop with the invective and epithet (that's what I assumed she was hurling at him) but to no avail. Once going, she was hard to restrain.

Shas, her eyes flashing, her hair thrown back angrily, ranted at him till the poor bus driver begged her forgiveness. I have no idea what she said but the passengers applauded.

I'm sure they didn't understand her either and were only clapping because it's very unusual to see a blonde-haired, blue-eyed girl yelling angrily in perfect Mandarin.

Shas usually got applause when she flew off the hook in Chinese.

I personally felt it was a bit much. She was over-reacting.

But then, I wasn't Swedish. Or Chinese. I was only Indian.

In India, people always arrived one to two hours late as a matter of habit. I'd read a tourist guide once, from a city called Bangalore where it clearly stated, 'If you're invited to a party at eight p.m., don't show up until ten. That's the norm. Whatever you do, don't show up early. You'll catch your hosts still wearing their underwear and it could be quite embarrassing. You may not get invited again.'

All that aside, I still had to face the wrath of Shas. I had stretched our relationship as far as it could go. I fully expected her to snap it off then and there, on the most important day in her life.

But I was prepared to grovel. I was prepared to beg for her forgiveness. I was even prepared to grovel and beg for Klaus's forgiveness even though, as you know, I didn't care for him much. He was a bit of a bore.

I dashed into the church as the bride was putting on the final touches to her face. She looked beautiful. Like a snowy princess about to make her grand entrance in a fairytale. Her dress was perfect.

'I'm sorry Shas, forgive me,' I wailed before she could speak. 'I love you, I love you, I love you. I'll do your laundry for a month. Even Klaus's. I'll go grocery shopping. I'll baby sit for free. Forgive me. Say you will.'

She wouldn't look at me for a few minutes. A very long few minutes from my perspective. Then she turned and glared at me as evilly as she could. I can't possibly repeat what she said with her eyes, it was foul.

She couldn't plunge into a full-on verbal attack because that would involve tossing her hair back and forth. I couldn't walk and smoke at the same time and she hadn't learned how to be angry and still.

It had taken the hairdresser about two hours to comb, tease, curl and spray her hair into position, in an upswept chignon. It was meant to withstand the pressure of the normal 'I do' and 'you may kiss the bride'. It would most certainly fall apart if Shas were to give me the third degree.

So luckily for all present, a smiling bride and groom were joined in holy matrimony while Hiro's band played 'Here Comes the Bride'. The happy couple left straight from the church to go and live happily ever after.

Or so I hoped.

She flung her bouquet at me with one last, fiery look that said, 'You haven't heard the end of this.'

I was counting on the fact that the honeymoon would have a soporific effect and she'd come back smiles and happiness, ready to tell me all about it. I was her best friend after all.

♦

I went back to Potato Print as usual, but things weren't the same.

Customers would walk in and ask for this and that, requests I normally obliged with a beaming smile followed by the kaching of the cash register.

But now, I mostly had to apologise.

We were always 'out of stock'.

It's a term that can be understood in two ways. The good way and the bad. 'Out of stock' could mean that the item was such a hot seller that it had flown off the shelves. 'Come back in a week,' a happy merchant could tell the customer in such a case. You could even go so far as to say, 'Leave me a deposit, I'll hold it for you as soon as it comes in.'

In my case, it wasn't that. Plain and simple, Harry and Manpreete weren't sending me enough items to restock. The shelves were beginning to look bare. 'Spread the merchandise around to make it look full,' Manpreete had instructed me on the phone from India.

'But what do I tell the customers?' I asked her.

'Tell them the consignment's delayed at customs,' she said. 'Indefinitely.'

It didn't look good.

Next door, at La Rive Gauche, Fabio had taken my hints seriously and found himself a new girlfriend. A gorgeous looking girl from Senegal who was hoping to be a model in New York. She looked like a walking magazine cover, even when she was chewing gum.

Pedro, my dishwashing mole told me that Fabio had bumped into her at a fender bender. Ma si, as they say in Italian. But yes.

I was happy for him, her, their dented cars and mostly for myself.

I'd taken to hanging around with Hiro, who as it turned out, was a terrific composer of songs. But when it came to writing lyrics in English, he had a few problems. He showed me the words to a song he'd come up with.

'A moon, it fly, near to sky
I try to catch star, it too far.
Love to me, love to me
I you see, I you see.'

It was set to a lovely minor bluesy tune that could have created wonderful imagery had Hiro not so resolutely done away with the articles and prepositions that are the thread holding the English language together.

I explained this to him as gently as I could.

'So you? I? We collaborate? We make music together?' he asked. 'We work on album?'

'We do,' I replied. I was delighted. I wanted to work on an album more than anything else.

◆

Rue called me up. 'Let's meet,' she said.

We met downtown in the East Village, her favourite hangout.

'Ready to quit your job and come see the world?' she asked me gaily.

'Been there, done that,' I replied wryly. If there was one thing I could do very well without, it was the world. Seeing it that is. I'd done plenty of that.

Rue told me breathlessly that the theatre company was taking a pared-down cast of the play The Ramayana, on a performing tour of various countries in Eastern Europe. Apparently Tabitha, Rue's on again director-lover had come back to her senses after the identical twins from Holland had tossed her aside without so much as a 'doei' (by your leave). Not only had she resumed carnal relations with Rue, but had managed to get funding for the play. While no one would be getting paid, all their expenses would be met. It was going to be a grand holiday.

I wondered what audiences in Moldova, Tbilisi and Baku and a few other places would think of Rue as she performed in her naked glory.

'Tabby's dying to have you come sing with us. Yes?' she asked me hopefully, we had fun together, Rue and I.

'No thanks,' I relied. 'I've got a new project going on right here in New York. With a Japanese musician. Don't be surprised if the next time you hear me sing, it's at Madison Square Garden.' I was kidding of course. Jazz musicians didn't make it to Madison Square Garden.

'Well you won't see me for a while, but I'll call you as soon as I'm back,' she said and we hugged each other goodbye.

◆

A couple of days after Rue left, on a Monday morning, bright and sunny, I decided to walk to work. I was feeling a little lonely all of a sudden. All my girlfriends had left, I had no boyfriend and I didn't know what to do with myself.

At least I have a job, I told myself. Maybe I should find out how to make a flyer and splatter it around in the vicinity of the store (without littering), I idly thought to myself. Maybe I ought to write Harry a letter and seriously complain about the lack of saleable merchandise. There was only so much I could fake.

As I approached the store, I noticed some odd activity.

A big moving van stood in front, blocking the view of the entrance. Such things were bad for business. The whole point of a storefront and window displays were so that people could be tempted to come in from all the way across the street, or even avenue.

I stepped up the pace so I could yell at the driver of the van. But as I came abreast of it I noticed something else.

The store was being robbed. Cleaned out. In broad daylight.

'Help, help,' I screamed as loudly as I could as I ran to the store. The meagre merchandise on all the shelves was gone. An electrician was unscrewing the light bulbs and a carpenter was dismantling the shelves. There were about four or five men who'd formed a relay chain to cart heavy boxes from inside the store to inside the truck.

'Police, help,' I screamed again.

'Look miss, we have orders to pack up everything in this store and ship it to India. Here, look at this,' he said and thrust a letter in my hands. 'We're not thieves, we're movers. Packers and movers.'

I looked at the familiar letterhead. The same one that had once contained my appointment letter. Tears welled up in my eyes. It was official. Harry was closing down the store but hadn't seen fit to give me a notice. He hadn't breathed a word of it to me. Rat, I thought to myself. After all I've suffered under him.

I looked a little closely at the letter. It was signed by Manpreete. Not Harry. There were a few sentences in it that made it all very clear. No one, even the so-called manager of the store, was permitted to stop the proceedings. Especially the so-called manager of the store, the letter said.

'Step aside miss,' the mover said to me as nicely as he could. 'We have other stops and a deadline. Take it up with the owners. But let us do our job.'

I ran next door to see if I could cry on Fabio's shoulders. He was there of course, but was deep in conversation with his Senegalese beauty. He looked at me dismissively. 'I knew you shouldn't have had an affair with that bearded man,' he said loftily. 'I told you a long time ago that he was tasteless and classless.'

There was no sympathy there.

Or with the other merchants on the street. Sherry, Aileen and Dona treated me as if I was dead to them already. So I trudged back home, called the aunt and told her I'd be coming over. I had nowhere else to go.

'Oh don't worry,' she said brightly. 'I knew this was going to happen. I was just waiting. We'll just have to dust ourselves off and start all over again won't we.'

Chapter 26

NO LAUNDRY ON SUNDAYS

Fortunately, I'd saved a tiny sliver of the seventy-five thou (which had eventually worked out to only a paltry five thou a month in hand after deductions) that Harry had promised me. Most of it had gone in acquiring a lifestyle, something I deserved.

What was left wasn't much, just enough to pay rent for another three months, if I ate Wonder Bread and drank tap water.

I'd burned my other bridge, Fabio, tearing him down rudely. I'd told him to join a gym (implying that he was out of shape) and leave me alone. I'd pretty much delivered him gift-wrapped with a pretty pink bow into the arms of a Senegalese beauty who loped elegantly around the city attracting attention wherever she went.

Long and the short was that I couldn't get free food from La Rive Gauche anymore. No more grilled salmon skins and fresh pesto. No more baked Brie. No more Russian caviar in avocado shell. No more fine wine.

Fabio's brother Luigi had a steady girlfriend already, a nurse who was handy with the Band Aid when Fabio went ballistic, so he was out too. There was no way I was going to stoop to beg for leftovers from Pedro the dishwasher. I had a little bit of dignity left and some of my wits.

I would use those to figure out what I'd do next. Something would turn up, I was confident. It always did.

The aunt offered me a job, a home, food of course, even a car. But I knew that she didn't really need me to work in the store. She had it well covered. Besides, I didn't want to move back to Long Island to wriggle uncomfortably under her judgemental eye, much as I loved being around her.

I thanked her kindly and sweetly, and said I'd think about it. Of course I did no such thing.

◆

Hiro called.

'We need collaborate fast. I going tour. Germany. With band,' he said in his rather sexy, low-pitched growl, which made up for his lack of English-speaking skills. 'You come?'

'Of course I come,' I said happily. Fate must have liked the sound of music.

It had been a really long time since I'd travelled with a band. I remembered how much fun it had been back in Arizona. Then I remembered the trouble I'd gotten into. And how it had led me directly to France and then onto the rest of my life.

One thing was definitely connected to the next. What a pity one had to wait till it was all done before getting the bigger picture. It would be so dandy if you could see it all at once, in advance.

I wondered if the fortune-tellers with their colourful neon-lit storefronts down in the East Village would be of any help unravelling my future.

I discarded that idea as soon as it entered my mind.

The horoscope columns in the newspaper were bad enough. Filled with veiled instruction and nuanced threat, they could drive a person insane trying to figure out what the phrase, 'You'll receive unexpected news that will make you think about the path you've chosen,' actually meant. And if, 'Be cautious while setting out this week as unexpected obstacles could obstruct your path,' meant anything more than, 'Watch the closing doors,' which is what you heard on the subway.

Astrology was way too difficult for me to figure out.

◆

The toss-up was whether I should use my last three months of financial independence to look for a proper paying job or take a risk on stardom to go off to Germany with Hiro.

Playing music professionally, even in Germany, wasn't going to top up my bank account. Especially not jazz. I knew this from experience. It was the very reason I wasn't a full-time singer.

But there was the tiniest sliver of a chance that I'd become as famous as Ella Fitzgerald. I liked singing to audiences at least as much as she did.

What the hell, I said to myself. I might as well have a good time. Who knew what lay ahead? Life was short. Getting shorter by the moment.

◆

The other musicians in the band were from New York City. They spoke full sentences in English. No staccato. Bass, drums, saxophone. No keyboards this time, Hiro didn't like competition from other chordal instruments.

We spent three weeks rehearsing in Hiro's apartment, playing very softly so that his neighbours wouldn't complain to the cops and have him evicted. It was against the law for musicians to kick up a racket in an apartment building in Manhattan.

But we were still in the learning stage with the music, so it was a mental process. The noise was mostly inside one's own head.

I wrote a ton of lyrics for his songs, trying to rhyme in an original, clever, witty, funny and rhythmic way.

But try as I might, I was unable to get away from love, heartache and pain. No thoughts came to me on the subject of nuclear disarmament or of human cloning. Of space exploration or the cure for cancer.

I understood finally why poets mostly write about the tragedy of love. Probably in every language, but most definitely in English and in Urdu. I felt a pang of sympathy for Urdu poets, the one's I was so fond of trashing as I viewed their job from a different angle. I now had personal insight into their limitations and restrictions.

As a result, I ended up with a lot of:

'My love, my love, from above, gentle dove, in my hands like a glove', and some, 'the rain, brings such pain, what do I gain, all alone I have lain', and plenty of 'moon light, stars shining bright, piercing the night, consider my plight'.

It was silly and extremely soppy when you took the words out of context without the melody. But reviewing some famous jazz standards through the decades, I discovered that people far more eloquent than me wrote lyrics like, 'Night and day you are the one, only you under the moon, beneath the sun.'

Cole Porter who is credited with writing over a thousand songs (music and lyrics), famously wrote the words, 'You're the top. You're Mahatma Gandhi. You're the top. You're Napoleon Brandy.'

But to his credit he prefaced the song with the following disclaimer:

'At words poetic, I'm so pathetic
That I always have found it best,
Instead of getting 'em off my chest,
To let 'em rest unexpressed,
I hate parading my serenading
As I'll probably miss a bar,
But if this ditty is not so pretty
At least it'll tell you
How great you are.'

♦

Finally we'd hammered out the tunes, the intros, the outros, the arrangements, the tempos, the solos and all the other things one needs to have in place before a song becomes a song.

In the final couple of days before we left for Germany, Hiro rented an actual performance studio so we could amp. the up volume and listen to ourselves the way audiences in Deutschland would.

The louder the music, generally the better. That's a rule of thumb.

It was rumoured that German audiences loved experimental and avant-garde music. And that they treated musicians with utmost respect and reverence. This was encouraging.

We'd concocted a brew of Japanese folk melodies stirred with Indian classical music and boiled over a low flame of jazz. It was delicious or disgusting depending on your point of view, art being most subjective as everyone knows.

American audiences were most certainly not all-forgiving. The level of excellence they expected from entertainment was merciless. We had to bring our A game all the time because they would think nothing of rudely walking out in the middle of a solo, if they didn't like it. They treated all manner of artists this way. From stand-up comics to stage actors to dancers to musicians.

So it was with a sense of relief that we were looking forward to Germany. We could have a few 'off' nights. No one would leave. They were too polite.

◆

I'd never been to Germany and knew very little about it except blutwurst, knackwurst and strudel. I was looking forward to eating a lot of that. Mostly low carb. Except the strudel.

We would be arriving in Frankfurt, we'd pick up a rent-a-bus, a Volkswagen of course and drive it ourselves to a number of cities. Germany isn't a huge country so it was possible for us to complete a tour of this sort in a few days. The Bundesautobahnen does not mandate speed limits. They only post polite advisories hinting that one ought not to exceed the speed of sound.

We'd be staying at cheap hotels, stopping where we chose, drinking in the Bavarian air and beer.

That was the plan outlined by Hiro.

Nooooooo, I said in my head. Why me?

While I'd had a marvellous time working on his music (despite the difficulties with the lyric) the whole trip sounded extraordinarily uncomfortable and unglamorous. It was the kind of thing hippies in the 60s did, with flowers in their hair and no bra to hold up their breasts.

My travels in the Orient, as you know, had been refined and civilized. Airlines, and star hotels followed by hefty tips. I liked taking my aperitifs and après dinner Cognacs in civilized restaurants.

I was knocking on the doors of three-oh, not a teenager anymore, so it was hard to convince myself that adventure lay ahead of me.

Oddly, the other members of the band had no issue with the arrangements at all. They were not in the least put out by the hardships they were about to undergo. They made no demands. They smiled happily. Maybe they'd become accustomed to the tragedy that is the life of a travelling American jazz musician.

'Why can't we record in a studio in New York, become really famous and then fly first class everywhere and stay in five star hotels,' I whined at Hiro, who had the added headache of being bandleader and manager.

Besides composing all the music, he set up the gigs, planned the itinerary, booked the tickets, figured out accommodation and maintained a lively atmosphere keeping morale up, so our music wouldn't sound funereal or robotic. It was extra hard for him because his English vocabulary was so austere. So he smiled a lot.

He didn't tell me to shut up. He didn't ask me to be grateful that we were getting paid, at all. I suppose he liked me just a little more than the other members in the band because he just stroked my hair and said, 'Soon we in lap of luxury. Soon.'

The way he said 'we' caused my toe to tingle a little. The left one. I am left-handed so I guess that makes me left-footed too.

◆

We circled around Germany in our almost new VW bus, which thankfully, didn't have any flowers or peace signs painted on the side. I would have died of shame. We were an intellectual jazz quintet after all, not some guitar-twanging Grateful Dead tribute band.

We began in Frankfurt. The Jazzkeller is a brick and stone piece of history where some of the greatest jazz musicians in the world have performed. 'And now some not so great musicians are about to sully its stages,' I said jokingly to the band, but I was met with rude and disgusted glares. They lacked a sense of humour. It turned out that while it was a first for me, these guys had been there, done that. Often. Even Hiro.

Legend has it that Dizzy Gillespie spilled red wine all over himself there. I made especially sure not to follow suit. The last time I'd spilled red wine in a jazz club, I'd ended up with trichomoniasis. No fun at all.

We had a great gig. And everything I'd heard about German audiences was true. They sat quietly through everything, and applauded lustily at the end. I made a few mistakes (that they either didn't catch or were too refined to point out) and the saxophone player was very nervous, but all in all we came away feeling good.

I discovered that America's national food, the frankfurter (a.k.a. hotdog) came from Frankfurt, way back in the 1600s when the Germans first began pouring into the United States, carrying with them a taste of the fatherland. They continued their exodus well into the 1900s, only serving to solidify America's passion for German food.

I wondered why hotdogs were also called 'wieners' and was told that those weren't German, but Austrian as in 'Wien' (Vienna). There were lots of Austrians in America as well.

We stayed in a B&B that night. Five separate rooms.

Hiro knocked on my door shortly after I'd brushed my teeth.

Hmmm, I thought. Here we go again. Not that I minded, but mixing business and pleasure had a nasty way of backfiring on me as I'd discovered very recently with Harry, despite loud and clear warnings from my two friends, Ego and Alter Ego. You may recall a lengthy conversation where one of them, I forget which, told me not to mess around where I worked.

I didn't want to make the same mistake with Hiro, who was the boss, but I knew it was going to be tough. He was the only halfway decent looking person in the band.

The drummer had long dreadlocks that came down to his feet and while he looked great in photographs, in real life he didn't tickle my hormones. They remained dormant.

The bass player was an overweight, jolly old chap who carried spare safety pins in case his buttons popped. How did you put the moves on a man who carried safety pins, I wondered? The saxophone player was an eighteen-year old prodigy who inspired maternal feelings in me, leaving only Hiro, cute and sexy.

'What's up?' I said opening the door, unsure whether I was supposed to let him in or say good night.

'Nothing,' he said. 'I want see you ok. You ok? You sleep. Tomorrow Köln,' he said in a kindly voice.

'Yes, I'm fine,' I replied and hit the sack.

'What a gentleman,' said the E immediately.

'Why's he being a gentleman?' wondered the AE suspiciously.

I shut them both up and fell asleep. There wasn't too much jetlag between the US and Germany.

The next morning following a hefty breakfast of all types of sausages, we set off for Cologne (Köln), which is most famous for its Kölnisch Wasser, 'Water of Cologne'. My grandma's favourite Eau De Cologne, which she used not only to make herself smell good, but to cure the headaches, fevers, stomach upsets and other ailments her grandchildren came down with.

The club we played at was called Stadtgarten. The more

experimental the jazz, the more avant-garde, the wilder, the weirder, the more they liked it at Stadtgarten.

It struck me that Rue and I would have probably been a huge hit in Germany, with our hard-to-define act. I wondered how she was faring over in Tajikistan or Herzegovina or wherever she was performing for only room, board and applause.

When the show was over, after two thunderous encores, we sat down to dinner. It didn't escape my notice that Hiro made a beeline for me, leaning unnecessarily more than once for salt, pepper, mustard and other condiments he barely used, just so his body scraped mine.

I was an expert on the subject of body language, so I knew the inevitable was ringing my doorbell, metaphorically. Whether I would let it in that night remained to be seen. I wasn't a 100 per cent ready. I resolved my conflict by drinking a lot of beer, declaring that I needed to sleep soundly if I was to put up any sort of believable show in Hamburg.

Hiro, his inscrutable eyes not giving away a thing said solicitously, 'Rest voice. Sleep good.'

I did. There would be plenty of time for Indo-Japanese fusion.

If shiploads of people from Frankfurt had arrived at Ellis Island with hot dogs in their hands, an equal number of people from Hamburg had docked at the shores of America with a penchant for seared chopped meat patties sandwiched between buns.

The famous hamburger.

I was learning so much about the history and the geography and the cuisine of Germany, between enthralling audiences.

We played in a fantastic place called Birdland named after a jazz club in New York City, where I hadn't yet had the pleasure of performing. Soon, I said to myself. Soon.

Birdland in Hamburg was a small and intimate club located in a basement. We outdid ourselves there and received three encores and one standing ovation when we finally got off stage; it was a record for me. Heady stuff.

Hiro didn't follow me to my room in Hamburg so I slept soundly and woke up looking forward to breakfast. The Germans were not cereal eaters, fruit and yogurt eaters. They liked a hearty egg-and-bacon-and-sausage breakfast which I loved too. I was going to toss out all the lite and low-cal boxes of rubbish I had in my apartment the moment I got back, I decided.

Our next stop was Berlin, which once had a wall separating the East Side from the West Side. The wall wasn't there anymore, but I was struck by the irony of the invisible wall that separated the East Side from the West Side of New York City as well. The successful, the educated, the moneyed. They lived on the Upper East. While the Upper West was artsy, cultural and generally not so gitzy. At least, back then. Today, there's hardly a spot in Manhattan that doesn't cost the earth to rent or own.

The nightclub was the fabled Quasimodo, one of Berlin's oldest and most prestigious clubs where jazz is performed, again, in the basement.

I think it's peculiar that club owners all over the world feel the need to have jazz in the basement rather than at street level, where it's easier to lug a large double bass or a tuba. But according to Hiro, huffing up and down staircases lugging the grand piano over the shoulder was part of the charm of the art form. He was kidding of course.

Berlin is also the city where Hiro first held my hand (before the show, quickly and quietly) and then kissed me after as we walked back to the hotel, dawdling a little behind the others.

He kissed me right out on Kantstrasse, named after Immanuel Kant the philosopher. I remembered him well. With distaste. He had written a bestseller back in 1781 called *The Critique of Pure Reason* and the aunt's husband Max, who was a professor of philosophy, was most fond of quoting from it at every opportunity. He had memorized it from cover to cover. Max was of German descent, so he knew the book both in English and in German. Double whammy.

It bored us (the aunt and me) to tears but we learned to say things like, 'We all shape our experience of things through the filter of our mind,' and, 'Let us once try whether we do not get farther with the problems of metaphysics by assuming that the objects must conform to our cognition,' which the aunt knew how to say in German as well.

But it made sense, in a sort of zeitgeist way, to be blatantly kissing out on said Kantrsrasse, without worrying about metaphysics, epistemology or ethics.

There was nothing unethical about what we were going to do. We were breaking no law when we sealed the deal without hesitation in a B&B in B.

The next day we decided that there was no point in spending money on two rooms so we gave up one. The other band members smiled knowingly. Was I so transparent?

We made our final stop in Munich, where the food was as excellent as it was everywhere else in the country. Our gig was at a small club called the Unterfahrt, (deep in the basement, naturally) packed to the walls with an appreciative audience. The view of the stage was obstructed by the odd way in which the place was constructed but the clientele didn't seem to mind at all. They cheered raucously after every tune, especially on my solos.

If not for the B&Bs, the VW bus and our travelling standards I considered to be only slightly above that of a homeless hobo, I might have considered moving to Germany to sing for a living. The response we were getting was fabulous.

But if French threw me for a loop, the German language had me twisted like an intestine. To say the number 777,777 you need sixty-five letters: Siebenhundertsiebenundsiebzigtausendsiebenhundertsiebenundsiebzi.

Aside from language difficulties, it was also possible that once

I'd settled down in Germany, become a 'local' so to speak, they may have tired of my singing.

Anyway, it was our last night.

I learned some unusual facts about Germany from a very drunken fan, who swore he was speaking the truth. I have no way of making sure but he claimed that one could not hang laundry out to dry on a Sunday and that it was illegal to run out of gas on the Autobahn. These were two disparate facts that may have served me far better at the beginning of our trip. Especially, the running out of gas part.

We were ready to go zuruck (back, in German) to New York where you could do laundry any day of the week and run out of gas anywhere you pleased. The AAA would come to your rescue, for a fee of course.

Chapter 27

ON HIS KNEES

Except for the fact that we were still as impoverished after our tour in Germany as we'd been before we left, the band's foray in the land of the Schwarzwälder Kirschtorte (Black Forest Cake) was an out and out success.

From the way audiences reacted to our music, to the applause at the end of each set, to the way the German club owners treated us, it was an experience we ought to have filmed for posterity, but didn't.

Instead we ate our last bratwurst and drank our last lager as if there would be no German food in New York City, which isn't the case at all.

But there was something special about the way food tasted in the Fatherland, a certain, 'das gewisse etwas' or je ne sais quoi if you will. Something in the air that made the wurst zing a little more and the lager pop just a bit louder.

Hiro sat next to me on the flight holding my hand. We partook generously of the little bottles they have on the plane (it was a habit with me) and I fell asleep on his shoulder.

We were quite the couple by then. He was even carrying my bags.

◆

But while I'd successfully pushed the dark and stormy clouds of my future to deep recesses of my subconscious all through Germany, I knew I couldn't put off the subject of finding a decent job much longer.

It was not possible to live in NYC without a job or a sugar daddy.

I had thought it was kind of clever of me to combine both into one specimen, saving cab fare, in a man called Harpreet. But then in one feral swoop, fate (whose name incidentally is Manpreete) struck me with the swiftness of a stock market collapse, and I lost everything all at once.

But soldier that I was, I picked myself up from the rubble, flicked off the insult and ignominy and went looking for work. I pulled out the old office wear, the pumps and the refreshed resume and made a round of calls to the employment agencies. I even went to a few interviews.

One of them was at a department store. The job was as one of the many floor managers. I came out of that interview completely depressed. They wanted me to be a bee in a hive. Another was a secretary in a law firm. An ant in a hill.

The job market wasn't brimming over with opportunity for someone like me who could only:

Sing jazz (kind of)

Organize exhibitions in China (appeal for that particular skill-set was severely limited)

Manage a boutique store (store managers were a dime a dozen. I was very lucky to have landed Potato Print. The going rate, sans sugar daddy, was only about twenty-five thou a year.)

I felt very much like Sisyphus, the poor king of Ephyra, who was condemned by Zeus to spend a futile rest-of-his-life pushing a boulder uphill, only to have it roll back on him. The price of hubris. I wondered if I'd spend the rest of my life hopelessly as well.

Indian gods were as capricious as Greek ones. One could never dismiss them and their vengefulness.

◆

Between the pounding of pavements, I spent time with Hiro,

understanding both music and the anatomy of the Japanese male.

'You move my apartment?' asked Hiro one day, a while after we'd returned from Deutchland.

For a second I was puzzled. He wanted me to move his apartment? Why couldn't he hire a company to do that? Or even a U-Haul? Why couldn't some of the other hefty band members hoist his amplifiers and guitars on their shoulders? It wasn't a job for a woman.

Then I realised that he was asking me to move in with him. Live with him. Make our collaboration more than musical.

He had told me when we first met, that Sony's A&R (Artists and Repertoire) people wanted to sign him up to produce an album, a full-length feature with at least eight songs.

He was now saying that he wanted me to be an integral part of the plan. There would be stinging guitar solos of course, it was his album after all. But both Sony and Hiro wanted to feature the vocals of one yours truly, a girl who could flip between the pathos of the blues, the intellectual complexities of jazz and the gymnastics of Indian classical music with the ease of a schizophrenic.

I couldn't believe it at first. It seemed too good to be true. Would that mean I wouldn't need a job? A real job? Could I do music full-time?

It was most flattering.

Hiro explained that they would first release this gem in Japan, to be followed by a worldwide release. A global tour would come close on the heels of the release and we would be playing to packed clubs from the very top of Japan to the bottom. Then on to the rest of the world.

The Sony chaps were confident that the songs we had composed would take the mellow jazz world by storm. We'd be played on every radio station in the world in a year, they'd told him. The sky is the limit. Or Ao-Tenjo. In Japanese.

It sounded excellent. Maybe the chaps at Sony had a clear

view into the blue beyond unlike me.

'You move my apartment,' he said again bringing me into the present, making the sentence declarative this time. 'We practise day night. You no need job. We make platinum record,' he smiled confidently.

'No Hiro,' I said. 'No can do.'

I wasn't moving into anyone's apartment. It was too dangerous. What would happen when I got kicked out, which was always step two in the two-step dance? Where would I go? My apartment was my only sanctuary, the only thing I could call mine.

Besides, I had just decorated it from top to bottom with stuff from PP. Harry had given me run of the store in a generous moment before the iron lady Manpreete had struck, so the curtains, bedspreads and cushions matched each other in careless grace and chaotic symmetry, just the way I liked it.

I had no desire to wake up to a roomful of wires and blinky-blinks even if the sex was great the night before. Even if I was beginning to develop a taste for the traditional Japanese breakfast of rice and smelly cold fish in the morning.

'I can't move in with you. Let's leave things as they are, Hiro,' I said firmly. 'Let's make the album. I'm here all the time anyway, so what's the difference?'

'But I want care you,' he said, sounding a little peevish. 'You my woman.'

'That's so sweet,' I gurgled. It was.

'Hiro, I have to get permission from my parents. They will be horrified that I've moved in with someone who's not Indian. From another country. (I said the word 'country' as if I was saying 'bubonic plague'.) I can't upset my mother. She has a heart condition,' I exaggerated dramatically, buying a little time.

It was blatantly untrue of course, she was as healthy as a buffalo. As a matter of fact, she would have been way more surprised if I'd called her up saying I was about to have a temple wedding with a Tamilian software engineer, the traditional seven-day affair, complete with horse. That may have caused a coronary.

But I didn't want to discourage him either because my musical future was so imminent and so dependent on him. 'I'll ask them,' I promised dishonestly. 'When I think the time's right.'

It's a habit I'd picked up quite early in life. Lying to get out of a jam. I had no qualms of conscience or ethical dilemma.

Unfortunately, very often there were disastrous consequences because one lie always led to another and another and it was hard to keep track, to remember what I'd said to whom and when, and the reason I'd been compelled to do so.

I guess Walter Scott, of the 'Sir' fame must have been faced with a similar predicament, propelling him to write in his renowned epic poem 'Marmion' the unforgettable lines, 'Oh what a tangled web we weave, when first we practise to deceive!'

Hiro seemed to believe me because he smiled happily.

♦

'Let's get to this album. I'm so excited. It's my first album. I can't believe it. Are you going to put my name on it? Really?' I said, distracting Hiro with my charm and naiveté.

He smiled indulgently. 'Of course,' he said. 'Picture also.'

I got lost in the image for a few minutes. An album. With my picture and name. What would I wear? What about the hair and make-up?

I needed to call someone for help. Rue. She was an expert on make-up, being a stage actress and all, she'd have it covered. I was barely listening to the rest of Hiro's conversation, so far gone was I in my fantasy.

'You advance,' he cut in to my thoughts, grinning widely.

As usual I wondered what in the world he talking about. Advance to where? Advance what? Advance how?

Then I looked down at his hands and found them clutching

an envelope with the Sony logo on it.

'What is it?' I asked him alarmed. Why was Sony writing to me? Complaining? Already? I hadn't even met the buggers yet. And there I was thinking they liked me.

But I needn't have worried. It was a cheque for five thousand dollars and I realised that it was payment for collaborating on the album. Hiro spoke shinjitsu. The truth.

Things were getting better and better. Brighter and brighter.

◆

We plunged right into preparing for the album.

Since recording studios in New York City are prohibitively expensive, you have to use them as sparingly as possible.

Very few people can afford to first rent the studio and then think about composing the music. Unless you're already a platinum record artist of course, in which case you can buy a studio for yourself, complete with recording engineers, cleaning crew and vending machine.

Hiro fell into the have-not category.

Our work was created in his apartment, which as I've already said, consisted mostly of recording equipment punctuated with musical instruments, underscored by computers.

There was no hint of the Japanese minimalist in his studio.

No ikebana, no artistic calligraphy, no rice paper screens and lanterns, no cherry blossoms. It's as if he wanted to forget all about Japan, aside from the food. His focus, always only on music, had now expanded to include me.

He shyly revealed to me that he'd dedicated an entire three-part piece in the album to me, with my name. I would not be singing on that one, he explained, because it was an homage, a dedication.

One didn't snatch the microphone from the emcee to sing in one's own tribute, I gathered.

Recording an album was a great experience. Using his computer and guitar mainly, he recorded synthesized sounds of all the parts played by the assorted instrumentalists, creating a starting point; a base on which we could begin.

When that was done, I sang my lyrics over that.

Now we had a 'rough' track, which the musicians could listen to, as they laid down their real instruments. Each time the bass, or the drums, or the saxophone would finish, Hiro would be deleting his electronic track.

It was fascinating.

I realised that very little was 'live' in the studio. A bunch of musicians did not thump an empty bottle of Jack down on the table before counting off One-Two-Three-Four.

It was serious business.

For that month, it was as if I'd moved into another world where nothing but the sound of music existed. I lost track of time. Hiro's intensity was exciting and his focus left me breathless, wanting more.

Watching him hard at work, observing his meticulous attention to detail, and listening to the results of his impressive thought processes, I realised I was almost one-third in love.

It's funny, that thing called love. Strikes you when you least expect it and for the strangest of reasons. But I knew it could disappear as quickly as it came. Like a nice dream. Or a bad cold.

It took a month of recording, re-recording, adjusting, re-adjusting and getting each song as close to perfection as possible before we could get to the studio.

We survived on take-out. Chinese, Japanese, Indian, Korean and good old pastrami and rye. It was great fun to be part of a creative and intuitive process with someone who was so experienced. It made me feel sophisticated and cool.

It was completely different from being in the theatre with a multi-cultural, multi-lingual cast, where perfection gave way to occasional flashes of genius.

And it was nothing like rehearsing with Rue. She and I winged it, hoping for the best. Since very few people knew what we were doing, having a clue about 'it' wasn't necessary.

But in this challenging environment, I shone. I sparkled. I didn't mind sleeping only five hours a night. I didn't mind being bedraggled and shop-worn. That's what creative genius looked like.

But I looked forward to the few nights I went back uptown alone, to soak in the luxury of my bathtub, with a glass of red wine, listening to the sounds we'd recorded just that day. Analysing, critiquing, making mental notes, perfecting.

I realised that while I'd always loved singing and done quite a bit of it, there had been no specific plan. It was all random and ad hoc.

It was as if until then I'd only been fooling around, waiting for someone to take my career in hand to guide me on a tarred road instead of the cobblestones I'd been hobbling on.

I was becoming a serious musician.

This was a career-changing point in my life. I was headed in a new direction. Hiro was my beacon. He had the experience, expertise, connections and musical brilliance to showcase me to the world.

'Me, you, we far go,' he told me more than once. He had stardust in his eyes when he spoke.

Of course I knew the danger of sleeping with the boss. Something I had sternly told myself barely a month ago, I would never, ever do.

I had to separate the two, but the time for that hadn't come yet. I'd have to go along until the proper moment presented itself.

Along with lying, procrastination was another one of my virtues.

◆

Shas called me a few times to find out how I was doing. I tried explaining the finer points of rhythm, melody, syncopation and harmony to her, but she wasn't interested. She was being tormented by technicalities of her own, in the Swedish food business.

Klaus and she had expanded their line to include assorted every-day, regular food items (besides Christmas food), and that included various jars and tubes and boxes of fish, caviar, crisp bread and whatnot. Stuff that the average Swede craved for, apparently. So much so that she announced gleefully, 'We're moving to Connecticut. We've just bought a house. Four bedrooms and a pool.'

I sat down hard. It was not fair. Here I was, wondering how I'd make rent and the cow was buying a house?

'What?' I said as if she'd just won the lottery. 'Please repeat what you said.'

She gurgled. 'Business is really good. We've decided to get out of the city and live in the 'burbs. We've got a warehouse and an office and a staff of ten. We'll be all settled in by next week so you better get your butt over there.'

The envy gave way to pity. I felt a little sorry for her. House? Pool? Bedrooms? Office? Staff? Warehouse? Sounded as boring as old Klaus himself. My life was way more exciting. Our album was almost ready. I'd be a household name soon. Like Ella. While Shas mowed the lawn.

'I will, I will,' I said to her. 'Kiss, kiss. Don't you dare call me about the pitter-patter of little feet,' I warned her.

'Not any time soon,' she said. 'Oh and we've bought a Saab and a Volvo. Guess which one for whom? Klaus wants a boat next.'

Indeed, I thought. Maybe it'll spring a leak.

◆

Hiro was eventually satisfied with the prep work we had done and declared it was time to call the musicians in for the real thing.

If I had been excited up to this point, I was positively agog by the time we arrived at the studio. We had only three days to record about twenty instruments (including the voice), and it had to be precise.

It went off like clockwork.

The musicians, high-calibre men from the city of New York, with years of experience and thousands of recordings under their belts, were able to whip it out in one or two takes each. That's why they got the big bucks. They didn't waste anyone's time.

On day three, after everyone else was done, I recorded my voice. I was nervous but Hiro put me at ease, smiling, hugging me, kissing me, bringing me hot water and honey, encouraging me and applauding me. I felt like a princess.

We got done around six in the evening that day.

I was exhausted and ecstatic.

'So when can I listen to it all?' I asked Hiro. 'When will the album be out? When can I send it home?'

He laughed. 'Month. Two month. Maybe more,' he said. 'Mixing, mastering, much work left. But next week, I play first cut you,' he said.

'Ok then,' I said a little deflated that after all the rush and hurry, I'd have to wait so long to see the results.

Shas had told me a joke once about some aliens who'd landed on earth to find out how earthlings reproduced. They came upon a couple that agreed to demonstrate. The humans whipped off their clothes and gave a convincing performance while the aliens stood by, taking notes. When the human couple was done, they got up to take a bow and then put on their clothes.

'Where are the offspring?' enquired the head alien, looking puzzled.

'Oh we have to wait another nine months for that,' replied the male humanoid, as the female was putting her bra back on.

'So what was all the hurry at the end then,' asked the alien, quite annoyed.

That's how I felt.

Ah well, I thought. One lives and one learns.

'Tonight you stay?' Hiro asked me.

My laundry had piled up. I hadn't vacuumed in a month. Dust bunnies and other furries were all over the place. I suddenly felt the need to be alone. It was probably time for me to take stock of where I was and where I'd be going. And what to wear when I went. It was 'me' time.

'Hmm,' I said to him. 'Tomorrow?'

'No tonight,' he said, insisting somewhat uncharacteristically.

'What's so special about tonight?' I asked him, surprised. He was the most undemanding of men usually.

'Surprise,' he said. That dreadful word men are so fond of springing on you. A word I had come to hate because it never led to anything good.

'For you. Surprise,' he said cheerfully.

I was tired. Arguing with someone who didn't catch nuance was exhausting work. It was easier to agree.

So we took a cab back to his apartment in Chelsea.

◆

We trudged up to the third floor and I dragged my feet behind me. He flung the door open and I was taken aback.

The place was sparkling. All the wires were gone from plain sight. His computer screens gleamed as someone had polished them. There was a new bedspread, flowers and twigs artistically sticking out of a vase, soft Japanese music in the background and at least twenty scented candles flickering in the pale evening light. On the table there was a bottle of champagne. Two flutes. Bags from Zabar's on the kitchen counter indicated that someone had done their homework. Not Indian and not Japanese, but some New York epicurean chic.

Wow, I thought. What's going on?

'Sit down, sit down,' said Hiro as if I was visiting him for the first time and not the fifty-first. 'I come back.'

He dashed into the bathroom. I didn't mind. A man had the right to rush to the loo in his own house. I just hoped I wasn't going to hear funny noises. That would be a turn off.

I sat down and looked around, marvelling at the transformation. I wondered what had gotten into Hiro. I was hungry and couldn't wait to open up the bags from Zabar's. And drink some champagne.

The bathroom door opened.

Out came Hiro wearing a black velvet suit (yes, black velvet) with a white shirt and a red tie. On his feet were black-and-white wingtips. His long, black silky hair was tied up. He looked like a ninja gangster at a cocktail party. He was holding a small black box. I recognised the logo from HW. Harry Winston. Probably one of the world's most expensive jewellers.

Hells bells.

My eyes flew wide open.

'We call parents tonight. Tell them news,' he said with a charming, confident smile and sank down on one knee, flipping the box open.

There was a diamond ring in it, empire cut. It looked like platinum. I personally liked 22 karat gold, but that wasn't the point.

'Will you be honour and…' he began, after clearing his throat a couple of times.

'Noooooo,' I blurted out before I could stop myself, my hands clapped to my mouth like a B grade Bollywood actress spurning the unwanted advances of some balding pervert.

'What mean you, no? You no marry me?' asked Hiro, looking genuinely puzzled. He was not expecting me to disagree, by the look on his face. And not so vehemently either.

'No Hiro, I'm not ready to get married. We hardly know each other,' I tried.

'But music? So beautiful? You no love?' he looked like he was going to cry. 'I want marry you. You marry me. No refuse.'

'Hiro, I love the music. It's fabulous. We make amazing music together but that's different from being married. Can't we just leave things the way they are?' I begged. I didn't like the way this was going one bit. I hadn't expected it at all.

'No,' he said angrily, standing up. He put the ring back in the box and then in his pocket. 'No go back. You marry me. We go on tour. We release record.'

His mind was made up. He sounded like he wouldn't listen to anything I said.

I tried again. 'This is a mutual decision isn't it, Hiro? I like you a lot. And I want to play music and do all the things we've been talking about. But marriage? Love? This isn't something we've discussed. I don't think it's fair for you to make up my mind for me.'

'No!' He said loudly. His eyes grew angry. 'I say marry. You marry. You listen me.'

'Ok, Hiro,' I said standing up. 'Now you're not being very nice. I don't like being yelled at. I'm sorry but I don't think I want to stay here right now, I'm going home. Maybe in the morning you'll think more clearly and we can talk about this again,' I said, now in tears myself.

I picked up my handbag and walked to the door.

He rushed there before I could and locked it. Lock number one. Lock number two. And lock number three. And because this was New York City, he slammed the police lock down too and bolted it.

'What are you doing? You're scaring me. Are you locking me in? What is this?' I said my voice squeaking.

'You not anywhere. You sit. You think. You agree. You marry,' and with that he walked to the kitchen towards the bags from Zabar's, like he was going to get dinner ready. On his way he popped open the champagne as if nothing had happened.

'You drink champagne. You have Zabar's dinner. You marry,' the man was insane. How had I not seen it before? He was so calm, it was horrifying. I expected him to whip out the steak knife any moment, to plunge it into my heart efficiently. Once I was dead, he'd wipe off the blood on his napkin and then fold it back neatly and get on with dinner, I imagined.

'No, Hiro, no,' I wailed. 'I don't want dinner. I don't want champagne. I want to go home. Unlock the door. Let me out. Please. Stop this,' I was crying loudly now. I was at the door, banging on it, hoping someone would hear the caterwauling and come in to investigate. 'Let me go. It's not funny. Please.'

I was trembling and shaking. Hiro's third floor walk-up had two other apartments on the floor, but I'd never seen anyone either go in or out. Who knew if they were even occupied? Hiro could murder me and no one would find me for a week. My heart was thumping and I felt I would faint.

How was I going to get away?

I decided to calm myself down. First things first. I downed two glasses of champagne. Gulp. Gulp.

'You eat,' said Hiro. 'You get sick champagne,' his concern was creepy. I considered slamming the champagne bottle on his head but discarded the idea immediately. He was bigger, stronger, faster and madder. Not worth the risk.

'I'm not hungry. Where's the whiskey?' I said rudely. Maybe that's what he needed to see. The mean and nasty me. The one who wasn't worthy of his name or his bed.

'We drink,' he said in a jolly way. 'You be happy. You marry.'

The man was a certified maniac.

I knew there was only one thing for me to do. Get him drunk enough so he had to pee, and while he was in the loo, I could get on the phone to call someone to come and rescue me. Someone who wouldn't ask any questions. Someone who would do the job and then milk it for a few months at least, but I could live with that.

I had to wait for two hours before that moment arrived. I managed to get five drinks into him, drinking only two myself.

Alcohol weakened my resolve and I didn't want to end up in bed with him.

The hours were spent mostly in silence. Hiro played some of the music we'd just recorded and once in a while made as if to come across to get into a snuzzle, but I wasn't having any of that. I was furious. I was mad.

Finally, he got up to the loo. The bugger had a bladder that could hold a lot, but it also meant he would be gone at least five minutes, giving me plenty of time to call Shas.

She got it immediately. 'Give me the address,' she said efficiently. 'Klaus and his friend Ulf will drive from Connecticut and get you. It's going to take an hour. Stay calm.'

'Thank you, thank you, thank you,' I whispered gratefully. I didn't want Hiro to hear me.

'One more thing,' said Shas.

'What's that? Anything,' I hissed. 'Anything.'

'I told you so,' she said smugly and hung up.

Chapter 28

RUY LOPEZ

It was one of the longest hours in my life. But I knew I could count on Shas. She was trustworthy and reliable even if she claimed to have something she called 'a Swedish sixth sense'. Oddly, no one else ever spoke of such a national trait, but I humoured her. She was an excellent friend to have, especially in times of trouble, as I was now. I knew she wouldn't abandon me.

So I was feeling far more positive when Hiro came out of the bathroom, fresh as a daisy.

'You want eat? You feeling better? You love? You marry?' he asked with the cheery breeziness of a nikuya satsu (butcher) asking you how you wanted your beef cut. Fortunately he hadn't heard my SOS to Shas and didn't know that two sturdy Swedish men would be coming to my rescue shortly and they would easily be able to take down one skinny Japanese ninja.

'Hiro, you are a maniac. I don't want to have anything to do with you. I don't even like you. I'm sorry I met you. I wish I'd never set eyes on you. You are my worst nightmare. I don't want to come on tour with you. I don't care if I spend the rest of my life working for Roto-Rooter. I never want to see you again,' I said in one stuttering breath, ending in a gulp of whiskey that I felt I deserved.

'What means?' he asked, as if we were making casual conversation.

Roto-Rooter is a company that clears up clogged drains and frees up sewer lines. But I didn't explain that to him.

'Hrrrrrrmph,' is what I said angrily. I couldn't believe that I was being held hostage. I couldn't believe I didn't have the guts to kick and scream and throw things around or even get into a hair-pulling match (his was longer than mine). I realised I was a ninny.

'You fine in morning,' he said with the certainty of a psychopath.

◆

The doorbell rang.

I sent a thank you prayer up to my gods. They never forsook me even if they scared me to death very often.

Hiro looked puzzled. It was 3.30 in the a.m. Not the time for a neighbourly drop by.

He peered through the keyhole. He must have seen Thor 1 and Thor 2, all blonde and thunderous, muscled and beefy. It must have unnerved him a little. But then he recognised Klaus. I could tell by the way his back stiffened. The same Klaus who had paid him big bucks recently to play at his wedding. The same Klaus, whose wife, Shas's best friend, was little ole moi. His hostage.

He turned to me, shaking his head. 'How could you be so dastardly,' he seemed to be thinking, in Japanese.

I sneered at him. 'I haff my vayys,' I replied in my head, in German.

He meekly opened the door.

'Klaus, nice see you. How Shas? Come in. Come in,' he said like a chatty host at an afternoon tea party. 'You pass neighbourhood?'

'Shas is waiting for her, and yes, we were driving around so we thought we'd take her along,' said Klaus obligingly. No one wanted any confrontation. No one was in the mood for fisticuffs, which I was half hoping for. It might have been fun to see guitars flying and jaws cracking. A little blood maybe.

'Hope the music is going well,' said Klaus solicitously. 'Oh meet my friend Ulf, he's just moved here from Sweden. He is my partner in the food business.'

They shook hands formally. You might have thought they were sealing the deal on a corporate merger.

No one spoke of why they'd driven all the way from Connecticut to New York City in the dead of night.

Hiro acted like he hadn't just locked me up, threatening not to let me go unless I agreed to marry him.

We were all very civilized.

'Bye Hiro,' said Klaus. 'Let us know when you're playing next in Connecticut.'

I didn't say anything. I didn't look at him.

We walked down the stairs and got into Klaus's Saab. Me in the back and Ulf in the front.

'We're taking you back to Connecticut,' said Klaus. 'Shas is expecting you. I think we could all use some sleep. Are you ok?'

'I am, I am, I am. I can't thank you enough Klaus. I'm so sorry to have woken you up. I'm really sorry. I had no idea this would happen. Things were going so well. And suddenly…' my voice trailed off. I had been truly frightened. There was a look in Hiro's eyes that I wouldn't be able to forget. The look of a sharp object slicing through skin.

But I snapped out of it.

'Meet Uffe,' said Klaus. Ulf. Uffe.

I noticed as we were walking out onto the street from Hiro's apartment that Uffe was a mighty fine specimen of Swedish manhood. He was taller and broader than Klaus and yet he wasn't a muscleman. He wore glasses, giving him an intellectual air and sported a five-day stubble. His hair was curly, a deep auburn, you could even call it russet. His eyes were a bright blue and he had a nice timbre to his voice. What a cutie, I thought. He probably can't speak a word of English.

'Good to know you're ok,' said Uffe in perfect English. 'Shas was worried.'

I was embarrassed. I wondered what Shas had fed him about me.

'I'm fine,' I said and slumped into the back seat. Suddenly, a wave of tiredness swept over me and the next thing I knew Shas was waking me up. It was still dark outside but in the streetlight I could see that their home was beautiful. Surrounded by trees and flowers, a lawn and a curved driveway, it was the picture of suburban bliss.

I felt secure and happy that I was coming home to Shas.

'I've made some hot chocolate for you,' she said. 'And then you go to sleep, my drama queen. We'll talk in the morning.'

What a darling she was. I obeyed, drinking the sweet cocoa with marshmallow bits and then followed her up the stairs to a pretty bedroom in shades of pink and purple. The wallpaper matched the curtains matched the bedspread matched the tables matched the lights. There were even flowers. It was perfect. She was perfect.

The bed was soft and fluffy and I sank into it gratefully.

I woke up the next morning not too late. It was about 10.00 a.m. Because it was a Saturday, everyone was home and I heard the sounds of hustle bustle downstairs. Shas had laid out some clothes for me, jeans, a T-shirt, underwear (she was my best friend after all and she'd been lending me her clothes for years) and I hit the shower, washing away the nightmare of the prior evening, along with my musical career.

As I lathered up I thought about the turn of events and it made me very sad. I wouldn't be touring Japan, I wouldn't be playing to packed houses and I wouldn't be a household name like Ella Fitzgerald. Or even Helen Merrill, who wasn't a household name, but someone you'd know if you were a die-hard jazz fan.

I wondered if I'd ever sing again. I wondered what would happen to all the songs on the album. Would he delete them? Would he get someone else to come and redo the vocals because he couldn't stand the sound of my voice?

I wept heart-breaking sobs in the shower and didn't realise I was so loud until Shas poked her head in.

'Stop it,' she said. 'Stop it right now. The world hasn't ended.

Come down and have breakfast.'

She was right. Besides, I was hungry. I'd only observed the bags of gourmet delicacies from Zabar's from afar, but hadn't actually partaken of them the night before.

I put on her clothes which as usual were a little tight for me, what's with her being all svelte and toned, but I felt I looked good enough to face the world.

After Eggs Florentine à la Shas, orange juice and fresh-brewed coffee, the four of us got into Shas's Volvo, and went down to their factory warehouse, a short fifteen-minutes ride.

A backlit sign proclaimed that we'd arrived at Scandinavian Suppers. It was impressive. Rows and rows of shelves, some of them freezers, neatly stacked with items all labelled in Swedish. Kalles Kaviar and Wasabröd and Felix Lingonberries. There were a few boys and girls in white lab coats with nets over their hair even though all the food was pre-packaged and there wasn't a chance in Valhalla that vermin could get in. But, being thoroughbred Swedes, Klaus, Shas and Uffe were taking no chances with the USFDA.

'It's fantastic,' I exclaimed. I meant it.

'Shall I take you on a tour?' asked Uffe. 'I'll explain Swedish food to you. Have you ever been to Sweden?'

'Nope,' I replied. 'But Shas gave me the edited version. I know about the babies.'

'What babies?' he asked, scratching his head.

'The angels that scream their heads off in the hospitals,' I explained.

He smiled at me indulgently. As if to say, 'you've been through a traumatic time. You're not to be held responsible for the things you say.'

'Where did you find all these kids who speak Swedish?' I wondered.

'Hmmm?' he asked 'They're local kids. They don't speak Swedish.'

'But what about these names?' I persisted. 'I mean, how are they going to be able to run to the right "Falukorv", and "Ansjovis", and "Glasmastarsill", when it's not in English?' I was reading off the names on the shelves.

'We train them. With flash cards. Images. It's not that difficult. But the phones are answered by Swedish-speaking people since all our customers are Swedish,' he explained.

'I love Swedish food,' I declared. I'd eaten plenty of it at Shas's apartment and way preferred it to Indian food. Especially pannkakor (pancakes) with hjortron (cloudberry sauce) and generous dollops of vispad grädde (whipped cream). I usually doused it with powdered sugar too, which wasn't part of the recipe but I had a sweet tooth. The bite marks showed up clearly on my middle section.

Pretty soon it was lunch-time. We sat in their office, opening up this can and that packet. It was a delicious meal.

'Let's go out for a smoke,' I said to Shas. She raised her eyebrows nervously. 'Shas doesn't smoke anymore,' said Klaus, with the confident smirk of a conqueror that has subjugated the enemy.

'Oh,' I said. 'Really? Wow! That's great Shas. But why? Don't tell me you're exercising? (We had smoked and drunk our way through China, swearing never to approach anything that came even close to exercise.) I haven't given up and I need one after this excellent lunch.'

She agreed to stand with me, and we strolled outside. I could feel Klaus glaring at us behind our backs.

'Want a quick drag?' I tempted her. 'I have mints.'

'No,' she said. 'I've really quit smoking. But listen to me. I want you to stay the weekend. Don't go back to the city yet. Relax a little. Sleep a little. Chill a little. I don't like the way things have been going for you and you need to unwind.' She wasn't being bossy or demanding. She was being mature, caring and reasonable. I didn't quite know what to make of it. No snide remarks. No exasperated shaking of the head. No, 'I told you so'.

'Besides Uffe is going back to the city on Monday and you guys can take the train out together.' Suburbia had morphed her into some sort of parental unit.

'What does he do in Manhattan?' I asked.

'He's running the city operations of Scandinavian Suppers.' she said. 'He has an apartment in Stuyvesant Town.' She referred to a large block of apartment buildings with parks and playgrounds and security, almost like a mini city, in downtown Manhattan.

I had nowhere to go anyhow. Shas was a good cook. They had a pool. Uffe was cute. I had no music, no job, only some dust bunnies and cobwebs to go back to. They'd still be there on Monday. My bank account had five thousand eight hundred and seventy six dollars and fifteen cents. Enough for two months, at the very end of the rubber band before it snapped back and took out my eye.

'Ok Shas. Thank you. You're my best friend. Forever. I'll stay, and Monday I gotta get back and look for a job,' I said.

Klaus and Shas's went to bed early in their lovely home in Connecticut on Sunday night. They wanted to be bright and chipper on Monday. Uffe and I were expected to hit the sack too. We were taking the 7.21 a.m. or 7.36 a.m. or some such inhuman train, so Uffe could be at work in his office by nine o' clock.

'Do you play chess?' he asked me, his eyes pointing at a transparent Plexiglas chess set on Shas's mantel, above her fireplace, alongside some framed photographs of the couple in their wedding finery.

You could see through the box to the translucent black and white rubber pieces inside. The box itself was etched in a way that resembled chess squares and you could deduce that once opened, the box served as the chessboard. Very classy. I would have expected nothing less of Shas.

'Hmmm,' I replied, the old hjärta (heart) sinking a little. If there was one word I hated more than 'surprise' it was 'chess'. But the brainier among men seemed to like it a lot and I couldn't understand why.

My strong anti-chess feelings may have had something to do with my grandfather, the gentleman who taught me the finer points of Chaucer by locking me up in a room and not letting me out until he was satisfied I had learned enough. The same not-so-gentle man also introduced me to chess. His method was to tell me what each piece did. Once. And then yell at me at the top of his lungs if I moved the knight in a straight line or castled after a check.

My throat always went dry when someone said chess.

I always wonder how he had succeeded in teaching my snotty brother how to play.

'Check mate,' I heard the brother say more than once, while the grandfather proudly and gracefully accepted defeat. My way of ending a game was to stand up in a huff when I saw I was about to lose and knock all the pieces over, pretending it was an accident. Both the grandfather and the brother stopped asking me to play after the fifteenth time I did that.

Chess players weren't the brightest votives at the altar, I figured.

But I could see Uffe liked it a lot. 'You know, I went to Iceland in 1972,' he said. If you knew anything about chess at all, then you'd know that the American Bobby Fischer beat the defending world champion Boris Spassky of the USSR in Reykjavík in what was known as 'The Match of the Century'. A knock-out match where only their fingers moved while the world stood still.

The grandfather spoke of it ad nauseam, so yes, I knew all about it. He hadn't actually gone to Iceland, what with it being really far away and extremely expensive, not to mention, the extreme climate change between Chennai (still Madras in 1972) and Reykjavik.

The people of South India didn't store astrakhans in their attics, awaiting winter. For two reasons. One, winter never made an appearance in Tamil Nadu. And two, because of what astrakhan really is. Foetal fur of the Karacul lamb, which furriers get by slaughtering its mommy, just when she's getting ready to give birth.

The grandfather was a non-violent vegetarian who took it all out on us with his loud voice.

It's another story that he wore leather shoes. And draped his wife, my grandmother, in the finest of silks. And silk as we all know is the product of boiling live silkworms so that the cocoon can be carefully disentangled into long, weavable strands.

You needed thousands of silkworms to make one 'pattu podavai' (silk saree). The grandmother, sweet and kind as she was, had at least three hundred silk sarees in her wardrobe.

A silk Nazi, you might call her.

Before I could debate the hypocrisy and merits of selective non-violence in my head, I heard Uffe say, 'My father took me there. I was a little kid. But it was very exciting,' said Uffe.

'I'm not good at it,' I admitted quickly, before he assumed I knew anything more than how to set up the board. 'My grandfather tried teaching me the Ruy Lopez but you know, I'm more into Jennifer Lopez.'

'I could teach you,' he said. 'Let's sit here.' He patted the spot next to him on the thick cotton navy and white striped sofa that Shas had placed in front of an elegantly carved, antique Chinese cinnabar table with a glass top. I folded my legs under and leaned on my arm, our faces close.

'You're white and I'm black,' he said.

I burst out laughing. 'I'm brown.'

'I mean you're white on the chessboard,' he explained unnecessarily. I knew what he meant.

'PK4,' he instructed. 'The pawn in front of the king moves up two paces.'

'I know what it means,' I said indignantly. I knew the names of the moves. It was just that they didn't pop into the mind at the appropriate moment, which is why I didn't like the game. Also because they didn't have a sniper piece. There were no wildcards in chess.

He moved his black PK4 in response.

I scratched my head.

'NKB3,' he said helpfully. He meant that I was to move my knight in front of my king's bishop.

He responded with an NQB3 of his own.

'Ummm,' I said, moving closer to him.

'BN5,' he said very close to my lips. I moved the bishop to the fifth square up from the knight.

He responded with his PQR3, and in the next moment our lips were locked in a passionate kiss. A few of the pieces, both his and mine went clattering to the floor but they were made of rubber so they didn't make a noise.

The game was over. But a new one was about to begin.

We tiptoed to Uffe's bedroom, luckily on the ground floor so there would be no creaking of stairs. Houses in Connecticut, indeed all over America, are made of wood. They're noisy.

I didn't want to have to explain to Klaus (who didn't like me much to begin with) why it was that he had been forced out of bed in the middle of the night to drive all the way into Manhattan to rescue me from the jaws of death, just so that barely forty-eight hours later, I could snuggle under the duntäcke (down comforter) with his brand new business partner.

I went back to my bedroom upstairs around 1.00 a.m., tired but fulfilled. No one heard me.

I fell asleep soundly and dreamed about babies with blue eyes.

Chapter 29

PINK STRIPS

There was too much morning activity for anyone to notice that Uffe and I were brushing up against each other unnecessarily, casting secret sidelong glances at each other in a way that suggested we'd done more than play with black and white chess pieces the night before.

I hugged Shas and Klaus as I said goodbye. 'I'll never be able to repay you. You saved me from jigoku,' I told Klaus. Japanese hell. 'No sushi ever again.'

My list of forbidden foods was growing. First French and now Japanese. He looked at me as if to say, ha, likely story.

I pushed aside thoughts of cherry blossoms and Shinto shrines, bullet trains and kimonos, platinum records and worldwide tours, spotlights and applause.

But for that Harry Winston ring, it could have been tengoku. Heaven.

Uffe held my hand on the train into Grand Central. It was nice. Then I remembered that Hiro had held my hand on the plane and I had thought that was nice too. You couldn't figure a man out by his hands, no matter what anyone said.

We didn't speak much. It was too early in the morning for conversation and besides, we were in that awkward period, just after the first time, when one didn't know for sure how the other person felt. When things hadn't yet been taken for granted and each person was waiting for the other to make the first move.

It was a delicious feeling, possibly because there was so much uncertainty and so much possibility.

The train deposited us in Grand Central so we would part ways. I was headed uptown to my apartment, while he was going downtown to his office.

I wondered if he'd call me. Ask me out on a date. Probably not, I concluded. It was probably just a *snabbt ligg*, a one-night stand, the kind Shas and I had been so partial to, back in China, oh, about a hundred years ago, when the world was still filled with hope and promise and we were in our early twenties.

The tears welled up in my eyes, but before I gave in to self-pity, Uffe pulled me into his arms and kissed me hard. Right there in front of the commuters. I noted a few indulgent smiles, also a few looks of disgust. It was practically the crack of dawn, a tad premature for romance.

'I'll see you tonight,' he declared. 'Do you want me to come uptown or do you want to come downtown?'

'I'll cook dinner,' I said smiling happily. 'Come to my apartment.'

I'd spend the day cleaning up. I'd get fresh flowers for a fresh start, I decided

'Don't bother cooking, I'll take you out,' said Uffe. 'See you at six.'

♦

He began coming over regularly after that. Sometimes I'd go down to his apartment in Stuyvesant Town.

But that was a bit of a downer because he was sharing it with another man. Another Swede.

It was bad enough that there was another human being around to thwart the spontaneity and excitement of new love (on kitchen counters, sofas, dining tables, living room floors, etc.) but to add to my discomfiture, Bjorn (Uffe's flatmate) liked to walk around naked.

The moment he'd get home from work (he owned a newspaper, a Swedish one of course), he'd toss his clothes all over the apartment and stride purposefully here and there, going about his business, butt naked as, they say, a jaybird. Starkers. Sky-clad like the Jains, if you prefer your analogies Indian.

He watched TV naked, cooked dinner naked, ate dinner naked and chit chatted with us naked. The only thing he didn't do naked was answer the doorbell. He'd pull on his underwear as a favour to the pizza delivery guy and the UPS guy.

It was horrifying. Uffe laughed at me. 'Its common in Sweden for people to be naked in their own homes. Don't worry about it.'

But I kept wondering about the sofa, the chairs, the kitchen counters and other areas his unmentionables had brushed-up against, the very same surfaces that Uffe and I used for our own naked activities.

I hoped fervently that I wasn't picking up the germs that Bjorn was shedding. After my encounter with Jerry and his trich, I was very careful.

It was all too unsanitary so I avoided going to Uffe's apartment as much as I could.

◆

'I'm starting my own business,' Uffe told me one day. 'Importing Swedish art from Sweden. For Swedish people in America to hang on their walls.'

'Really?' I asked. That surprised me. I wondered why Swedish people didn't just get used to the art and the food and the news one found locally in America. Why did they cling so lovingly to tradition from the homeland?

I suppose it was a good thing from Shas's and Scandinavian Suppers' point of view—nostalgia and homesickness meant big bucks. Four bedrooms and pool big bucks. Two-car big bucks. Boat big bucks. Maybe Uffe had locked onto something that would make him rich too.

Was there something wrong with me, I wondered. I never felt

like eating tandoori chicken or hanging up miniatures of Mughal princesses on my walls, their feet always pointing to the side. I never got the urge to decorate the apartment with gold foil Tanjore paintings embedded with semi-precious stones, or install Rajasthani wooden screens behind the diwan.

One of the reasons I had liked the bedspreads and curtains from Potato Print, was because although they were born and raised in India, Harry and Manpreete had ripped off Laura Ashley's designs as closely as they could without getting sued.

'Swedish art?' I asked him. I had never heard of it. Not that I knew much about art. One had heard of the odd Manet and Monet and Rembrandt. The Pollock and the Warhol. Even Norman Rockwell. I mentioned this to Uffe.

'Ah Rockwell. He stole everything from Carl Larsson,' he said huffily. 'All his ideas, all his concepts. That's why I want to set the record straight with Larsson prints from Sweden.'

'Oh,' I said, I had no idea what he was talking about. But I was confident he would make a ton of money like Shas and Klaus. The Swedes were a most clever lot even if they didn't exude the aroma of Mensa at first whiff.

'Do Klaus and Shas know?' I asked him.

'Of course,' he replied. 'It's no competition. Food and art. We'll all be friends. We'll share customers. It's going to be great.'

♦

Bit by bit, Uffe brought a few of his things over to my apartment. A toothbrush. Shaving items. Underwear and socks. A few shirts. And then a suitcase filled with more stuff. Finally, a crate of Glenfiddich. Pretty soon, he had moved in completely.

I loved it.

It had been a long time since I'd lived with a man and it was sort of nice to plan breakfast for two and dinner for two. Besides, Uffe was very handy around the apartment.

'Your walls need painting,' he declared and the next thing I knew he had bought a stepladder, some paint, a spackle knife and some putty. He set about doing all the work himself. In no time at all, my walls glistened in original eggshell with dove accents, as they were meant to.

The Swedish people are great DIYers. That's a major difference in our cultures. As an Indian, I tried to do as little as possible myself, palming off major responsibilities to others as soon as the opportunity presented itself.

It was hard living in America being as incompetent in the DIY department as I was, but somehow I'd managed to find someone to help me out every time. A wiggle of the tush, a little cleavage, a smile. Usually, that's all it took.

I still hadn't found a job.

Everything that came my way was either too boring or downright insulting. So I joined a gym, to help whittle the weight that was accumulating around my middle rather rapidly.

I also helped Uffe with his business a little bit. Writing down orders, making brochures, labelling his inventory and so on.

◆

And then suddenly, I started feeling sick. Nauseous. My head began to ache and I wanted to stay in bed. All day. I couldn't understand it. Not sick enough to go to the doctor but close to.

I took some over-the-counter medication but it didn't help.

I called Shas.

'I don't know what's the matter with me,' I wailed.

'Is it Uffe? Did he do something? What…' she began, but I stopped her.

'No it's not Uffe. He's a darling and I'm helping him set up his business. It's me. Something's wrong. I'm throwing up all the time.'

There was a silence at the other end.

'When did you get your last period?' she asked me.

Damned if I knew. It had been at least two months. Bloody hell. More accurately, non-bloody hell. My stomach and heart did a pole vault together.

'Wait,' I said to her and went into the bathroom to throw up again.

'Get a home pregnancy test from the drug store,' she said, when I came back. 'Call me when you're done.'

◆

I was sure Shas was over-reacting. But there was no harm in finding out. Uffe wasn't home yet. I went out and bought a little kit from the drugstore around the corner and rushed back to the loo, ripped open the box and read the instructions.

'Pee on strip,' it said (it may have actually said 'place a few drops of urine on the strip provided' or something official like that). At any rate it was simple enough.

I held my breath.

First there was nothing.

Then a thin pink line appeared.

And then another.

I burst into tears.

I called Shas back when I'd stopped crying. I'd been doing a lot of crying recently, I noted. It made my eyes swell up and it wasn't a pretty sight.

'Will you come with me to Planned Parenthood?' I asked Shas. 'Please? Now? Or tomorrow?'

'What are you talking about?' she said. 'Aren't you going to tell Uffe? I mean he has a right to know.' She stopped short and took a breath. 'If it is Uffe, that is, and not some other low-life from god-knows-where.'

'It is, it is, it is,' I wailed. 'But how can I tell him? He'll hate me.'

'You have to tell him or I will,' said Shas, the keeper of the universe's truths.

That evening, Uffe came home, carrying a big bag of goodies from Balducci's in the Village, a fabulous gourmet deli, which has since moved further uptown. Cheese, caviar, red wine, smoked salmon, goose liver pate and other delicacies. He was so sweet, that Uffe.

I didn't know how I was going to break the news.

'Uffe, we're going to have a baby,' was one option.

'Uffe, we're going to kill a baby,' was another.

'What's up?' he asked after kissing me probingly at the front door, the groceries still in his arms. He saw that I was troubled.

'Hmmm,' I began. 'I'm uhhh. I mean. You know I've been feeling a bit ill. Under the weather. Pukey. Queasy. Uncomfortable. Right?'

'Yes,' he agreed. He'd been witness to all of those things.

'Well the truth is, I'm pregnant,' I blurted out, stepping back to watch his reaction.

He set the groceries down on the kitchen table. He walked straight to my handbag where I kept my cigarettes. He pulled out the packet of Marlboro Lights that I'd switched to recently. He walked up to the sink and turned on the tap, drowning my cigarettes.

'We're having a baby,' he said joyfully and kissed me once again. 'You can't smoke anymore.'

I looked at the bottle of wine.

'No you can't drink anymore either,' he said rapturously.

I eyed the food.

'Now that you can have plenty of,' he said. 'In fact, you're going to be eating for two.'

And with that my turvy world turned topsy. Again.

Made in the USA
Monee, IL
03 May 2026

49438423R00173